'Glittering, engros...
HELEN OYEYEMI, author o...

'An unflinching look at how fo... ...
pursue their dreams and ambitions in Seoul'
NEW YORK TIMES BOOK REVIEW

'One of the buzziest debuts of the year.
If I Had Your Face transports readers to glittering,
futuristic Seoul. Essential reading'
VOGUE

'An endearing story of female friendship staged against
a backdrop of elitism, sexism and the relentless quest
for cosmetic perfection . . . Enthralling'
VANITY FAIR

'Hypnotizing . . . You won't want to put
it down until the very last page'
HARPER'S BAZAAR

'An eye-opening story of female friendship set against
the brutal beauty standards of South Korea'
GLAMOUR

'Immense fun . . . It isn't difficult to see why
it comes garlanded with praise'
IRISH TIMES

'If you loved *Crazy Rich Asians* or *Daisy Jones and the
Six* then this is going to be right up your street'
GRAZIA

'Troubling, kaleidoscopic and hugely enjoyable'
NELL ZINK, author of *Mislaid*

'A gripping portrait of four young women in South Korea . . . Its focus on the tangled and complicated nature of female friendship is universally familiar and fascinating'
REFINERY29

'Hilarious, cuttingly observant, feminist'
ROWAN HISAYO BUCHANAN, author of *Starling Days*

'Mesmerizing . . . weaves together the complexities and contradictions of modern-day Seoul, in an ultimately uplifting story of women living in defiance of oppressive customs'
DAZED

'I love the way Frances Cha rotates between mindsets to look at how beauty and privilege influence the way women live, whilst maintaining a sly lightness'
REBECCA WATSON, author of *Little Scratch*

'Cha writes beautifully about the hopes and dreams of her female protagonists as they try to navigate the oppressive structures of the world that seems set on keeping them in their place. Dark and fascinating'
DAILY MAIL

'Compelling, understated, casually brutal and very cynical. I love it'
HANNA JAMESON, bestselling author of *The Last*

'Powerful and provocative'
WASHINGTON POST

IF I
HAD
YOUR
FACE

Frances Cha

PENGUIN BOOKS

PENGUIN BOOKS

UK | USA | Canada | Ireland | Australia
India | New Zealand | South Africa

Penguin Books is part of the Penguin Random House group of companies
whose addresses can be found at global.penguinrandomhouse.com.

First published in the United States of America by Ballantine Books, an imprint of
Random House, a division of Penguin Random House LLC, New York 2020
First published in Great Britain by Viking 2020
Published in Penguin Books 2021

001

Printed and bound in Great Britain by Clays Ltd, Elcograf S.p.A.

The authorized representative in the EEA is Penguin Random House Ireland,
Morrison Chambers, 32 Nassau Street, Dublin D02 YH68

A CIP catalogue record for this book is available from the British Library

ISBN: 978–0–241–98635–6

www.greenpenguin.co.uk

For my mother,
who taught me how to hold on to a dream

If I Had Your Face

Ara

S ujin is hell-bent on becoming a room salon girl. She has invited Kyuri from across the hall to our tiny apartment, and the three of us are sitting on the floor in a little triangle, looking out the window over our bar-dotted street. Drunk men in suits stumble by, contemplating where to go for their next round of drinks. It is late and we are drinking soju in little paper cups.

Kyuri works at Ajax, the most expensive room salon in Non-hyeon. Men bring their clients there to discuss business in long dark rooms with marble tables. Sujin has told me how much these men pay a night to have girls like Kyuri sit next to them and pour them liquor, and it's taken me a long time to believe her.

I'd never heard of room salons before I met Kyuri, but now that I know what to look for, I see one on every side street. From the outside, they are nearly invisible. Nondescript signs hang above dark-ened stairways, leading to underground worlds where men pay to act like bloated kings.

Sujin wants to be a part of it all, for the money. Right now she is asking Kyuri where she got her eyes done.

"I got mine done back in Cheongju," says Sujin sorrowfully to Kyuri. "What a mistake. I mean, just look at me." She opens her eyes extra wide. And it's true, the fold on her right eyelid has been stitched just a little too high, giving her a sly, slanted look. Unfortunately, the truth is that even apart from her asymmetrical eyelids, Sujin's face is too square for her to ever be considered pretty in the true Korean sense. Her lower jaw also protrudes too much.

Kyuri, on the other hand, is one of those electrically beautiful girls. The stitches on her double eyelids look naturally faint, while her nose is raised, her cheekbones tapered, and her entire jaw re-aligned and shaved into a slim v-line. Long feathery eyelashes have been planted along her tattooed eye line, and she does routine light therapy on her skin, which glistens cloudy white, like skim milk. Earlier, she was waxing on about the benefits of lotus leaf masks and ceramide supplements for budding neck lines. The only unaltered part of her is surprisingly her hair, which unfolds like a dark river down her back.

"I was so stupid. I should have waited till I was older." With another envious look at Kyuri's perfect creases, Sujin sighs and peers at her eyes again in a little hand mirror. "What a waste of money," she says.

SUJIN AND I have been sharing an apartment for three years now. We went to middle school and high school together in Cheongju. Our high school was vocational so it was only two years long, but

- - - -

Sujin didn't even finish that. She was always itching to get to Seoul, to escape the orphanage that she grew up in, and after our first year she went to try her luck at a hair academy. She was clumsy with scissors though, and ruining wigs was expensive, so she dropped out of that too, but not before she called me to come take her spot.

I am now a full-fledged stylist and a few times a week Sujin comes into the salon where I work, at 10 A.M. sharp. I wash and blow-dry her hair before she goes to work at her nail salon. A few weeks ago, she brought Kyuri in as a new client for me. It is a big deal for smaller hair shops to snag a room salon girl as a client because room salon girls get their hair and makeup done professionally every day and bring in a lot of money.

The only thing that annoys me about Kyuri is that sometimes she speaks too loudly when she is talking to me, although Sujin has told her that there is nothing wrong with my hearing. Also, I often hear her whispering about my "condition" at the shop, when my back is turned.

I think she means well though.

SUJIN IS STILL COMPLAINING about her eyelids. She has been unhappy about them almost the entire time I have known her—before and after she had them stitched. The doctor who performed the surgery was the husband of one of our teachers, who ran a small plastic surgery practice in Cheongju. About a dozen girls got their eyes done there that year because the teacher offered us a 50 percent discount. The rest of us with monolids couldn't afford even that.

"I'm so glad I don't need any restitching done," says Kyuri. "The hospital I go to is the best. It is the oldest hospital on the Beauty Belt in Apgujeong and singers and actresses like Yoon Minji are regulars."

- - - -

"Yoon Minji! I love her! She's so pretty. And super nice in person, apparently." Sujin stares at Kyuri, rapt.

"Eh," says Kyuri, annoyance flitting across her face. "She's all right. I think she was just getting some simple lasering done, because of all the freckles she is getting on her new show. The one that films out in the country with all that sun?"

"Oh yeah, we love that show!" Sujin pokes me. "Especially Ara. She's obsessed with the kid from that boy band Crown, the one who's the youngest in the cast. You should see her mooning around the apartment after the show ends every week."

I pretend to slap her, and shake my head.

"Taein? I think he's so cute too!" Kyuri is talking loudly again, and Sujin gives her a pained look before glancing back at me.

"His manager comes to Ajax sometimes with men who wear the tightest suits I've ever seen. They're investors probably, because the manager is always bragging to them about how popular Taein is in China."

"That's crazy! You have to text us next time. Ara will drop everything and go running straight over to you." Sujin grins.

I frown and take out my notepad and my pen, which I prefer over typing into my phone. Writing down words by hand feels more akin to speaking.

Taein is too young to go somewhere like Ajax, I write.

Kyuri leans over to see what I've written. "Chung Taein? He's our age. Twenty-two," she says.

That's what I mean, I write. And Kyuri and Sujin both laugh at me.

SUJIN'S PET NAME for me is ineogongju, or little mermaid. She says it's because the little mermaid lost her voice but got it back later

----

and lived happily ever after. I don't tell her that that's the American cartoon version. In the original story, she kills herself.

Sujin and I first met when we were assigned to work a sweet potato cart together our first year of middle school. That was how a lot of teenagers made money back in Cheongju in the winters—we stood on street corners in the snow and roasted sweet potatoes over coals in little tin barrels and sold them for a few thousand won each. Of course, it was only the bad kids who did this, kids who were part of the iljin—the gangs of every school—and not the nerds, who were busy studying for entrance exams and eating cute little boxed lunches that their mothers packed for them every morning. But then again, the ones at the sweet potato carts were the *good* bad kids. At least we were giving people something for their money. The truly bad ones just took it from them.

AS PERILOUS BATTLES were fought over the best corners, I was lucky to have been paired up with Sujin, who could be ruthless when necessary.

The first thing Sujin taught me was how to use my fingernails. "You can blind someone, or punch a hole in their throat, if you want. But you have to keep your nails the optimal length and thickness, so that they don't break at a critical moment." She examined mine and shook her head. "Yeah, these won't do," she said, prescribing nail-strengthening vitamins and a particular brand of thickening polish.

That was back when I still spoke, and Sujin and I would joke around or sing as we manned our cart, and call out to passersby at the top of our lungs. "Sweet potatoes are good for your skin!" we'd yell. "Gives you health *and* beauty! And they're so delicious!"

A few times a month, Nana, the senior girl who gave us her coveted corner, would stop by to pick up her dues. She was a famous iljin member, and had conquered the entire local district in a series of legendary fights. She'd broken her pinkie finger in the last one however, and handed her territory off to us while she recovered.

Although she would slap around the other girls in the bathrooms at school, Nana liked me because I was the only girl in our school gang who didn't have a boyfriend. "You know what's important in life," she always said to me. "And you look innocent, which is great." I would say thank you and bow deeply, and then she would send me off to buy cigarettes. The man at the corner store wouldn't sell them to her because he didn't like her face.

I THINK I KNOW why Sujin is so obsessed with her looks. She grew up in the Loring Center, which everyone in Cheongju thought of as a circus. In addition to housing an orphanage, it was a home for the disabled and deformed. Sujin told me that her parents died when she was a baby, but recently it occurred to me that she must have been abandoned by a girl even younger than us. Perhaps Sujin's mother was a room salon girl too.

I told Sujin I liked going to visit her at the Center because no one was there to hover over us. We could drink all the expired drinks donated by grocery stores, and park our sweet potato cart there with no questions asked. But secretly, it scared me sometimes to see the disabled slowly roaming the grounds, their caregivers addressing them in singsong voices.

"I HATE TO TELL you this, but Taein has also had major work done at my hospital. The clinic manager told me." Kyuri looks at me

- - - -

slyly and shrugs when I glare at her. "I mean, they have the best surgical staff in the world. It would be stupid *not* to get your face fixed there if you want to be a star." She stands up slowly and stretches like a cat.

Sujin and I are watching her and we start yawning too, although secretly I resent her dig at Taein's face. I really don't think he's had anything done other than veneers. He doesn't even have double eyelids.

"Wait, you're not talking about Cinderella Clinic, are you?" Sujin's eyes narrow to slits.

Kyuri says yes.

"I heard all the doctors there graduated top of their class at Seoul National!" exclaims Sujin.

"Yeah, they have a wall covered with doctors' photos and every single bio includes Seoul National. The magazines call it the Pretty Factory."

"Isn't their head doctor really famous? Dr. Shin or something?"

"Dr. Shim Hyuk Sang," says Kyuri. "The waiting list to see him is *months* long. He really understands beauty trends before they even happen, and what girls want to look like. That's so important, you know?"

"That's him! I read all about him on BeautyHacker. They did a huge feature on him last week."

"He is a lovely man. And skilled, obviously."

Kyuri waves her hand over her face and winks. She sways a little too, and it's only when I get a good look at her that I realize she is completely drunk.

"Is he really your doctor?" Sujin leans forward. I know where this is going.

"Yes. I got one of my friends to introduce me without paying the

----

premium he usually charges. She's had her hairline and her calves done there."

"That's wonderful!" Sujin bounces up. "Can you refer me? I *really* need to fix my jaw and that article said that jaw surgery is his specialty." Only I know that she has been plotting how to ask Kyuri this for weeks and weeks—in fact, probably since they first met. Sujin has often told me that Kyuri's jawline is the prettiest she has ever seen.

Kyuri looks at Sujin for a long moment. The silence is awkward and she motions for more soju. I pour her another cup and mix in some cold, sweet Yakult for her. She makes a face at me for diluting it.

"Look, I am not saying I regret having jaw surgery. It was the turning point of my life. And I'm not saying that it won't change your life—in fact, it definitely will. But I *still* can't say I recommend it. Also, Dr. Shim's really busy and that hospital is really expensive. *Really* expensive, even without the premium. He only takes cash. They say they take cards, but they bait you with such a big discount if you pay cash that you can't possibly not pay cash. It's just too expensive, unless you're an actress who has signed with a major agency, and then he'll sponsor you." Kyuri downs the rest of the soju and blinks her feathery lashes. "Otherwise, you're going to have to borrow money from somewhere else. And then you have to pay off the interest forever."

"Well it's going to be the biggest investment of my life, and I've been saving for a while now." Sujin tosses her head and shoots a quick look at me as she says this. I've been doing her hair for free so that she could save up for her new surgery. It's the least I can do.

"I don't know how much you have saved, but you'll be surprised at the final bill. It never ends up being that one surgery you went in

----

to get," says Kyuri. Later, Sujin and I will discuss potential reasons for why Kyuri does not seem to want Sujin to get this surgery—does she feel uncomfortable asking Dr. Shim for a favor? Or does she think Sujin might end up looking too much like her? Why wouldn't she want Sujin's life to change?

Kyuri sighs and adds she wishes *she* could save more money. Sujin has told me that it's hard for room salon girls to save up because they are constantly getting into debt and blowing off steam from work by going to "ho-bars" and spending money on room boys. "I could pay for two surgeries with what most room salon girls spend on alcohol in one night," Sujin said to me once. "You don't understand the scale of the money they make and throw away every week. I *have* to get there. I just have to." She says she'll keep saving until she can stop worrying about how to get through another day, another month.

And whenever she says these things, I nod and smile so that she knows I believe her.

SOMETIMES, WHEN PEOPLE ASK me how it happened, I tell them that it was because of a boy. *He broke my heart and I lost my voice.* Romantic, don't you think?

I contemplated typing it up and having a little printout ready instead of writing something out every time. Then I realized it would be too reminiscent of beggars on subway cars.

Once in a while, I lie and write that I was born this way. But if I get a new customer that I like, I tell them the truth.

It was the price of surviving, I write. *Things are a little different outside of Seoul.*

Actually, it would have made more sense if I had become deaf. Most of the blows landed on my ears. Although my eardrums were

----

ruptured at the time, they have gained almost full recovery and I can hear fine. Sometimes I wonder if I can hear better than before. The wind, for instance. I don't remember it having so many shades of sound.

ON MONDAY, Kyuri comes into the salon a little late. She looks tired but waves at me from the makeup chair as I prepare my corner for her blowout. The girl who works at the chair next to mine uses far too much hairspray and I've written her many notes asking her to please cut down on the products because the cloying smell and fog from the spray make my head ache, but she just blinks at me placidly and does not change her ways.

After I wash Kyuri's hair, I bring her iced yuja tea. She sinks into the chair.

"The usual please, Ara." She peers at herself in the mirror as she takes a sip. "Oh my God, look at my dark circles. I'm a monster today. I drank too much last night."

I take out the straightener and show it to her, my eyebrows raised.

"No, just waves, please." She absently combs her fingers through her hair. "I guess I haven't told you, but it's actually a rule at Ajax. They can't have too many girls in the room with the same hairstyle, so we get assigned a look for the season. I'm lucky because I got the waves. That's what men like, you know."

Smiling and nodding at her in the mirror, I put away the straightener and take out the curling tongs instead.

"I make it a point to ask every man—just because I want to know for sure. And they all say that they like long, wavy hair. I really think it's because of Cho Sehee from that movie *My Dove*. She was so beau-

----

tiful in it, you know? And her hair is completely natural, did you know that? She hasn't dyed it or permed it in ten years because of her contract with Shampureen."

Kyuri prattles on with her eyes closed while I gather her hair in small strips and pin them to her head. I start curling the sections on the left side first, inside out.

"The older girls have to try so hard with their hairstyles. It's really tragic, getting old. I look at our madam and she is just the ugliest creature I have ever seen. I think I would kill myself if I looked that ugly. But you know what? I think we must be the only room salon with an ugly madam. It really makes Ajax stand out. And I think it makes us girls look prettier too, because she is so horrifying."

She shudders.

"Sometimes I just can't stop thinking about how ugly she is. I mean, why doesn't she just get surgery? Why? I really don't understand ugly people. Especially if they have money. Are they stupid?" She studies herself in the mirror, tilting her head to the side until I right it again. "Are they perverted?"

AT HOME, the only time I ever hang out with Sujin is on Sundays, which are my only days off. During the weekdays, I go to work at 10:30 A.M. and come home exhausted at 11 P.M. So on Sundays, we lounge around the apartment and eat banana chips and ramen and watch TV on the computer. Sujin's favorite program is this variety show called *Extreme to Extreme,* where they feature several severely deformed (or sometimes just really ugly) people every week and have the public phone in their votes on who should win free plastic surgery from the best doctors in the country. She loves watching the

----

final makeover, when the chosen step out from behind a curtain while their families—who have not seen them in months while they recover from surgery—scream and cry and fall to their knees when they see how unrecognizably beautiful the winner has become. It is very dramatic. The MCs cry a lot.

Usually she watches it over and over but today she is too excited to stay still.

"Kyuri was actually so nice about it when she finally came around. She said that she would talk to the place where she sells her bags, and they would be willing to lend me money for the surgery. She says that's actually their main line of business—lending money to room salon girls! And then when I am better and everything is fixed, I can find work through her."

Sujin trembles with excitement as I pat her arm. "I can't wait," she says. "I am only going to eat ramen until I pay back that loan so fast that there won't be time for any interest to grow."

She looks giddy. "Wouldn't it be wonderful to go to sleep at night and wake up rich every day? But I won't spend it. Oh no. I will stay poor at heart. And that is what will keep me rich."

What will you buy me? I write. She laughs and pats my head.

"For ineogongju," she says, "her heart's desire." She walks over to the mirror and touches her chin with her fingertips. "Just make sure you know what it is by then."

ON THE DAY of Sujin's surgeries, Kyuri comes to the salon early so that she can take Sujin in to the hospital and talk to Dr. Shim before he operates. I am going to leave work at 5 P.M. today to be there when Sujin wakes up from the anesthesia.

- - - -

Thank you for introducing her to such a magician, I write. *She is going to be beautiful.*

Kyuri's face goes blank, but soon she smiles and says she likes the idea that she helped add more beauty to the world. "Isn't it so generous of him to fit her in like that for just a tiny premium? He's usually so busy that you can't schedule a surgery for months." I nod. At the consultation, Dr. Shim told Sujin that restitching her eyes will not be a problem, and she needs to get both double jaw surgery and square jaw surgery, desperately. He'll cut both the upper and lower jaws and relocate them, then shave down both sides so that she will no longer have such a masculine-looking jawline. He also recommended cheekbone reduction and some light chin liposuction. The surgeries will take a total of five to six hours and she will stay in the hospital for four days.

He was less forthcoming about how long it will take for her to look completely natural again. "Probably more than six months" was the most specific answer anyone gave us. Everyone's recovery time varies wildly, they said. But a girl at the salon whose cousin got it done told me it took over a year for her to look normal. Her cousin still couldn't feel her chin and had a hard time chewing, she said, but she had gotten a job in sales at a top-tier conglomerate.

When I finish curling Kyuri's hair, I fluff the curls and then squeeze some of my most expensive shine serum into my hands. I rub them together and comb them lightly through her hair. It smells lovely, like peppermint and roses.

When I tap her on the shoulder to let her know I'm done, Kyuri sits up straight. Her lashes flutter as she gazes at herself with her "mirror expression," sucking in her cheeks. She looks breathtaking, with her cascade of waves and carefully made-up face. Next to her,

----

I look even more faded, with my ordinary face and my ordinary hair, which Manager Kwon is constantly harping at me to style more dramatically.

"Thank you, Ara," she says, her face breaking into a slow, appreciative smile. She catches my eye in the mirror. "I love it. What a goddess!" We laugh together, but my laugh is soundless.

IN THE HOSPITAL, all I can do is hold Sujin's hand while she weeps silently, just her eyelashes and nose and lips visible in her bandaged head.

WHEN I GET home that night, I find a sheet of paper on the table. It is her will. We had read many news stories about patients who died from flecks of jaw bone getting lodged in arteries, causing them to choke to death on blood filling up in their throats while they slept. I made her stop after the first few articles, but secretly, I read them all.

I LEAVE EVERYTHING I own to my roommate, Park Ara, it says.

IN THE ORIGINAL STORY, the little mermaid endures unspeakable pain to gain her human legs. The Sea Witch warns her that her new feet will feel as if she is walking on whetted blades, but she will be able to dance like no human has ever danced before. And so she drinks the witch's potion, which slices through her body like a sword.

What I want to say, though, is that she danced divinely with her

----

beautiful legs, even through the pain of a thousand knives. She was able to walk and run and stay close to her beloved prince, and even when things didn't work out with him, that wasn't the point.

And in the end, after she said goodbye to her prince and flung herself into the sea, expecting to disintegrate into sea foam, she was carried away by the children of light and air.

ISN'T THAT a beautiful story?

Kyuri

Around 10 P.M., a girl who was not one of us entered our room at the room salon. She was small and expensively dressed, in a flowing bird-patterned silk dress and high heels edged with mink. I'd seen that exact dress in the latest issue of *Women's Love and Luxury* and it had been the same price as a year's rent. She stood there, dainty and scornful.

There were five of us girls sitting around the table, one for each of the men, and she stood in the doorway and stared in turn at each of us, her eyes alight with intense interest. Most of the men did not seem to register her entry—they were drinking and talking loudly—but us room salon girls, we froze. The other girls then looked away immediately, heads down, but I stopped myself and stared back at her.

She was quietly scrutinizing everything in the room—the dark marble walls, the long table laden with bottles and glasses and crystal plates of fruit, the light emanating from the bathroom in the corner, the karaoke machine, which had been switched off midsong because Bruce had received an important work call and couldn't be bothered to step outside. The fact that she was not escorted by one of the waiters meant someone had told her exactly which room to come to—which was not an easy feat given our deliberately confusing underground maze of hallways.

"Ji, over here!" Bruce, my partner, turned to see what I was looking at and called to her while giving my inner thigh a rough pinch under the table. "You came!"

The girl called Ji walked slowly toward us and sat down where Bruce had indicated. Up close, I could see that her face was devoid of surgery—her eyes were single-lidded and her nose was flat. I would not have been caught dead walking around with a face like that. But clearly, from the way she walked and held her head, she came from the kind of money that didn't need any.

"Hey, you," she said to Bruce. "Are you drunk? Why did you tell me to come here?" She sounded upset to be called to such a setting, but I knew that the opposite was true—she was delighted to see for herself what the inside of a room salon looked like. On their rare visits, women usually gape like fish, judging us. You can tell they are thinking, "I would never compromise my morals for money. You probably only do this to buy handbags."

I'm not sure who's worse, them or the men. Just kidding, the men are always worse.

A half-empty bottle of whiskey sat in front of me on the table. As always, Bruce had booked the largest room and had ordered the priciest bottles we had on the menu but tonight he and his friends were

----

taking longer than most parties to drink it. Bruce was a recent big catch for our room salon—not only was his family famous (his father owned a stem-cell clinic in Cheongdamdong) but he had started his own gaming company—and Madam was thrilled that he'd been here every week for going on two months now. "All because of you, Kyuri," she'd said to me a few nights ago, her toad-like face breaking into a smile. I smiled back. I happen to know that ours is the closest room salon to his office.

"Of course I'm not drunk," Bruce snapped at the girl. "I called you because Miae's not talking to me."

This was the first I had heard of a Miae, but why would I have heard of her?

"You had *another* fight?" she said. Shivering, she pulled a sand-colored cardigan out of her bag and put it on. That gesture in itself was another affront. Madam keeps the room cold and comfortable for men wearing suits, while we're in minidresses trying to hide our goosebumps.

"You need to talk to her, wake her up so she understands how the real world works." Bruce took off his glasses and rubbed his eyes, something he does when he's frustrated. Without his glasses, he looks like a lost little kid and the name Bruce seems ludicrous. I started calling him that after he told me he reached 3-dan in tae kwon do before he turned fifteen. We were at a hotel and I was teasing him about his skinny arms. I was too tired for sex that night, and had hoped he would get annoyed if I teased him.

I don't know at what age men become assholes—boyhood, teenage years? When they start earning some real money? It depends on their fathers, and their fathers' fathers, probably. Their grandfathers are usually the biggest assholes of all, if mine are any indication. Men these days are actually much better than previous generations—the ones who used to bring mistresses into the house and make their wives feed and care for their bastard children. I've just heard too many stories in my own family tree to have had any illusions to begin with, even before I started working in a room salon. If they don't die early, stranding you with kids and colossal childcare expenses, they fuck you over in other ways that are entirely boring.

The only gentlemen I ever see are in those dramas on TV. Those men are kind. They protect you and cry and stand up to their families for you, although I wouldn't want them to give up a family fortune of course. A poor man cannot help me when he cannot help himself. I know, because I was in love with a poor man once. He could not pay to spend time with me and I could not afford to spend time with him.

"You fight more than any couple I know," said the girl. "At this point, you need to break it off or propose." She was looking me up and down as she spoke.

Bitch, I thought, resisting the urge to tug at the hem of my dress.

"I know," Bruce said, reaching for the bottle. I let him pour himself another shot without offering to pour it for him. If Madam had seen me, she would have said something. "It's what every fight is really about these days. I'm not ready, I'm only thirty-three. None of our friends are married. Even the girls. Although what *they're* going to do is beyond me." He frowned. "Except you, Ji, of course," he added hastily. "You obviously have nothing to worry about."

The girl made a face. "I'm so sick of my family setting me up on these blind dates, trying to get me married. What century do they think this is?"

His expression turned solemn as he weighed her problem. I rolled my eyes but fortunately no one saw me.

"My grandmother has already picked a date for my wedding," she continued. "Next September fifth or something. They just need a

----

groom. She says she needs a lot of time to figure out which hotel I'm getting married in because she doesn't want to offend the owners of whatever hotel she *doesn't* choose."

I took out my compact and went back to retouching my face. How funny, the wild variety of shit some people are worrying about in life. In the past, I would have been fidgeting, ashamed and uncomfortable, while she stared at me. Now, I just wanted to slap her face. And Bruce's too, for good measure, for calling her here.

"Anyways, I think it's a good sign that you are actually this affected by Miae and that you're cut up about her," she said. Then she began talking rapidly in English, using wide hand gestures. It's a thing English speakers do, I've noticed. Their hands flail wildly and their heads move a lot when they talk. They look ridiculous.

"Bruce, what the hell?" The other men had all turned their heads sharply when they heard her speaking English. It was when they realized a girl from the outside world was among them.

"What the fuck?" said the plump, sweaty guy who'd been sitting on the other side of me. Earlier, I'd heard him bragging to Sejeong, the girl he'd picked, that he was a "top company lawyer." Sejeong hadn't been able to stop laughing at him and he'd blushed like a teenager.

His rotund face was now hostile as he looked from Bruce to the girl and back to Bruce.

"Guys, this is my friend Jihee, you met her before at Miae's birthday party, remember?" Bruce beamed, slurring his words. They all stared back at him. She probably knew a good third of their sisters and wives and co-workers. Probably their parents too.

The girl retreated further into her seat, looking as innocent as she could. She didn't want to leave, it was clear.

There was a silence, one that none of us girls cared to tide over. It was bad of Bruce to break the unspoken rule, but the guys couldn't stay angry at him. For one thing, he was too drunk to care, and more important, he was paying for the whole night, as he always did. The bill was probably equivalent to half of their monthly paychecks. So the men turned back to their girls, though they were much more restrained now.

If it had been like most other nights, I would have gotten up and left for another room, as I tend to have regulars asking for me at the same time and I rotate room to room. But Bruce is an exception and it was a slow Tuesday. Besides, I was hungry and no one had touched the plates of anju. Although it was against the salon's policy and I'd never done it before, I took a slice of dragon fruit and started eating. The flesh was silky but almost tasteless.

"So how did this fight actually start?" the girl asked.

"Miae wanted to have dinner tonight with her brother's new girl-friend," said Bruce. "I've been working so hard for this IPO I've been sleeping on my desk every night, and there's no way I'm going to sit down with some country girl her idiot brother is dating at his no-name university. I don't *give a shit*."

He nursed his whiskey and brooded. He ignored me completely, as if he hadn't fucked me over a chair two nights ago.

"She takes that kind of thing as you not caring about her family, you know. You should be careful."

He snorted. "Do you know that her brother actually asks me for *pocket money*?" He jerked his head in disgust. "And of course he's going to come to me for a job, when we don't hire anyone who's not from the top three schools. Or at least from KAIST. Or someone with parents that have direct power to help us."

"What does her dad do again? I think I heard once but I forgot."

"He's just some lawyer with his own tiny firm in some neighborhood I've never heard of that barely counts as Seoul."

He looked upset.

"Why don't you just break it off, then?" the girl said, impatient now. "She's become my friend too, and I'm saying this for her. Don't waste her time if she is going to have to meet someone new. It's going to take her another year to meet someone, maybe a year of dating to talk about marriage, then another few months to marriage and then another year to have kids. And she's thirty already!"

"Yeah, I know," he said gloomily. "So I agreed to have our parents meet. For dinner. And I'm freaking out right now. Life as I know it will end on March first. Independence Movement Day. Seven P.M. Even all the siblings are coming." His face was tragic.

"What?" she and I said at the same time. And then both Bruce and the girl looked at me, Bruce amused and the girl with a withering stare.

"A sangyeonrae?" she went on. "That's more final than a proposal."

I don't know why this news shocked me so, but I fashioned my lips into a teasing smile and joked, "You're getting *married*? I guess I'll be seeing you even more often!"

"That's why I was so pissed," continued Bruce, as if he didn't hear me. "I don't want her brother's girlfriend there at the dinner—my mother would have a stroke on the spot if she thought someone like her could become an in-law of our family. As if things aren't going to be difficult enough. But Miae is adamant that her brother will get so upset if we leave the girlfriend out."

"Why is it such a long way off?" she asked. "Three months? Where is it going to be?"

"I booked a private room at Seul-kuk, at the Reign Hotel," said

----

Bruce. "Her mom's been so damn aggressive in this whole process and my parents finally said yes. That's just the first night that both my parents are free. They're putting it off as long as possible too. And honestly, the reason this is happening at all is because my mom went to a fortune-teller. Apparently Miae is supposed to be an ideal daughter-in-law and wife and mother. Oh God." He shook his head. "I don't know if I can do this."

"Stop with the misery already," said the girl in a chiding voice. "Your parents have to meet Miae's family sooner or later."

Bruce groaned and fiddled with the strap of his shiny watch.

"At least they're respectable," she said after a pause. "It could be much worse."

Just from the tone of her voice, I could tell she was referring to me.

AS A MATTER of fact, I know all about respectability. My older sister, Haena, married into some wealth.

She graduated from a top women's university in Seoul with a degree in early childhood education, which is the only thing that made her marriage possible. At the wedding, which was held at one of the most expensive hotels in Seoul, the groom's side had more than eight hundred guests, mostly men in black suits and animal-patterned Ferragamo ties bearing their gifts of cash in white envelopes. His family had to hire fake guests to fill our side, so it didn't look like they were marrying down.

She's been divorced now for a year, and she has yet to tell our mother.

Her ex-husband, Jaesang, has been playing along with the farce by coming to our house for a day for the big festivals, Chuseok and

----

Lunar New Year, but recently he's been putting Haena in a panic by refusing to attend the weddings of any of our relatives. The pride of our mother's widowed life is showing off her rich son-in-law.

Jaesang's parents know about the divorce and are apparently torn, weighing the public shame of it all against the immediate urge to look for a better second wife for their son. They only met my mother twice throughout the entirety of the two-year marriage, and there is no danger of them telling her.

Haena got to stay in the Gangnam apartment, which is still in Jaesang's name. It remains strategically scattered with his things for when our mother visits bearing baskets of food she's cooked for her beloved son-in-law.

"It's the only thing I can do for him," our mother says whenever Haena protests that Jaesang barely eats at home. "It is my way of protecting you." So Haena just takes the food.

IT WAS ON one of those days last year after yet another frustrating phone call with my mother about Haena ("Kyuri-ya, what do you think I should buy Jaesang for his birthday? Make sure you send your present early and write a card") that I invited the two girls across the hall from me to have a drink. I had been meaning to talk to them for some time before I finally got around to it.

It says something about my frame of mind that I wanted to talk to them at all. Neither of them was particularly interesting to look at, nor did they seem to have interesting jobs or relevant hobbies or anything like that. No, what struck me each time I saw them was how close they were—how companionable and comfortable they were with each other. The giddy girl with the square face and the furtive girl with the pale face is how I thought of them. If they were together, their arms were linked, and I would see them around the neighborhood, eating at one of the corner vendors together or buying soju at the convenience store, the square-faced one always loud, both of them radiating tenderness. Sometimes they would leave their front door wide open to air out their apartment and I would see them lounging around in their pajamas, Pale Face playing with Square Face's hair as they dozed watching dramas. "Like sisters," I caught myself thinking in a melancholy way.

My own sister and I do not feature much in each other's lives except to align ourselves on one goal—to shelter our mother as much as we can.

I KNEW JAESANG had quite a reputation at room salons for years before Haena found out about his "girlfriend." Three years ago, I'd seen him doing something particularly disgusting at a room salon in Gangseo where I was working at the time. That was before I had my double jaw surgery, and the salon I worked at was one that had a connecting hotel upstairs.

I'd entered the room behind the other girls and saw Jaesang sitting in the far corner. I fled before he saw me and sought out the madam, who sent me home for the night because I was so nervous and she didn't want a scene. She later went in and introduced herself to Jaesang, pampered him into feeling extra-special all night, and made him promise to phone ahead every time he came so that I wouldn't accidentally be sent into his room. "I can't have one of our girls unhappy," she said to me, pinching my cheek. It made me want to puke, the way that she pretended to care about me when she kept me in such a state of ghastly anxiety every night about how much money I was bringing in.

- - - -

Of course I never told Haena. My normally levelheaded sister be-haved like a fool when she found out about the girlfriend, who worked at a Samseongdong room salon. But the divorce wasn't really because she kicked up a fuss. Jaesang wasn't in love with that girl or anything. He had just fallen out of love with Haena at that point and didn't feel the need to endure her agony of heartbreak. And our family wasn't one that would make him think twice about divorcing her.

THESE DAYS, it's nice to finally be working at a "10 percent"—a salon that supposedly employs the prettiest 10 percent of girls in the industry—where the madam isn't blatantly pushing us to have sex with clients for "round 2." There is still pressure to bring in money, but it's slightly more civilized. Whenever I get angry at Madam, the other girls whisper at me that she's not that bad, and to remember other madams of my past. We've all suffered under those far more treacherous.

OUR MOTHER HAS secrets too, only they are the harmless kind.

"Kyuri, the secret ingredient I put in every side dish is a few drops of Chinese plum sauce," she says, sweat forming in the deep wrinkles of her forehead as she fries anchovies with crushed peanuts and plum syrup. "You can put it in anything and it is so good for health!"

Whenever I travel home to Jeonju, I watch her toss them in the frying pan with her feeble wrists. She never lets me near the stove. The result is that Haena and I don't know how to cook a single dish, not even rice in the rice cooker.

"You will both have a better life than a housewife daughter-in-

----

law," she said to us growing up. "I would rather you not know how to cook at all."

Her body has been shutting down since our father died. She had to give up her corner at the market, where she's sold slabs of tofu for the past thirty-five years. They found and removed two large tumors in her right breast two years ago. They were benign but of alarming size. She's hovering dangerously on the edge of diabetes and her bones have started to crumble. Her left hand had an infection six months ago and is still swollen like a sponge. I massage it for hours whenever I make the trip to see her, and am taking her in for a surgeon consultation next month, the earliest I could get an appointment at the SeoLim Hospital.

SUJIN ALWAYS LIKES to say that I am the first real filial child she has ever met, and Ara nods vehemently in agreement. "Who knew a room salon girl would be the daughter of the century?" Sujin says. It's because I told her that I did not buy any of the bags I own, and that I do not have any money because I send it all to my mother.

MY MOTHER CALLS me hyo-nyeo—filial daughter—and strokes my hair with so much love it breaks my heart. But sometimes, she has spells when she shakes with anger toward me.

"There is no greater sorrow than not getting married!" she says. "The thought of you alone in life, no children, that is what is making me old and sick."

I tell her I am meeting scores of men at the office where she thinks I work as a secretary. It's just a matter of finding the right one.

"Isn't that why you suffered so much pain with your surgery?" she says, stabbing her finger into my cheek. "What is the point of having a beautiful face if you don't know how to use it?"

EVEN AS A GIRL, I knew the only chance I had was to change my face. When I looked into the mirror, I knew everything in it had to change, even before a fortune-teller told me so.

When I finally awoke the evening of my jaw surgery and the anesthesia began to wear off, I started screaming from the pain, but my mouth would not open and no sound came out. After hours of persistent agony, the only thing I could think was how I wanted to kill myself to stop it—I tried to find a balcony to jump from and when I couldn't, frantically searched for anything sharp or glass; a belt to hang on a showerhead. They told me later that I had not even made it to the door of my hospital room. My mother held me during the night as I wept, soaking the bandages that encased my face.

I am terrified of her dying. When my mind wanders, I think about her tumors spreading poison throughout her body.

THE OTHER DAY at my clinic, I finally saw the actual girl that I modeled my face after: Candy, the lead singer from that girl group Charming. She was sitting in the waiting room when I walked in, slumped in the corner with hair spilling messily out of a black cap.

I went to sit beside her because I wanted to see how clear the likeness was. I'd brought in photos of Candy's face when I had my first consultations with Dr. Shim. She has a slight upturned bump at the end of her nose that makes her so uniquely, startlingly beautiful. Dr.

Shim was the surgeon who gave it to her, which is the reason I had come to him.

Up close, I saw that her eyes were streaked with red, as if she had been crying, and she had ugly spots on her chin. She hasn't been having a good year, with all those rumors flying about how she has been bullying Xuna, the new girl in their group, and that she's busy running around with a new boyfriend and missing rehearsals. The comments on Internet portal sites have been merciless and torrential.

Sensing my staring, she pulled her cap down lower and started twisting her rings—a slender gold band on each of her ten fingers.

When the nurse called her name and she stood up to walk in, she turned to look at me and our eyes met, as if she could hear what I was thinking.

I wanted to reach over and shake her by the shoulders. Stop running around like a fool, I wanted to say. You have so much and you can do anything you want.

I would live your life so much better than you, if I had your face.

- - - -

Wonna

My grandmother died last year, in a hospital for the senile in Suwon. She was alone when she died—that is, no family members were with her—and the old woman in the next bed was the one who told the nurse to remove the body because it was starting to smell.

When I heard the news I became so distressed I had to leave work and go home to lie down.

My father was the one who had called to let me know. "You don't have to go to the funeral," he said. When I was a child, and then when I was older, I used to daydream about her dying. I told my father I had no intention of going to the funeral.

My father and I had never really spoken about the years I lived with her as a child, when he was working abroad. Sometimes, one of

----

us would obliquely refer to her things—"He looks like the dog your grandmother brought home one day when I was in middle school" or "That shed looks like the outhouse at Grandmother's house"—but these were comments to which neither of us expected a reply.

My husband came home early that day. My father must have called him at work. He came into the bedroom, where I was lying with my eyes open, and he sat down next to me and took me by the hand.

I don't know what he thought I was feeling. He knew that I had spent my childhood in the care of my grandmother, and also that I never talked about her and had never once gone to see her. So he must have understood *something*. But I cannot possibly discuss my memories with him. I can picture his round, well-meaning face puckering up in sympathy, and I would have to get up and leave.

"I have experienced terrible events in my life as well, you know," he said to me when he was first trying to ask questions about my childhood and I would just look at the floor and not respond. He was talking about the death of his mother, which I am sure was very sad and scarred him to a sympathy-inducing degree, but he would not understand what I went through living with my grandmother. Most people have no capacity for comprehending true darkness, and then they try to fix it anyway.

He is a person who expects people to be kind because he is kind. When he drinks or watches a movie, he will say sentimental things that will make me embarrassed for him. If we are in a group setting, I become deeply ashamed. I married him because I was tired and it was already too late for me, even though I was still so young.

AT NIGHT, when my husband is sleeping next to me, I often become so claustrophobic that I have to walk downstairs and go sit on the top

----

33

step of the front stairs of our office-tel. Our street is so full of life at night that it wipes my thoughts clean.

If it is a weekday, the girls who live above me usually start trickling home around 11 P.M. They look so quiet and cold no matter the weather and they nod at me and whisper hello under their breath. Sometimes I say hello back and sometimes I look away. They don't know that I have been waiting for them to come home.

On weekends, I occasionally catch them on their way out. But the best is when I hear them knocking on each other's doors to borrow makeup or order fried chicken together at strange hours of the day.

Until they come home, I sit on the stoop and watch passersby. During the day ours is an ugly street, washed out and dusty with trash piled up and cars honking and trying to park in odd corners, but at night, the bars light up brilliantly with neon signs and flashing televisions. In the summer, they set up blue plastic tables and stools outside and I can hear parts of people's conversations as they drink. Usually they are sharing anecdotes about the last time they drank together. Sometimes, men talk about the women they are seeing and vice versa, but a lot of times, conversation is about TV shows. It is astounding, how much people talk about TV.

Perhaps it's because I spent most of my childhood without one—my grandmother smashed her television in one of her rages—but I still don't know how to talk about dramas or actors, nor do I understand jokes from those reality shows. My husband thought this was charming when we first met and he would always try to work it into conversations somehow until I asked him to stop. Everyone who heard that small fact about me, though, assumed it was because my parents were focused on education—apparently there are many young parents these days who don't allow televisions in the house

----

because of their children. I understand how reality TV can damage your brain, because the way they replay the same punch line scenes with the laugh tracks over and over is enough to make one go mad. But when they hear the name of the provincial university I graduated from, they look at each other as if to say, *See, this is why progressive parenting is risky.*

IT'S NOT an original thought perhaps, but I think people watch so much TV because life would otherwise be unbearable. Unless you are born into a chaebol family or your parents were the fantastically lucky few who purchased land in Gangnam decades ago, you have to work and work and work for a salary that isn't even enough to buy a house or pay for childcare, and you sit at a desk until your spine twists, and your boss is somehow incompetent and a workaholic at the same time and at the end of the day you have to drink to bear it all.

But I grew up not knowing the difference between a bearable life and an unbearable life, and by the time I discovered there was such a thing, it was too late.

UNTIL I WAS EIGHT, I lived with my grandmother in a small stone house in Namyangju, northeast of Seoul. It had a low stone wall that ran around it, an outhouse with a leaky roof, and a pair of raised urns by the front door that my grandmother used to keep goldfish.

My grandmother slept in her room and I slept in the living room, on the floor next to a small white statue of the Virgin Mary, who had tears of blood painted down her cheeks. At night, when the rest of the world was asleep, the statue would seem to glow as it stared

----

down at me, with the tears turning black. When my grandmother's prayer group from church would meet at the house, she would sometimes tell the story of how I once tried to scrub the blood off the Virgin's cheeks with a kitchen brush, and she'd had to get the tears repainted.

The churchwomen chuckled and patted my head. But what she didn't tell them was that it had taken over a week for the cuts to fade from the backs of my legs after she beat me that night with a branch from a tree in the garden. I had loved that tree very much.

IN THE WINTERS, the house would get so cold that I would wear three or four sweaters at once and burrow under several of my grandmother's coats that still had the tags on them. Every fall, my aunt and uncle would send a new winter coat from America as a gift for my grandmother, but they were always too big for her, even though they were the smallest American size. Whenever she had company she would bring out the coats to show them off, and if the guests expressed admiration, she would shrug and say they weren't her size and she was hoping someone would buy them. I was always terrified that someone would rise to the bait, but I guess everyone thought a coat from America would cost too much.

OURS WAS NOT a wealthy neighborhood but the children who went to our school were usually dressed in neat clothes and had things like siblings and haircuts and change to spend in the stationery store. I didn't know this then, but when I look at the few photos I have from my childhood, I see I am dressed poorly, in my grandmother's old undershirts. I have never seen a photo of me wearing children's colors. It was not something I missed or craved or even noticed. The other children did not pick on me, but they did not seek my company either, and so it was a natural thing for me to play alone by the creek after school or in the garden of our church, where one of the nuns had given me a patch to plant things. The nuns, who saw my grandmother every week at services, had a better idea than most people what she was like.

IT WAS a pretty spring day when the letter arrived from America, I remember. Cherry blossoms had erupted over garden walls earlier that week, and my grandmother and I were walking back from the well on the mountain where we pumped our drinking water every few days. The mailman was at our gate.

"Letter from your son in America," he called, waving when he saw us.

"Really? He writes too often," said my grandmother merrily. She had not spoken to me for several days, but she was good at hiding her moods from others.

Because she wanted to brag more about the letter, she made a show of opening it on the spot.

"He's coming to visit this summer," she said, reading it slowly. "His wife and children too."

"My goodness! What an event. Is it his first time since he left for America?" The mailman, like the rest of our street, knew about my uncle, the prodigy who had been offered a job at a think tank in America after marrying my aunt, a treasured only child from a wealthy family.

My grandmother pursed her lips. "Yes," she replied, and then abruptly went inside the gate, leaving him puzzled.

- - - -

37

I flew in after her. My cousins were coming! The thought made me dizzy. My cousins, Somin and Hyungshik. I knew all about them from my aunt and uncle's letters. They were six and three to my eight years and they lived in Washington on a street where no other Asian people lived. Somin went to a school with American children and was learning wonderful things like ballet and soccer and violin while Hyungshik was starting a gymnastics class for toddlers.

My grandmother would plummet into her morose rages every time a letter came, but I would pore over the details in my aunt's graceful handwriting. My aunt would often include small gifts for me in her packages and letters, and every year she sent an American birthday card with flowers or animals. She also sent photos from Somin's birthday parties, which always showed her daughter in a frilly dress and a party hat, blowing out candles and surrounded by other little girls and boys, some with yellow or orange hair and skin the color of paper.

"Such ridiculous extravagance for a child!" my grandmother would say angrily before tossing the photos in the trash, or sometimes, if she was in a particularly dark mood, cutting them to pieces with scissors.

I didn't have high hopes for my younger cousin, Hyungshik—I only had a hazy idea of the physical capabilities of a three-and-a-half-year-old (could he even talk? I didn't know or care) and he would probably only serve to slow Somin and me down as we played. But I dreamed of taking Somin to my plot in the church garden to show her my flowering cucumber plants, which even my grandmother said made good oiji.

If things went really well, I would also take her to the stationery store next to the market, where the neighborhood children gathered

----

to play on the benches out front. I imagined them whispering to each other about how pretty and interesting she was, Wonna's cousin, the girl from America.

These were the daydreams I had in those days.

MY FATHER was the second of three sons, but it was my youngest uncle who lived in the big house in America. While my grandmother always belittled my aunt when speaking about her, she always made sure that the gifts my uncle sent from America were on display in the house when company came over. A shiny black camera would be left on the kitchen table, or a pouch of cosmetics would be spilling out on the living room floor.

One time, after her guests had left, she rummaged through her cosmetics bag and said that one of them must have taken her gold cream. At the time it was my grandmother's most prized possession—a heavy tub of face cream with a gold lid that my aunt had sent the previous month. E-suh-tae Ro-oo-duh was the name of the cream. After going through my little cupboard to make sure I hadn't taken it, she said that it must have been Mrs. Joo, who had always been bitter that her daughter had been rejected by all three of my grandmother's sons. My grandmother cursed the poor woman for days with a fearsome breadth of language that I have rarely heard since. I never saw Mrs. Joo at our house again, which saddened me as she tended to have a wrapped yeot candy in her purse and was one of the few women in the village who always had a lovely, motherly smile for me. She once saw me staring at the stationery store from the other side of the street and gave me an abrupt hug and a five-thousand-won bill.

- - - -

MY GRANDMOTHER often got into bitter fights over money. Sometimes it was with a shopkeeper who she said had cheated her, or sometimes it was with her sisters, who looked and talked like her and were just as nasty. Her only brother—the youngest of four siblings— had married a poor girl, and the abuse my grandmother and her sisters heaped upon her over the first few years of their marriage caused them to run away to China.

In contrast, my uncle in America not only had married rich but also was the only one of her sons who was making good money. The other sons she treated like idiots—I still to this day don't know what my oldest uncle did for a living—but she reserved the most contempt for my father, who had gone to a good college but worked at a sanitation company. It was the greatest irony in the world that she had taken in the child of the son who humiliated her the most, she often said to me.

On top of his poor choice of job, his most grievous offense was his choice of wife. "Insolent, stuck-up bitch" was how my grandmother referred to my mother. "I should have pushed her into the river long ago, when she was pregnant with you," she said to me.

Over the years, I gathered that my mother's family had erred in sending an insulting dowry that had not included the mink coat or the handbag my grandmother had hinted at throughout the engagement. My mother also had worn "unacceptable, arrogant" expressions on her face during her first year of marriage, when my parents lived with my grandmother.

When people asked why I lived with her, my grandmother said my parents had asked her to take me for a few years while my father

----

went to work in South America. "He's an international project man-ager, you know," she said. "They couldn't have a baby girl where there are wild animals in the jungle!"

When I was particularly bad, she told me that she would send me to the orphanage in the next town over and no one—especially my parents—would even notice. "When the boy is born, the daughter is cold rice anyway," she said. "Time to throw away."

Her eyes would fold into a smile when she said these things.

THE WEEK my cousins finally arrived, my grandmother hid every present that aunt and uncle had sent her over the years. I don't even know where she put them all—she must have taken them to her sisters' houses.

I don't know if she was born like this, or if my grandfather's early death had made her go a little insane.

BUT HOW EXCITED I was! Tremors ran up and down my small body when I woke up on the day they were supposed to arrive. I waited in the garden for hours in the morning, imagining I heard the footsteps. But it was only when I finally went back into the house in the afternoon that I heard the noise of a car outside our gate.

Through the window, I watched them open the gate and walk down our stone path—my stylish young aunt holding Hyungshik as if he were a baby, and Somin, in a sun-colored dress, skipping from one slab to the next. The three of them—my aunt, Hyungshik, and Somin—I could see their unusual brightness even from inside the house. There is something about happy people—their eyes are clear and their shoulders hang lower on their bodies.

My uncle, however—as he closed the gate and looked toward the house, I saw from his expression that he was one of us. He stood at the gate for a minute and I could see that he did not want to come in.

I STILL REMEMBER the sunflower dress my cousin was wearing that day. It flared out at the waist in a way I had never seen a dress do, and she had a matching yellow and red hairband adorned with a tiny sunflower. And her gold shoes! I think that was the first time I was ever struck speechless by the power of clothing.

WHILE MY AUNT was opening the suitcase of gifts they had brought from America, my grandmother had a look on her face that I knew meant serious trouble.

"Can I show Somin my vegetable garden in the churchyard?" I asked quickly. My uncle said yes and patted my head. He felt very sorry for me, I could see that.

"It's not too far, is it?" my aunt asked, a little worried. "Will they be okay on their own?"

"This isn't America," my grandmother said in a steely voice. "There are no madmen with guns. The children will be fine."

"Me too!" said Hyungshik, tugging at Somin's hand.

"Yes, you too," said my uncle, gazing at him with such fondness that it made me look away. Then my uncle met my eye and he and I knew that a scene was coming. He wanted both of his children out of the house when it happened.

"Let's go then," I said, springing up.

- - - -

I TOOK the long way to the church, up the little hill behind our house and past the shops at the end of the street. It was my aim to spend as much time out, and to have as many people see my expensively dressed cousins, as possible—this was a way of thinking that I had picked up from my grandmother, perhaps.

To my disappointment we only passed two or three people I did not know, and no one I wanted to see. The only thing I had accomplished by taking the long way was to make Hyungshik tired.

"My feet hurt," he whined, kicking at the curb. "I want to go back to my daddy. This is boring."

I looked at him with hatred welling in my chest. The walk was not going anything like I had hoped. Somin had not been very responsive as I'd chattered nervously about the nuns at the church, especially Sister Maria, who was my favorite. She was more preoccupied with getting Hyungshik to behave. He was walking erratically—lurching along for a few steps, then swaying from side to side. "Look, I'm a dead elephant," he would say with a giggle. And then he would whine again about being tired.

Instead of yelling at him, Somin laughed too. I couldn't understand why she was being so nice to him. She kept taking Hyungshik's hand, even as he would shake it off, and she would make a game out of it. "Look, I caught you!" she said.

I gave up talking to her while she was so preoccupied with her brother and sullenly led the way to the church. When we finally reached the church garden, I could have cried with relief. My small plot was in the far corner, right on the stream bank, and I had spent the entire summer making it into an orderly vision of beauty, with geometrically strung cucumbers and green peppers and squash.

"Here it is," I said with a dramatic sweep of the arm. Sister Maria had told me kindly the week before that she had never seen so many cucumbers from one flowering plant.

"This is your garden?" Somin was looking at me with her eyebrow raised. "This is why you made us walk that entire way? My garden in Washington is twenty times bigger than this," she said, starting to laugh. When she saw my face, she must have felt bad because she stopped talking, but Hyungshik had started to laugh too and then he broke away from her grip and ran toward my cucumber plants at top speed.

"Oiiii!" he yelled and reached for a particularly large one that I had been watching for days, grasping it with all his might. He did not see that it was covered with spikes.

The pain must have been delayed because he didn't start shrieking until a few seconds later, and then I watched as he clutched the thorny cucumber even tighter.

We both started running toward him—Somin and I—but I got to him first and wrenched his hand free and pulled him toward me by the back of his shirt. But he began screaming even louder, startling me, so I let go abruptly, causing him to trip and fall face-forward into my cucumber plant.

THE SCENE—I CAN see it, perfectly, in its entirety—the sky, the garden, Hyungshik's eyes, the gashes—it comes to me often. The horror of it all. I cannot wish it away.

Hyungshik gets up, and as he lifts his face, crying hysterically, we

- - - -

can see that it is bleeding. His face has gotten caught on some of the wires I'd rigged to support the vines. He puts his hands to his face and then sees the blood on his hands. When I start toward him again, he begins backing away, even as he keeps screaming.

A FEW YEARS AGO, during my junior year of college, my father actually took me to a mental health clinic. It was a small second-floor office in Itaewon, across the street from the tree-shielded American base. There were still prostitutes and hawkers and late-night murders in Itaewon back then, but it was the only neighborhood with a handful of psychiatrists who would accept cash on the spot and no questions asked about insurance or patients' names.

After circling to find a spot, my father finally parked the car in a hotel lot, something I had never seen him do before. It was a sign that he had resigned himself to spend some serious money that afternoon.

He had recently discovered that I had stopped going to classes, and instead was spending my days in a comic book café, immersed in piles of comic books. One of the ladies who worked in the supermarket next door tattled on me—she lived in our apartment and told my father that I was hanging out all the time looking homeless.

I had no answer for my parents when they asked, then yelled about why I had stopped attending classes. "You know exactly how much tuition is!" my father stammered in his anger. "Do you think we have money to throw away like that!" My stepmother just rocked back and forth in silent agitation.

I had no desire anymore to go to school. My major was a joke and so was my school. I would not be able to find a job since my father

----

had been forced into retirement from his company at fifty-five and so had no "pull" anymore, which was what anyone needed to get employment. So what was the point?

Leave me alone, I wanted to say. Besides, you owe me. But I didn't say it—I didn't say anything at all when he slapped me hard across the face and threatened to shave off my hair.

At night, I heard them discussing me in low tones in their bedroom. It was about a week after that that he told me he was taking me to talk to somebody in Itaewon.

"Do I have to speak English?" I asked, alarmed when I saw the English signs on the building and a heavy blond American woman emerging from the door that said, MENTAL HEALTH COUNSELING AVAILABLE.

"She speaks Korean," he said. "I'll wait here." He pointed to the fast-food restaurant across the street. "Call me when it's time to pay."

I thought about just walking away, but in the end curiosity propelled me. I had never seen a therapist before and haven't since, and I was curious what sorcery elicited these precipitous prices.

So we sat there, the therapist and I, for an hour of valiant, gentle parrying on her part. She was a disappointment to the imagination in both looks and speech, from the moment she walked into the small room wearing a cheap nylon sweater and faded pants that hardly inspired any respect, let alone soul-sharing.

"Would you like to talk about school? Why do you feel like you can't go to class?"

"I don't know."

She consulted her pad of paper. "Do you think you can talk to me about the blinding of your cousin when you were a child? I understand it was a freak accident."

"What? *No.*"

46

My father paid for the hour, cash, in a fat wad of ten-thousand-won bills that made me flinch, but he looked relieved. For that much money, copious fixing must have taken place. I could see him recommending this to his friends in the future—an instant solution! An American-educated therapist!

He did not respond when the receptionist asked what day I would be returning for my second session, and I was the one who said we would call to schedule later that week.

IF YOU ASKED me why I married my husband, I would say it was because his mother was dead.

I found out the second time I met him—our first had been a blind date—and when he described his mother's brain cancer and her daily radiation therapy and metastasis and ultimately her death, surrounded by her children in her hospital bed, he did not see the flash that must have leapt into my eyes. He was bent over his dish of pasta, his face closed in sorrow as he told me of her pain and his, while I listened, electrified.

There was actually another thing that made up my mind that day; the fact that he had chosen a restaurant near my house so it would be convenient for me. I had been on many a blind date at restaurants that were near the man's work, or near the man's favorite bar, or, the very worst, near the man's home. The better he looked on paper, the more selfish he was, that much I knew.

But this man, not only was he kind, but he had a dead mother. If we had a child—and I wanted a baby, a wee creature who would be completely mine—she would not interfere with its upbringing. Nor could she ever take it away from me. It was too good to be true.

You see, I have long understood what most women learn by fire

----

after they are married—that the hate mothers-in-law harbor toward their daughters-in-law is built into the genes of all women in this country. The bile festers below the surface, dormant but still lurking, until the son becomes of marriageable age; the resentment at being pushed aside, the anger of becoming second in their sons' affections. It was not just my grandmother; I have seen it time and time again. That is the one storyline of every Korean drama that I recognize and understand, if I do not comprehend much else. So I rose from my torpor and jumped at my chance to avoid it.

That was what was most important to me. At the time.

Miho

I wake up to the sound of rain on our roof. After years of living in soundproof, prewar student apartments in New York, the sound reminds me of my childhood dorm room at the Loring Center. There, my bed was by the window and I would often go to sleep to the sound of rain hitting the pavement. Now, I live on the top floor of a small cheaply built four-story office-tel. The building is called Color House, although the outside is painted gray and the lettering is white. There isn't a speck of color anywhere across the entire four stories and the rent is dirt cheap, but only on our floor. I didn't realize the aversion to the number 4 was only an Asian superstition until I went to America, where they have an aversion to the number 13 because of some horror movie with a clown. Or a vampire, I forget. Anyway, the owner can't hide the fourth floor of a four-story build-

----

ing like you can in tall apartments by just skipping the elevator buttons from three to five, and so I'm one of the small group of girls living in the two tiny apartments on this floor, grateful for the zip code and the subway station two blocks away.

As a child, I could not have imagined that I would one day live in the busiest part of Seoul, with its shimmering skyline and whimsical sculptures that stand guard outside each skyscraper. It is still amazing to me how comfortable people my age look as they walk in and out of marbled lobbies with disposable coffee cups in hand and employee passes dangling from their necks.

My life before I went to New York was a small restaurant in a field of flowers and then an orphanage in the middle of a forest. A provincial arts school in the mountains.

When Sujin wrote to me to come live with her after my New York fellowship ended, I leapt at the suggestion. She had left the Loring Center shortly before I had and we'd corresponded avidly over the years, swapping stories of Seoul and New York. We did not talk about the past much.

Sujin had told me that as office-tels go, hers was very small—usually they are dense high-rises with hundreds of units—and I told her to keep an eye out for a room opening up, so that I could book my plane ticket as soon as she gave the word.

She had been worried that I would be let down after my New York experience, but I told her I love the building, and it's true. It was built for the unfettered.

It's mostly girls who live here—apart from a married couple who live in the apartment below us. All day long girls go in and out in clean, pretty outfits. I think I'm the only girl in the entire office-tel who doesn't wear full makeup or have dyed or permed hair. The first time Ara saw my hair she gasped and she hasn't been able to stop

- - - -

touching it whenever she sees me. I took it for flattery (usually people in the States would exclaim how much they envied my hair) until I saw her shaking her head sorrowfully at Sujin as she ran her fingers through it. *So raw,* she wrote in her small notepad.

BECAUSE MY BEDROOM is next to the front door, which is next to the stairs, which echo loudly, each morning I hear the conversation of the married couple downstairs when they leave for the day. They are older, in their thirties, and the husband is desperately affectionate to the wife, who always sounds like she is somewhere far away.

"Wonna, do you want me to pick anything up from the store today?" he asks eagerly. "Are you craving anything in particular?" Three seconds later the wife responds, "What? Oh, whatever," before they clickety-clack down the loudest stairs in the world.

Sometimes, I see the wife sitting on the steps when I come back late at night from the studio. She never raises her head as I walk past. It's all very rude but I am used to her.

I listen to the rain a little while longer, trying to remember why I feel more agitated than normal this morning. Then it washes over me—today I'm supposed to meet my boyfriend, Hanbin, for lunch. At his parents' house.

It is a momentous occasion of epic implications.

His mother will be there, and perhaps—and I can't spend too long thinking about it as it makes me so anxious—his father too, who is usually busy playing golf or meeting famous people from other countries.

"I want to show you the Ishii, it finally came last week," Hanbin said last night, when he came to pick me up from my studio at school.

It seems indecent, somehow, that someone can just own an Ishii fish sculpture to put in their house, to touch if they want, whenever they want. The only times I have ever seen one were at the Gagosian in New York, from a distance, and at the National Gallery in D.C. after waiting two torturous hours in line with a full bladder because Ruby wanted to see it.

"And don't worry, Mr. Choi will be there too," he said when he saw my face. He was referring to his mother's driver, who has picked us up several times before and has always been very polite to me. I looked at him in utter exasperation, my handsome, confident, clue-less boy, who thinks that his family's elderly driver pottering about his national treasure of a house would be the source of any comfort.

I stood up. "I need to go back to my work," I said. We were in the empty café downstairs because I don't allow him in my actual studio. He hasn't seen anything I've been working on in the year that I have been back in Korea.

"Can I come see?" he said. "It's so ridiculous that you won't show me."

I shook my head and frowned.

"No, not now," I said. "Besides, my studio mate is there working too and she will get so upset if anyone else comes in."

This was a lie, as the girl who shared my studio left months ago for a new fellowship at another university. And even if she had still been here, she would have loved nothing more than a chance to gos-sip with a good-looking older guy with lots of questions. She had been so chatty while she was working—she usually worked on fluo-rescent reproductions of Silla Dynasty crowns and belts that re-quired no thinking, apparently—that I had been on the verge of complaining to the department head when she told me she'd been offered the fellowship, which awarded ten million won more

----

than what we got at our current university. She had bragged with intent to sting, but when I understood she'd be leaving immediately, I enveloped her in such a heartfelt hug that she was visibly discomfited.

"I will see you tomorrow," I said to Hanbin firmly.

"I'll pick you up at your apartment?" he asked. He knew I didn't like him coming to the office-tel either. I don't want him around the other girls, especially my roommate.

"No, that's silly. Let's just meet at Gyeongbokgung and you can pick me up there. Why would you come all the way down south? It's a waste of time."

Hanbin sighed and took my hand.

"You drive me nuts," he said. "I must be a sick masochist, drawn to this."

I don't say anything because it must be true. He was that way with Ruby too, before me.

IN THE LIVING ROOM, my painfully plastic roommate, Kyuri, is watching her favorite drama. It's clear from her makeup and hair that she hasn't gone to sleep yet from the night before. In her lap, she's caressing a red lambskin jumbo Chanel bag like it's a puppy, while staring at the TV with bloodshot, unseeing eyes. This is odd behavior—usually she keeps her bags covered and enshrined in her closet, rarely taking them out unless there's some pressing occasion.

"That's pretty," I say, eyeing the bag as I make myself a cup of coffee. "Was it another present?"

"Yeah, it's from my gaming company CEO," Kyuri says without taking her eyes off the TV. "Isn't it gorgeous?"

Kyuri keeps a meticulous log of her presents and how much she

----

sells them for, so that she doesn't lose track of who gave her what. She has an arrangement with one of the luxury resale shops at the corner of Rodeo Drive in Apgujeong—they know she'll hand the bags over to them completely new, and she knows she's getting the best price in the neighborhood for them. And sometimes, when she has to see a client who's been asking about his present, she'll run and borrow a bag from the store for a night—they always have every kind in stock, the kinds that clients give their girls anyway. She tends to ask for the same exact one from all her men so that it's less confusing to keep track of them, and she can just keep one and sell the rest that come in.

I know that anyone who is remotely respectable would die of horror before they would be seen with her. But she makes a lot of money and saves a lot of it too, unlike other room salon girls apparently—or anyone our age for that matter—and it's hard not to respect her for that. Kyuri doesn't drink Starbucks.

As roommates go, she and I get along pretty well, but mostly it's because we don't see each other too much. During the day I'm usually at the studio and she leaves for the salon and then work in the late afternoon. When she comes home I'm either still in the studio or asleep.

The one time we almost got into a fight was a few months ago, when we were drinking together on the weekend and she accused me of feeling superior to her because I was pretty without having surgery.

"You know, you're just lucky that your kind of face is trendy these days," she said, her eyes clouded over from anger and too much drink. "But you don't have to be such a condescending snob about surgery."

When I protested that I didn't know what she was talking about, she fired off examples of criticisms I had voiced when we were watching dramas together.

"That was about Jeon Seul! You agreed with me!" I said. "You said her new nose looked like Michael Jackson's!"

"No, I *know*," she said, slumping onto her side. "I know what you think. You're a stuck-up bitch."

She fell asleep on the table and I was so vexed I didn't even move her to her bed. The next morning, she didn't remember our spat and came to my room to ask if I had an ice pack—in the night she had fallen off the chair and bruised her expensive face.

BUT I DO have to admit I feel a pinch of pride when someone asks if I have had surgery and I can say no. Our department head has gone so far as to make me promise not to cut my hair, which is really torturously unmanageable now that it hits my waist. Whenever I talk about cutting it off, department chair be damned, Hanbin gathers it in his hands and starts speaking to it tenderly as if it is a threatened child. "I won't let her do it, don't you worry," he croons. And Kyuri hasn't even read the articles and reviews of my work that unfailingly describe me as "the naturally beautiful artist-in-residence."

"So I'm supposed to have lunch with Hanbin's mother at their house today," I tell Kyuri, against my better judgment. "Not sure what I'm going to wear."

Kyuri sits up straight, her red eyes suddenly aglitter.

"Really? I thought she hated you!" she says.

I make a face.

"Well, it might not happen, but that's the plan, anyway. Do you think my black long-sleeved dress is too . . . black?" I ask, sipping my coffee.

She shakes her head. "It's not the fact that it's black—didn't you buy it at the market in Itaewon? You have to wear something *really*

- - - -

expensive. It's more about your attitude when you wear it. You have to have that confidence you get from wearing something that costs too much."

Kyuri gets up and slings the Chanel bag over her shoulder like she's going out.

"You can borrow something of mine! Let me check what I have right now."

For her work clothes, Kyuri uses a clothing rental store that specializes in room salon girls. This means a lot of short skirts and tight polyester dresses. I highly doubt she'll have anything I will want to wear, but when I follow her into her room, she pulls three surprisingly demure dresses from her closet that still have Joye department store tags attached.

I run my fingers over a high-necked cobalt sheath in admiration. Whose taste is this? Certainly not Kyuri's. She doesn't offer an explanation though, and I don't ask.

"I think this one is perfect," she says, holding up an olive silk dress with cap sleeves and a chiffon belt. "It's got color *and* sleeves."

I take it from her and hold it up in the mirror, and I have to admit, the dress looks beautiful. I read the price tag and shudder. "No way, what if I spill something on this?"

She wrinkles her perfect, upturned nose. "That's okay—this is really important! I want you to marry Im Ga-yoon's son and introduce me to celebrities all the time."

She doesn't see the horror on my face as she gives me the dress on the hanger.

"Just try it on while I go wash my face. I have to start getting ready for my skin appointment," she says and heads for her bathroom.

I laugh because I know that she will put on a full face of makeup just to have the nurses at the dermatologist's wash it all off for her

----

facials and treatments. Meanwhile, she shudders at my freckles and general lack of skin care, for refusing to implement her ten-step regimen twice a day. Sujin loves to compare the latest face masks and serums with her—Kyuri has what seems like a hundred bottles and jars on her vanity—but I barely remember to wash my face before going to sleep.

Slipping out of my pajamas, I try on the dress and am buttoning up the back when she returns, her face damp and shiny, and helps me fasten it. "Don't you love it?" she asks before sitting at her vanity. "It looks amazing on you," she says with approval, looking at me through the mirror over her collection of vials and face masks of all shapes and sizes. She pulls her hair back with a fluffy band and starts her ritual by applying drops of serum on her skin with her fingertips. Then she takes out a small syringe and pumps a honey-colored fluid over her face.

"What's that?" I ask. I am always fascinated by how much time she spends on skin care.

"Ampoule with stem-cell extract," she says matter-of-factly. "My skin is so dry this morning because I drank so much yesterday. This ampoule is just to tide me over until I get the full treatment at the clinic. You know, you should go with me this morning, so that you'll look your best for his mom. I can probably squeeze you in because I'm such a favorite customer."

I'm tempted, because Kyuri's skin gleams like pure glass right now, but the thought of lying still on a spa table flares my anxiety. I shake my head. She sighs at the look on my face and then starts applying tiny dots of eye cream with her fourth finger.

"So this is why you've been so jittery," she says. "You know, I was going to make you drink this weekend to cheer up. It's been so depressing around here because of your nervous energy, you know

----

that? Now, what about this Bottega to go with the dress?" She pulls out an intricately woven bag from her closet and pushes it into my hands.

HANBIN'S MOTHER, or Im Ga-yoon, as the rest of the country knows her, was one of "the Triumvirate" of the 1970s—three Miss Koreas turned actresses that starred in most of the movies, dramas, and commercials during that decade. She was the oldest of the three and the most prolific, with an iconic role as a nun turned femme fatale in the hit series *My Name Is Star*. They used to say that you couldn't spot a car on the road in the entire country when *My Name Is Star* was on. After a brief but damaging affair with her younger costar, she disappeared from the public eye for a few years until it came out that she had secretly married the younger son of the KS Group, a second-tier conglomerate that manufactured water tanks and heaters. And a decade after that, she opened an art gallery near Gyeongbokgung Palace and reinvented herself as the first dealer to bridge the celebrity world and the art world in Korea. Celebrities flocked to her to decorate their homes, and it's been conjectured that she's made more money than her father-in-law.

All these things I found out by reading obsessively about Hanbin's family online and in the gossip pages of women's magazines. The titles of the articles ranged from "Im Ga-yoon and Husband Snap Up Land on Jeju Island" to "Is Im Ga-yoon's Gallery Inflating Prices to Celebrities?" and "KS Group Whistle-Blower's Accusations: Will Im Ga-yoon's Brother-in-Law Go to Jail?" Usually they were accompanied by paparazzi shots of Im Ga-yoon in snowy furs and sunglasses emerging from a car outside her gallery.

I've met her a few times now. The first time was in New York, at

----

Hanbin's graduation from Columbia. Since returning to Korea, Hanbin has ambushed her twice, once by taking me to the airport to greet her on the way back from a gallery sales trip to Hong Kong, the second, arranging for the three of us to have lunch for his birthday at his favorite restaurant at the Reign Hotel. The first time, the only things she said to me were "Oh, hello" and "Goodbye," answering Hanbin's questions in the car with monosyllables. The second time, at the lunch, she asked me gentle questions about my family, questions that showed she knew all about me already and I shouldn't attempt to gentrify myself. "So, how old were you when you last saw your parents?" "And your uncle, he ran a . . . taxi restaurant?" (with a shudder). And the kicker, "It's just so wonderful how there are so many opportunities these days for people like you, isn't it? Our country has become such an encouraging place."

I could have looked hurt or angry, I know, but I settled on chirpy as my default state a while ago, because I remembered something Ruby said to me once back in New York.

"Rich people are fascinated by happiness," she said. "It's something they find maddening."

I STOP BY Joye department store to buy miniature orchids from the flower shop on the first floor. It costs ten times more than the flower market near my apartment, but the pot bears the Joye logo and name. When I meet Hanbin outside the subway station nearest to his house, he sees the shopping bag and says there was no need to buy a gift, but I can tell he approves.

Hanbin's house is modern and astonishing—all gray slate and glass and slanted roofs—atop a hill in Sungbukdong behind a tall brick wall. When the gate opens for us, my heart drops in an in-

----

credulous lurch that takes my breath. He has only told me about the inconveniences, of how cold it can get in the winters, how tourists and journalists tramp about the neighborhood to catch a glimpse beyond the gate, how friends of the house's famous Dutch architect show up for impromptu calls to examine his first commission in Asia. The architecture reminds me of Japanese museums that I studied in school, all stark lines and muted beauty.

But it's not until I am standing on the lawn—and what house in Seoul, let alone one in the most coveted arts neighborhood, has a *lawn of real grass*?—that I realize I almost despise Hanbin right now. Certainly his mother.

The inside of the house seems to be bursting with even more white flowers than the gardens. Heaps of orchids and peonies in unusual arrangements are everywhere and I look at my little pot sadly.

"I will go tell your mother that you are here," says the man who opened the front door for us. He bows, takes my coat, and hands me a pair of leather slippers from the marble shoe closet. Despite his formal speech to Hanbin, he is dressed casually—just a long-sleeved (striped!) T-shirt and wrinkled khakis, not the suit or uniform I realize I'd been expecting.

"That's all right—I'll go up and tell her myself," says Hanbin. He asks me to wait in the living room to the left of the foyer, then bounds down the hallway to the right.

The living room is cavernous—about the height and size of a basketball court, with groupings of chairs and coffee tables in each corner. In the center is the Ishii fish, the size and color of a baby elephant—a beautiful thing that glistens as I draw near. The art on the walls is also modern Japanese, a mix of Tsunoda, Ohira, and Sakurai. I sit down in the far corner, next to another tiny Ishii the color of an angry cloud.

The man who opened the door brings me some tea on a tray. The tea is a small mauve flower that opens in the water as it steeps. He adjusts the flowers on the coffee table without saying a word, and I realize that Hanbin was right, Mr. Choi the driver would have been a comfort to me if he'd been here, which he's not.

"Mother's actually not feeling well so it'll just be us today," says Hanbin, coming toward me. "She has a terrible headache and she's lying down."

He's looking at me a little too earnestly as he is saying this, as if he's forcing himself not to look away. Either he's lying or he thinks she's lying and my heart begins pounding loudly. Acid starts to trickle through my veins. He does not say she apologizes for not coming down.

"That's terrible. I hope she feels better soon." What else is there to say, really? We stare into our cooling teas, then he clears his throat.

"I'll show you the gardens while they're getting lunch ready. Unless you want cake or ddeok? Are you hungry?"

I shake my head and he takes my hand and leads me back outside through the foyer. On the way out, I see two uniformed women peeping at me from a doorway and I jerk my head so that they are not in my line of vision. When we reach the door, the man who opened it for us earlier materializes with our coats.

The gardens stretch around the house, unfolding into a series of miniature landscapes. My favorite is the pine grove in the back, a maze of carefully designed and pruned pine trees. The scent has a calming effect on my nerves.

Through the trees, the view floats up toward us. I can see other massive houses scattered on the hill and the rest of the city sprawled out beneath them.

As Hanbin walks in front of me, stooping beneath low-hanging

- - - -

branches, my heart burns. It is too much, this house, his mother, the art. What was he thinking, bringing me here?

"That's my grandmother's house," Hanbin says, pointing to a white two-story house in the distance. It's a Western-style house surrounded by rosebushes and more pine trees. His paternal grandmother is on the brink of dementia, and has lately taken to accusing the servants of stealing her money.

"And over there, that's Ruby's father's house," he says. My head snaps toward where he is pointing, to the right of his grandmother's house. Even from a distance it looms like a fortress, morose and dark, the gardens a sinister moat. But perhaps it's because I am seeing it with Ruby's voice whispering in my head.

We stand there, saying nothing, until he's the one who starts walking back first.

After lunch—a painfully awkward affair served in a spectacular sunlit dining room by two silent men—I ask Hanbin to drop me off at my studio. He doesn't protest, although I know he wanted to see a movie, and in the car we are both quiet.

"Can I come in?" he asks again when he pulls up in front of the art studios on the university campus.

"Absolutely not," I say, giving him a quick kiss on the cheek before getting out of the car. "I don't know why you keep asking."

Scowling, he drives away.

IN THE STUDIO, I feel the great wash of relief I always feel when I walk in through the door. Tying my hair back, I head into the bathroom to change into my work clothes and hang Kyuri's dress carefully on the door.

The terrible drumming in my heart subsides as I pick up my small

----

chisels and sit down at my workstation. The scéne that I have been trying to bring to form—the picture that's so clear in my head—is that of a night sea with a girl on a boat. Her long hair covering her face, she's leaning forward over the water, wearing a sheer nightgown and a blood-red ruby ring on her left ring finger. She is riveted by something in the water.

Last week, I started to carve her out of plaster. Her face was the easiest part—it's the hair that will take the longest. I think I will make the sea out of ostrich feathers and the boat will be a real boat—a wooden rowboat, I am thinking, with faded red paint.

After a few hours of carving, I have to set the chisels aside to start working on a watercolor of the same scene. I just want a rendering of what I had in my head before I forget anything, although such loss is hard to imagine. This is going to be the sixth in my latest Ruby series. The other five pieces—paintings and sculptures—are sitting in the back of my studio, in the shadows. They were pathetic manifestations of what I had in my head, of course, but they are as finished as they can be for now.

IN A SHOE BOX somewhere under my bed is a stack of black-and-white photographs—my first Ruby series, if I choose to think about it that way. My favorite shows Ruby in a white fur coat, a preposterous thing of shorn mink with cream silk lining and a matching hat. She is standing on our school library steps (how I miss winter in New York!), snow piled up on either side of her, lights glowing in the windows. Underneath the coat, she is wearing a knee-length ink black dress, stockings, and precarious high heels. She looks happy, her eyes crinkled in a rare, crooked smile.

We were on our way to a gallery opening that evening and we had

----

stopped by the library to see if they had any books on the featured artist—a German painter who specialized in neon-tinted birch trees. "All we need to read is the introduction," she said authoritatively as she ran a finger along the spine of the book we found in the European wing. "That's all you need," she said. When she found the book, she skimmed the introduction twice and made me memorize the titles of three of the artist's most noted works.

Hanbin picked us up that night in front of the library. Or did we meet him at the gallery? He picked us up most nights, anyway, and he was certainly there for that particular exhibition. He bought a painting for Ruby and surprised her with it for her birthday a month later. It was the cheapest one at the exhibition, he whispered to me at her party. She loved that painting so much—a fluorescent forest of birches, streaked with shocking pink and yellow, in a thick gold frame inscribed with her name. RUBY SO-WON LEE.

I wonder where the painting is now, maybe up on a wall at her father's house, or in some closet crowded with skeletons.

THERE WAS a short article about Ruby's younger brother in the news the other day—the American news, not Korean news. His exotic car rental start-up had just received funding from the second-biggest venture capital firm in San Francisco. I found this puzzling for many reasons—why would Mu-cheon need funding at all, why was he trying to work on something as insignificant as a car rental company in America, in English no less, and what happened to law school?

But when I asked Hanbin about it, he just shrugged and said, "Why not?" which effectively stopped any further line of conjecturing. Hanbin did say that he thought the funding thing was more

----

about publicity than about actual need, and that the Silicon Valley investors probably needed Mu-cheon's connections more than Mu-cheon needed them. An illegitimate son is still an heir, potent and wary, a prize to be carefully wooed over long periods of time.

WHEN I THINK about Ruby, I remember her best just lounging on her white sofa in her Tribeca apartment, caressing a piece of jewelry she had bought that day, surrounded by impossibly beautiful things. She was a born collector with a devastating eye, who could make harmony out of the myriad pieces she purchased. We would walk into an antiques store and she would home in on seemingly incongruous, heart-poundingly extravagant knickknacks—a century-old ebony jewelry box encrusted with uncut gemstones, gold-edged teacups from Russia, a woebegone nineteenth-century doll with ash blond curls and a wardrobe of miniature, exquisite dresses—but when they came home to her apartment they looked as if they had been grown there, sown from other seeds of beauty. Her apartment nourished a part of me I didn't know I had—a desolate craving to touch and see and luxuriate in objects.

The thing about her was that she knew I was entranced by her things, but she didn't mind. I was already firmly categorized in her mind as an artist, a creator and lover of beauty. My worshipping of her taste fed her vanity as a collector.

"Just because you buy a bunch of expensive things doesn't mean you have a *collection*," she said contemptuously once while reading an article in the *Times* about the latest spending habits of the new rich in China.

I understood what she meant though. Her eye wasn't exactly a gift, but more of an instinct, as natural to her as melancholia, or distrust.

- - - -

I MET THEM all in New York—Ruby, Hanbin, their group of friends. It had been an unfathomable step for me, going to New York to start a program at SVA. It was my first time on a plane, my first time out of the country, my first time stepping out from under the umbrella of the Loring Center, my first time following a star. Among other shocks, I had been bewildered to find so many Koreans so at home in the streets and cafés and stores of New York—and in the hallways and classrooms of SVA—for whom studying abroad and traveling back and forth by themselves were commonplace occurrences. For some, it was something they had been doing since they were children.

I was there on a SeoLim visual arts scholarship, a fact that Ruby found amusing when she interviewed me for a job at her gallery. I didn't understand why she laughed until another girl who was there on the same scholarship told me months later that Ruby's father was Lim Jun Myeong, the CEO of SeoLim Group and one of the most famous men in Korea. Ruby and her brother Mu-cheon were younger than his other children by more than two decades, and so it was rumored that Lady Lim was not their mother and they were illegitimate by way of a receptionist in a SeoLim office building.

I'd responded to an ad on the bulletin board in our department building—a forlorn, empty square occasionally punctuated by ads for babysitting jobs posted by our cash-strapped professors. I'd needed a job desperately—the scholarship covered my tuition, my room and board, and the plane fare but not much else—and an ad in Korean looked like a lifeline. I plucked it off the board and retreated to my room to study it.

It was remarkable not only for its contents but for its appearance—gold-foil-pressed script on thick olive-colored paper—which looked more like a wedding invitation than a student flyer.

"Art Assistant Wanted for New Gallery Opening" was the header, and underneath, in smaller script, it said, "Thorough knowledge of contemporary art and fluency in Korean and English a plus."

I imagine there wasn't much competition for the job, but I was ecstatic when she hired me along with four other girls from various universities throughout the city. I was put in charge of designing the gallery's catalogs, flyers, and postcards. The printing costs alone astounded me but she paid them without even glancing at the bills I would nervously hand over.

For nearly three weeks, our small group worked into the night, Ruby and I usually staying the latest as I would help her with anything she needed, even running out to bring back coffee and croissants, all bought on Ruby's credit card, of course. The other girls tried to befriend her, but she would only respond coolly and monosyllabically to anything that wasn't work-related, and this bred resentment. I didn't realize until later that these girls all came from wealthy families and didn't need the money like I did—they took the jobs so that they could meet Ruby.

Sometimes, I would just stare at her as she was working. She cut a striking figure, no matter what she was doing. She wore only lipstick and no other makeup, although I suspected she had had her eyeliner tattooed, and her clothes were always a marvel, consistently stunning in both style and cut in unusual color combinations. She had a low voice and a rare smile, which sometimes flashed across her face like a comet.

"The dean loves her because of all the donations her father made," said one of the Parsons girls after Ruby asked us to work on Sunday

- - - -

morning. "And he only made them because she didn't get into Stanford like everyone else in their family."

"I heard it was the biggest disgrace—even all the cousins-in-laws' neighbors get in if they're connected to the SeoLim family," said another girl, who went to Tisch. "Then apparently she wanted to go to Yale, but her boyfriend's ex is going there so she threw a fit and decided to come here."

"No, no, it was because of a huge drug bust at Ashby," said the first girl, flipping her hair. "She was supposed to get kicked out, but they let her graduate because her dad donated a new gym. My cousin goes to Ashby and she said it cost twenty million dollars and it's outfitted with all the latest SeoLim technology."

Ruby came in and glanced around the room until she saw me. "Miho, can you come help with these flyers?" Without a word to anyone else she stalked back out immediately and I could see the other girls' dissatisfaction printed on their faces. Which pleased me, because they had been ignoring me once they discovered I was on scholarship and hadn't gone to a boarding school in America.

"I've never heard of it," said another SVA girl when I told her the name of my public middle school in Korea. "Which neighborhood is it in again?" And when I told her it was in Cheongju, her eyebrows bounced sky high before she turned swiftly back to her phone.

But I didn't care, and it wasn't like I could have lied about my schools anyway. For all its millions of people, Korea is the size of a fishbowl and someone is always looking down on someone else. That's just the way it is in this country, and the reason why people ask a series of rapid-fire questions the minute they meet you. Which neighborhood do you live in? Where did you go to school? Where do you work? Do you know so-and-so? They pinpoint where you are on the national scale of status, then spit you out in a heartbeat.

THE THING ABOUT Ruby was, it wasn't only me or other Koreans who found her fascinating. I would be sitting with her in a coffee shop or even a library and people would just steal glances at her the entire time. I couldn't quite figure out what it was—the sheen of her skin and her eclectic, expensive clothes or stony expression, I did not know. But it was only the most oblivious of men who would try to talk to her. Once, we were eating dinner in a new salad place near her apartment when a man approached her. He looked foreign— Italian?—and he was young and slickly dressed in a well-cut suit, clearly a finance type stepping out for a quick take-out dinner to eat at his desk. He had been looking in our direction while standing in line, and after he had picked up his bag of food, he came and stood by our table.

"Excuse me, sorry to interrupt," he said with a slight accent, looking both cute and confident. "I have to tell you that you are very beautiful."

Ruby didn't look up from her food and kept eating slowly, not saying anything.

"Can I ask if you live in this neighborhood? I live and work around the corner," he said, pointing to the window at a building that he clearly thought we should know.

His smile began to falter when neither of us responded.

"Okay, well, have a good dinner," he said, almost sullen now, and headed for the exit. As he opened the door, I distinctly heard the word "bitch" muttered under his breath.

"So ridiculous!" I said lightly to Ruby.

"Maybe I can have him killed," she said, her eyes slitted.

I laughed, then stopped when she glared at me.

"Next time this happens, take a photo of the guy," she said. "How dare he think he can just walk up and talk to me?" She clenched her jaw and continued to eat, eyes flashing wildly now.

I nodded and murmured agreement. I was still learning what to say and how to react around her.

RUBY DID TELL me, a few months later, after the gallery had opened and the other girls had quit and we'd had to find replacements who were not Korean, that my behavior was now passing muster.

We were drinking at a bar in K-Town, waiting for Hanbin and one of his friends to join us. Ruby had wordlessly handed me a real-looking fake ID with my gallery staff photo earlier that evening and I was still heady from the rush of finally ordering my first real drink at a New York bar. It was such a different world from Korea, where alcohol flowed freely for underage drinkers with only the most half-hearted of pretenses to uphold any restrictions.

"You know, I like that you're a quick study," she said suddenly, smiling a crooked smile.

"What do you mean?" I asked.

She waved an airy hand over my outfit. I was wearing a black cashmere sweater and a long, tight leather skirt that I'd bought at a thrift store in Brooklyn. I'd heard that designers donated their unsold samples from last season there, and I'd sift through the racks for hours, searching for designer pieces with tags still attached.

"Remember when you'd wear *pink fake suede*?" she said with a peal of laughter.

I blushed and pretended to slap her lightly on the arm. "So what?

Lots of designers use pink every season! Stop being such a boring New Yorker."

"And you're so easy to tease!" She choked with more amusement. Then Hanbin came in with another good-looking, well-dressed boy from Columbia and we were fortunately diverted. But afterward, her mirth would come back to me and I would sit up in bed abruptly in the middle of the night, my cheeks aflame.

BACK THEN, Hanbin constituted the third of our trio, trailing behind us while Ruby and I would walk a few steps ahead. He was a quiet but attentive boyfriend to Ruby, always driving us places, getting us into clubs with lines, arranging front-row tickets to plays and exhibitions and fashion shows that Ruby wanted to see. The two of them never displayed any affection publicly and never took any photos together, which I thought was strange. Only once did I see them embrace, and that was late one night when I was leaving her apartment after the three of us had been watching a movie. I looked behind me as the door closed and Ruby was laying her head against Hanbin's chest as he put his arms around her. They looked so peaceful and complete and so utterly content that I stood transfixed until the door slowly shut. I never saw them touch again.

Every time I had a show—part of my scholarship requirement was that I had to exhibit as much as I could—Ruby and Hanbin both came and stayed a long time, which meant a great deal to me. They even came for the freshman show, in which I was only exhibiting two pieces. Ruby never said much—just posed questions about other students' work—but Hanbin was surprisingly interested in my process. He would always ask, "How long did this one take you?" and "What was the inspiration for this piece?" He looked sweetly unsure about

----

what was appropriate to ask and I would have to resist the urge to reach up and touch the small wrinkles that formed on his forehead.

Sometimes, and I lived for these moments, Ruby would be late or she would text and cancel altogether when Hanbin and I would already be waiting for her. He would frown and sigh a little—he was unfailingly disappointed when she stood him up, even as often as it was—but then he would turn to me and say with a shrug, "So, do you still want to get something to eat?" And my heart would rise and I would nod a little too enthusiastically, and later in secret writhe with self-loathing.

"We don't have an artistic bone in our entire family, even my gallerist mother," he said to me once when he and Ruby came over to my studio to see renderings of my final project.

I was showing him some sketches, which I was planning to turn into a series.

"I really love what you're doing with this one," he said reverently, holding up a rough sketch of a girl in a well, looking upward with her hands outstretched. It had been buried under a pile of other sketches and he had gone through them all. "This is quite incredible."

"It's all very morbid," I mumbled, embarrassed. I'd forgotten that sketch was in the pile, and the girl's eyes had turned out so differently from what I had envisioned in my head. It had been a class assignment on family that I had never turned in.

"But that's why we like you," said Ruby, from the corner where she had been studying one of my sculptures of blind children. "That's why *I* like you," she said. "I think you can see things very clearly that others can't because they are so easily distracted."

I had no idea what she was talking about, but I smiled so as not to dispel such heightened notions of me.

IN THE WINTER, it was a thing among the rich Korean kids to book a hotel suite for the night and drink there, even though all of them lived in beautiful apartments. One time, we drove to Boston because Ruby wanted to. "I'm so bored here," she said, and collected her brother Mu-cheon, who went to Columbia with Hanbin and lived uptown, and a few other friends from boarding school. And off we went to stay at the Corycian Hotel on Boylston Street, with plans of shopping and clubbing.

Ruby insisted on driving herself in her red Maserati and Hanbin sat up front while Mu-cheon and I sat in the back. He was passed out because he was hungover from the night before, and I sat quietly, staring out the window at the snow-covered trees whizzing by.

I had been trying not to think about the scene I had witnessed the week before. I had been walking out of the library, wondering why Ruby had not contacted me for over a week, when I saw her and another Korean SVA girl—Jenny—getting out of a taxi with oversize shopping bags. They were laughing as they grappled with the bags and the driver had to get out of his car to help them. I could see from the logos on the bags that it had been a Fifth Avenue day. A few weeks before that, she had left me out of dinner at her house with several other study-abroad friends. I had found out about it when I overheard two girls raving about the private chef she had hired.

Only stopping twice, Ruby drove all the way to a little restaurant in Boston's Koreatown, where we ate dinner and started drinking; the owner knew Hanbin and didn't bother us for ID. The place got louder and louder as it became packed with drunk students.

- - - -

There were six of us to start with, but soon more people started coming as everyone began calling and getting calls from their friends in Boston.

Around 1 A.M. we ordered more soju for takeout, and with plastic pails in hand, we left. Ruby drove slowly and jerkily.

Back at the hotel, someone put on some music and we continued drinking. Our suite number had been given out at the restaurant and people started arriving in groups of two and three, all carrying more drinks. Some had booked rooms on our floor, so we started wandering in and out of them, drinks in hand, whispering and laughing in the hallways. I didn't know any of the newcomers but we were all giddy and drunk. I listened to their banter and smiled and drank some more. In the corner Mu-cheon started nuzzling some Wellesley girl.

I don't know what time it was—3 or 4 A.M.—when I went to lie down on the bed in one of the suites. My head was hurting and my body felt like it was buoyed on waves, rising and sinking. I heard murmurs and music outside but was relieved to just close my eyes.

The door opened and shut and a hand brushed against my forehead. It was Hanbin, looming over me. "My head hurts," I said. "Do you have any Tylenol?"

He shook his head.

"Then can you just press my temples a little? Like this." I put my fingers on my own temples where they were pulsing.

He had big hands and he clumsily tried to do what I'd shown him, but soon just started stroking my hair.

I rolled my body a little closer to his and he leaned down and somehow, suddenly, he was kissing me.

It was over so quickly but I loved it terribly, the feel of his broad, strong body against mine. His shoulders were so wide and appealing and his mouth was warm. He got up abruptly, looked down at me for

- - - -

a second, and then left. We have never talked about it since, but I remember everything.

WHEN RUBY KILLED herself two months later, I could not talk to anyone. I stopped going to classes. I could not leave my room. I did not know how to live.

I wish she could have told me more about her family, about the grief that her father caused her on a daily basis, the demons she inherited. She had alluded to these things, but I had not asked for more, and I knew that that was how I had failed her, by not asking for more details, by not telling her repeatedly about how her life was so spectacular compared to mine. I assumed she knew that, I assumed that she felt lucky compared with me, that that was why she kept me around as a friend. I should have told her more stories of my own sorrows.

I then proceeded to betray her in the worst possible way, by loving and taking Hanbin, and I know that in the next life, I will pay. But for now, I can't help it, I cannot stop going down this path, even though I know the wreckage that it will leave of my heart. All of this—Hanbin, my job, my frenzied productivity—is very temporary, I know. All I can offer her is proof she haunts me still, every day.

Ara

Every night before I go to sleep, I call in to SwitchBox to hear Crown's message of the day, hoping to hear Taein. Technically, one-fifth of the messages of the day should be recorded by Taein, since Crown has five members and at the SwitchBox launch press conference—to which Taein wore those limited-edition Louis Vuitton Bronze Splatter High-Tops that then sold out across the world in twenty-four hours—they did promise that a different member would record a message every day. But in reality, only about a tenth of the messages of the day are by Taein, which makes sense because he is the most popular and therefore the busiest, with his solo contracts for two new reality TV shows and all those endorsements he films by himself as well.

Bestie ends up recording the most messages. He is the most an-

----

noying member of the group because not only is he the least popular but he doesn't seem to understand that he's the least popular. He always talks like every girl in the country is fawning over him, when honestly, all they want to do is see and hear Taein, and also maybe JB, while Bestie is just filler. Why Bestie doesn't understand this is beyond me—he keeps monopolizing precious time in interviews and talk shows. I can't help complaining about Bestie on the Taein fan boards, but then I get bombarded with comments to shut up about Bestie on a Taein fan board. Everyone on the board hates Bestie for being such a mooch and a copycat. It's true, in the last three red-carpet events, Bestie wore a black tattoo choker and a gold link bracelet, which is what Taein wore to the latest X-Men movie premiere, where he arm-wrestled Hugh Jackman and Hugh Jackman let him win.

My favorite message on SwitchBox so far has been the one where Taein talked about what he does when he is lonely on the road.

"I don't think a lot of people realize this because our lives look so glamorous from the outside, but usually we just spend all day and night at the concert halls rehearsing and then we come back to our hotel and each of us goes into our room and we stay there alone watching TV until we go to sleep," he said in his deep, magnetic voice. "It's a little embarrassing, but I've been watching so many period dramas in my hotel room that I've been dreaming about them. Bestie caught me talking to myself in a period-piece accent the other day!"

I love hearing his voice on my phone. And I love that it doesn't matter that I can't say anything back.

AT WORK, I am having trouble with the girls—the assistants who are supposed to do the prepping and washing and sweeping and even

----

some blow-drying if I am busy with another client. They are meant to be as unremarkable as background music, which is why the salon has them all dress the same, in uniforms mimicking schoolgirl outfits of white button-down shirts and short red plaid skirts.

The problem started when the new girl came. There are always new girls coming and going—they are saucy and bored and mumble at the ground whenever they are addressed. But this one, Cherry, she came with a malicious glint in her eye. And she was assigned to me.

Even before Cherry, I would do a lot more of the grunt work than the other stylists because I cannot call out orders and am forced to physically find the girls and touch them on the shoulder to gesture what I want done. So if I can't find them right away, I end up just doing whatever needs to be done myself. Which is fine most of the time but there are always days when several clients arrive in a row and fume when I can't attend to them immediately. It is always in these moments that Cherry disappears altogether and I am at my wit's end, trying to pull other people's assistants for just a few minutes, and then the other stylists complain to Manager Kwon afterward, even though they are so sugary nice to me in person.

Monday was particularly trying. I had one of my most important clients—the KBC producer—come in for a blowout at the same time as my oldest client, Mrs. Oh, who wanted a color and a perm. Mrs. Oh always tips at least thirty thousand won, which is unheard of at my salon, while I am always hoping the KBC producer will get me into a *Music Pop* taping, or even, in my wildest hopes, backstage at one of the end-of-year music award shows. Cherry was nowhere to be found and I was running back and forth between chairs, trying to blow-dry while mixing the dyes, and I dripped some cold dye on the back of the KBC producer's neck, which I wiped off quickly enough, but she winced.

It is hard to scold someone in writing.

Where were you earlier? I wrote on my notepad at the end of the night, when Cherry was sweeping the floors. On the page, my words did not convey any of the fury I was feeling.

"What do you mean?" said Cherry, the picture of innocence. "I was working." She threw the other girls a look that was almost an eye roll.

I couldn't find you for 20 minutes! I underlined "20 minutes" three times.

"I was probably doing an errand for you," she said. "I was around the whole time, you can ask the other girls." She looked at them again and the girls nodded vehemently. She has them wrapped around her finger, the little witch.

I WOULD HAVE the salon fire her, except that I already asked Manager Kwon to replace an assistant just three months ago. That one wasn't a bad egg, just dim-witted and prone to accidents. After the third time she spilled hot coffee on a customer, I requested a switch. Manager Kwon was understanding, but I know he won't like it if I do it again, especially since Cherry takes great care to be alert and respectful around him. I can't have the salon thinking I am difficult to work with, when it would be almost impossible for me to find another job like this. The only reason they took me in here is because Sujin badgered the owner for months about giving me a try, and then I worked without pay for three months in gratitude for giving me a chance. If I'd had any inkling, I would have just stuck with the other girl.

The thing is, I remember how I used to be even worse than Cherry when I was young, back when I had my voice and my confidence. My friends and I, we terrorized the streets and knew no fear of money or the future. I know how she thinks. And that's the problem. Because I know there isn't anything that can change her except time and inevitable misfortune. Those girls I used to roam with, they all live with despair now, I can tell you that. I just hope that whatever calamity she has coming her way, it strikes sooner, rather than later.

WHAT'S NOT BEEN helping my mood this week is the rumor that Taein is dating Candy, the lead singer of Charming. Of course, there are ludicrous rumors every month about who Taein is dating, but for the past two years the paparazzi photos have consistently showed some no-name Japanese model whom all the fans tolerate because the body language clearly shows that she is the one who is following him around rather than him being more into her. Besides, she is weird looking, with eyes that are too far apart and lips puffier than a blowfish's.

But Candy, Candy would be a different story altogether. She is the type of insolently beautiful that's offensive, and everyone knows she's been bullying the new girl in her group. People hated her even before this scandal and the Crown fan portals are jittery with disbelief and unease. "There's no way Taein would go for Candy—he's always said he wouldn't date other idol stars!" "I saw her once in the restaurant in Itaewon and she was being a complete bitch to her manager." "Who else is going to go to INU Entertainment HQ tonight to wait for her to come out? Charming is supposed to have rehearsal until they have to go to Star Plus Radio for the guest appearance at ten P.M."

Photos of Taein and Candy together have not surfaced yet, but on its home page, LastNews has been hinting for weeks at the biggest idol scandal it's ever scooped. On the portals, people are saying the

- - - -

reason it's taking so long for them to release the photos is because they're negotiating with each star's agency about which ones to publish. The more scandalous the photos, the more money they can extort from the agency. Usually only the tamest ones end up being released—just some light handholding or a shot of a couple in a car together.

Neither Taein's nor Candy's agency has released a statement yet, but there is an announcement that Crown will be wrapping up their promotions for the album this week to start preparing for their world tour. "We are so excited to kick off in L.A. this time!" says Bestie on social media, and then there's a mad scramble on the portals about what the various fan clubs are going to do about the last music show this week. The club president decides on the chant "See you soon, Crown!" and chooses the messages that are to be painted on ribbons for the flower wreaths that will be delivered backstage to the members at that last show. Five separate donations will be made to each of the members' favorite charities in their names. There is a brief scuffle about the amount of each donation (Taein fans insisting that our amount exceed the other members' because there are more of us), but a conclusion is reached swiftly (same amount for each member) and the comments die down for the night.

I'm reeling, however, from a comment that a Taein fan writes about how she'll miss seeing him for years, since they'll be heading out on tour for at least a year and then they'll need another year to make a new album. Years? How am I supposed to wait that long? What will I be living for? I need to see him. I need to.

I'VE BEEN JUMPING every time Manager Kwon calls for me with a client, but the KBC producer doesn't come in until Friday morning.

I smile extra-wide as soon as I see her and give her a little squeeze on the shoulder. Cherry sees this and surveys me with speculation.

"*Someone's* in a good mood today, Miss Ara," says the producer with a pleased smile back at me. I shake my head and touch her hair with a question on my face. She's always kept the color dark and changed the style only slightly in the three years I've done her hair. The clients who come to me are the ones who do not have many demands—they are the type to give themselves over, with trust. But today, she seems restless, tapping her loafer on the floor as she stares at herself in the mirror with displeasure.

"I think I want to go lighter this time," she says, fingering her hair self-consciously. "I'm sick of black, you know?"

I nod and smile and bring her a book of color swatches to choose from and she picks a medium chestnut with a brassy tint. It's a bold choice for her and I write so on my notepad and show her.

"I know, but I have a blind date this weekend so I kind of want to shake things up," she says with a toss of her head. A lot of my customers do this before blind dates and I've seen it both work and fail. Sometimes they are imbued with new light, other times, they are distraught and ask that I return their hair to the old style and I have to frantically reschedule other customers.

I nod and smile again and retreat to the coloring closet. In my head I am writing and rewriting what I want to ask her and the anxiety is making my hands tremble. Today is my only chance.

As I'm blending the dyes in a bowl with a brush, I hear Manager Kwon calling my name again and I rush out to see who it is. It's one of Mrs. Oh's friends who wants her roots dyed black. Of course, Cherry is nowhere to be seen and I sit my new client down next to the producer before going to pick up the dyes again. As I run to retrieve my dye bowl, I see another of my regulars, Mrs. Chin, walk in

----

with her daughter, and Manager Kwon waves to catch my eye as he asks them to sit for a second to wait for me. While I whirl around frantically, trying to find some help, I see the girls scattering helter-skelter, avoiding my eye.

My head is pounding and I breathe in to try to steady my nerves, but the fumes from the dye and hair products just make my apprehension worse. I've learned to control my reaction to the fumes over the years, but today, I feel like I am being smothered.

I cannot blow this opportunity. After this week, Taein will be gone, perhaps for years, singing and dancing in America and the rest of Asia, for those who can afford to travel to see him in concert.

My hands shaking, I take out my notepad and start composing my request, but Manager Kwon appears in front of me.

"What are you *doing*?" he hisses, grabbing my elbow. "You are keeping three customers waiting and they're starting to complain, especially when they can see you just standing around doodling! Go see to them *immediately*."

I bow an apology and hurry to escort Mrs. Chin and her daughter to empty chairs. By the time Mrs. Chin has finished telling me what she wants for her daughter—a toned-down color that's not too somber and a layered trim starting from her cheekbones—Mrs. Oh's friend has called for me in a high-pitched, complaining voice. "How long am I going to be kept waiting like this? This is outrageous!" And by the time I go through color swatches with *her,* I see in the mirror that the KBC producer is standing up in *her* chair with an enraged look on her face.

"Look, Miss Ara," she says in a cold, steely voice when I go to her side. "Isn't this just too much? I usually never complain when you keep me waiting because I know things must be a bit harder for you and everything, but enough is enough. I told you how important this

----

hair appointment is going to be, and I took precious time off work today to be here since my blind date is lunchtime tomorrow, and I just waited and watched you attend to everyone else who came in after me, and you still haven't even applied the dye! I can't wait any longer, I'm going to have to leave." She starts taking off the black salon robe and gathering her things from the side table.

I am shaking my head and bowing and clutching to find my note-pad to write her an apology, but she is already gone. The glass doors close behind her and I stand there in shock, staring.

"Isn't this yours?" says a voice behind me, and when I turn around, I see Cherry, holding out my dye bowl and notepad. Her smile is both sly and hard, glittering with mockery and derision, and she is holding the notepad in a way so that we can both see my writing as clear as day.

Would it be possible for you to let me come to the taping of KBC's idol music show this weekend? I am such a fan of Crown and would really really appreciate seeing them one last time before they go out on tour, it reads in my spidery handwriting, my words quavering with hope.

"I told your customers you always need a little more time," says Cherry, watching me. "I tried to calm Manager Kwon down too. But he's asking for you. He looks mad. You don't need this anymore, right? I'll go wash it." She takes the dye bowl back to the dye closet, a skip in her step, for all the world looking like a happy schoolgirl in her little plaid skirt and bouncing ponytail.

A FEW HOURS LATER, around dinnertime, the news breaks all over the portals. The top ten trending keywords on every site per-tain to Taein and Candy.

"Taein and Candy photos," "Taein and Candy car," "Taein and

Candy dating," then, about an hour after that, "Taein's management agency acknowledges Candy relationship, asks fans for understanding," "Taein's official statement."

The photos don't show much—both of them are heavily camouflaged in hats and masks, but Taein's lanky silhouette is unmistakable and so is Candy's signature bleached hair jammed under the hood of her sweatshirt. There is a photo of them walking to Taein's car together, a few feet apart but clearly together, and then there is another of Candy supposedly leaving the parking lot of Taein's apartment, and yet another shot of Taein exiting a few minutes after that. Rumors swirl in the comments that there were photos of them checking in to a hotel together in Japan but Candy's agency paid an astronomical sum for those to stay under wraps.

I eat my dinner of take-out dumplings in the rec room, reading and refreshing the LastNews home page, which keeps rolling out more articles to accompany the same photos.

I see Cherry and the other assistant girls huddling together and giggling out of the corner of my eye but I ignore them as I keep reading. Charming is now going to have to wrap up their promotions too, until this dies down. Taein's fans are already gearing up to swarm Charming's performances at KBC and BCN tonight. They will not take this well, to say the least. She may have to leave the country for a few days until the next celebrity scandal takes over the media.

I finish my dumplings and throw out the styrofoam box, then go find Manager Kwon. *I'll clean and lock up tonight,* I write on my notepad with a smiley face. *Send the other girls home except Cherry.*

Manager Kwon looks at me and sighs.

"Okay, Miss Ara. I know you're trying and I am not heartless."

I bow in thanks and go to brush my teeth, and on the way I see

----

him talking to the girls, Cherry turning to look across at me as he gives instructions.

AT 10 P.M., the last customers leave and the stylists are not far behind, having already touched up their hair and makeup in a flurry of anticipation of Friday night revelry. "Thanks, Miss Ara!" some of them call as they hurry out, and the girls stay only the shortest amount of required time before they leave too. They don't say anything to me as they go, just bow halfheartedly and mumble unintelligible sounds. They can't get out of the salon fast enough. "See you tomorrow, Cherry!" they yell, but Cherry is wiping the closet doors so she doesn't hear them. She started cleaning crazily about half an hour ago—she must have plans tonight.

I make sure the floors are mopped and the mirrors and counters spotless before getting my coat and keys. Cherry comes running with rags in hand as I start turning off the lights in the back.

"I'm done with the bathrooms and the rec rooms and the closets," she says, panting. "Do you need to check them?"

I shake my head and gesture for her to get her things and stand by the front door, waiting until she comes out to turn off the last light and lock the double door carefully.

"Well, that was pretty fast," Cherry says cheerfully, all smiles now, and she turns toward the stairs. That is when I reach out and yank her by her ponytail so hard that she falls on her back.

"What the fuck?" she screams in shock, and she is still screaming when I kick her hard in the stomach. Earlier, I'd changed into my boots with metal tips. As she writhes on the ground, I reach again and pull her up by her ponytail and then drag her over to the bathroom in the hallway. She is heavier than she looks, but no matter.

Flipping the toilet seat up, I smash her face into the bowl. I'm happy to see that it's quite dirty. She is thrashing ferociously now, but she's still in pain from the fall and the kick so she's no match for me. She chokes bubbles into the toilet water and seems to swallow a good amount before I'm satisfied. My friends and I, we used to pull this toilet bowl trick a lot when I was in middle school.

I give her ponytail a final yank and shove her to the floor of the bathroom. Hunching over her, I fish her phone out of her pocket, then throw it into the toilet, the water splattering on her hair. Then I take off her shoes and leave with them, slamming the door shut behind me. After I've walked a few blocks, I fling them into an alley, one after the other, as far as I can throw.

BACK AT HOME, Sujin is waiting for me with my favorite green tea cake from the bakery near her work. She's still wearing a dark brown scarf wrapped around the lower half of her face, even when I protest that she should take it off when she's home with me, but she has vowed to live behind a mask until all her swelling goes down.

"Sweetie, I'm so sorry about Taein," she says, her voice muffled through the scarf as she gives me a big hug and steps back to survey my face.

"Wait, why do you look so excited?" she says suspiciously, and I shrug, opening the kitchen drawer for two forks. I will my body to stop trembling.

"I was going to save this as a birthday present, but I figured you need some cheering up so . . ." She opens her bag and takes out a small white envelope. Inside, there is a ticket to the final Seoul show of the Crown World Tour.

"I got it through one of my customers who works for that ticket-

- - - -

ing company! It was apparently so hard to get, but she's been a regular of mine for years and she only charged me a ten percent premium, which was really nice of her. Although, with this scandal, do you think people are going to start refunding tickets?" Sujin chatters on as she opens the refrigerator, taking out two beers.

I stare at the ticket and stare some more because it is too improbable to be believed. I finger the thick green paper incredulously. And then I start to cry.

Sujin lurches, spilling her beer, and automatically reaches over to rub my shoulders. "What's wrong, Ara? What's wrong?" she asks in a panic as I sit there with tears dropping onto my hands and the precious ticket. "What is the matter? You can tell me," she soothes, the way she always has, ever since we were children.

Kyuri

My young friend Nami and I are drinking again. I'm avoiding Sujin, who I know will be home soon and knocking on my door.

We are sitting at my favorite pocha, where the fish cakes in the fish cake soup are just the right marriage of chewy and salty, and the owner always brings us free plates of food to go with our soju because he has a crush on me. Last weekend, he sat and drank a round with us and then had some fried chicken delivered from another store because I said I was craving gochujang wings. He's one of those shrinking, gawky types that knows he doesn't have a chance in hell with me, which is the only way I like them.

Nami and I—we drink together at least every other weekend. Getting drunk by ourselves is completely different from getting

----

drunk when we are working. When the two of us are drinking, it's "game over" from the beginning. Nobody else can keep up, although sometimes men try to join us, but they give up when we drink shot after shot while ignoring them. We see enough men at work, Nami and I. They need to leave us alone on the weekends. We wear baggy sweatshirts and baseball caps pulled down low and no lipstick, just eyeliner, but still they come talk to us. "You're too pretty to drink by yourselves," they say. "Can we join you?" And then when we ignore them, they turn nasty. "What the fuck," they say, real manly, muttering under their breath as they slink away. "Stuck-up cunts."

Nami is the only girl I still talk to from my red-light-district days. None of the other girls at Ajax know that I used to work in Miari, and if they knew, many of them would likely never talk to me again. It's ridiculous—we are all doing some variation of the same work, even if you're one of the "prettiest 10 percent" and don't actually sleep with the clients. But they'd judge me all the same. It's basic human nature, this need to look down on someone to feel better about yourself. There is no point in getting upset about it.

I wish I could share this sort of wisdom with Sujin but for now I'm avoiding her. She is wild-eyed these days because her nail salon has been flailing and her boss told her that she will probably have to let her go soon. It's only been two months since her surgery and parts of her face are still inflated and she talks funny because she can't open her mouth very wide, but she's already hounding me about next steps to getting a job at a room salon. I have told her to just look for another nail salon job for now where she can wear a dust mask and no one looks at her anyway.

The problem is that Sujin feels obligated to take care of Ara. Yes, Ara is handicapped but she also has a job, even if the hair salon probably doesn't pay much. But when I tell Sujin she should learn to look out for herself before worrying about anyone else, she tears up and says Ara cannot adjust to the real world and must be protected and Sujin has to make as much money as she can for both of them.

What she doesn't understand is that I am trying to save her. Once money exchanges hands and you step into our world, things turn bad really quickly.

One minute, you are accepting loans from madams and pimps and bloodsucking moneylenders for a quick surgery to fix your face, and the next minute the debt has ballooned to a staggering, unpayable sum. You work, work, work until your body is ruined and there is no way out but to keep working. Even though you will seemingly make a lot of money, you will never be able to save because of the interest you have to repay. You will never be able to get out of it entirely. You will move to a different shop in a different city with a different madam and a different set of rules and times and expectations, but it will still be the same, and there is no escape.

I WOULDN'T HAVE made it out of Miari myself if it wasn't for one of my oldest customers—a balding, stooped grandfather, who fell in love with me and actually gave me the money that I needed to pay off my debts—fifty million won cash. The owners of the place I worked, they would have tried to scam me into working there even after taking the money, but the grandfather was a retired lawyer and he made them sign all these documents confirming that I was debt free. The mixture of the two—cash and fear of the law—was the reason they let me go.

The grandfather still comes around every few months, but I always make sure my roommate, Miho, isn't at home when he does. All he asks is that I do a little show removing my clothes and then stay

----

FRANCES CHA

naked during our time together so that he can touch me and look at me. He doesn't even want to have sex or a blow job. He's too old to take that kind of excitement, he says, adding that he doesn't want to die on top of me. I don't know if that's out of consideration for me, or to save face for his family. It's nice to have him look at me so fondly and call me "art," without me having to do anything.

He doesn't know, though, that I've started racking up debts again because of my recent touch-up surgeries. They're just small ones here and there but they add up. I've decided not to tell him. He thinks I am going to school to become a teacher. He is so proud of how he has changed my life, and often, his eyes water when he looks at me. He loves the story that he saved me.

WHEN NAMI FIRST came into that place I worked in Miari, I tried to tell her not to take money from the pimps. That money was never the casual gift they always made it seem. But she had already started and like the rest of us, she couldn't stop.

She was just a kid, one of the youngest at that joint, and she looked even younger because of her dumpling cheeks and buck teeth. I think she was thirteen or fourteen when she first showed up. She wasn't attractive at all back then, just a chubby kid with no breasts whatsoever. But men would choose her again and again because of her age, if nothing else.

I don't know why I took a liking to her. I usually don't like the girls I work with, but Nami was so homely and so young that it was hard not to feel for her. It bothered me, the fact that she sat with no smile on her face and she would just stare at us, the girls and the men. And I could tell that the men who chose her were the types who wanted to punish her for looking like that.

- - - -

WE BOTH LOOK so different now, Nami and I. Sometimes she says she wishes she had a photo of us from those days. "Are you joking? Why would you want any evidence?" I say, appalled. I would kill someone and rot in jail before I'd let them see what I looked like pre-surgery.

Now that I've been working for a few years in Gangnam, where everything is so chic and subtle and the goal of every surgery is to look as natural as possible, I cringe to see some of her recent choices. Her breasts, for example, are cartoonish, jutting out like grapefruits on her otherwise boyish body. The entire effect makes people ogle openly or look away in embarrassment, especially when she has that hangdog expression on her face, her mouth slightly open as she stares at everyone around her.

"I want them to think I'm stupid," she said to me once. "No expectations is nice. It gives you a lot of time to think."

Well, you've certainly got everyone convinced, I wanted to tell her.

My roommate, Miho, joins us around 10 P.M. Our rooms were originally one bigger office-tel with one side the "office" and the other side the living quarters, connected with an adjoining door that was locked so that they could turn it into two small, separate apartments. Before Miho, a creepy thirty-something man used to live next door, and at night, I would hear his whimpers when he jerked off. I was relieved when he moved out and Miho moved in a few weeks later. I invited her over to drink a few times and she invited me over to see the paintings she was working on. I personally do not care for her style of art—the world is depressing enough already. There is no

------

need to add more freakish misery. Meanwhile, Miho thinks all my regimens are a waste of time and money. But there was something to be said for staving off loneliness, and to have someone there to respond to. So after a few months of getting to know each other, we asked the building to unlock the connecting door between our apartments.

Nami is very intimidated by Miho, because Miho lived in America until recently and she has a real job at a university being an artist. Somehow, she gets *paid* to fuck around with paint and wood and clay all day. Most of the time, though, she seems to be just staring at the wall.

When Miho arrives, she sinks into a chair at our table with a big sigh and starts drumming her fingers on the table. They are truly disturbing——blisters all over with splotches of paint that has dried inside old cuts. And the state of her nails!——I don't think she has ever had a gel manicure in her life. I shudder and Nami gapes at her.

"I'm so hungry," says Miho. "Did you order any more food?" She twists her long ponytail around her wrist like a rope.

"When's the last time you ate?" I ask. Miho will forget about food when she is working. I get jealous because it is so hard for me to diet but she doesn't even spend a thought on her weight and remains impossibly slender.

"I think I ate this morning. And then I had, like, a pitcher of coffee every hour."

I push some of the leftover fish cakes on my plate toward her and wave at the pocha owner, who comes rushing over from the counter.

"Hi, can we get an order of kimchijeon? And what else do you want?" I ask.

"Whatever you think is the best thing on the menu," Miho tells

- - - -

the owner, who scratches his head. But she has already turned back to me and he hurries to the kitchen.

"Hanbin's on his way too but it's going to take at least an hour with the traffic. Don't say anything about his mother, okay?" Miho's tone prickles with warning. She is so sensitive when it comes to her boyfriend.

"Of course I won't," I say witheringly. "You think I'm crazy?"

"How have you been, Nami?" Miho turns to Nami and looks at her kindly. This is the third or fourth time they've met, and after every time, Miho tells me that Nami seems much too young to be having so much surgery. "Won't she regret it later, when she's older?"

For someone who grew up in an orphanage herself, Miho can be so naïve. As if there's a chance Nami is thinking about the future! She hasn't seen her parents since she ran away at twelve. She lives one night at a time. Anyone with half a day of real life experience would be able to see that in a heartbeat. But Miho also thinks working in a room salon is something I do because I want to make a lot of money. She could never imagine the type of place Nami and I started in. Even though Nami has also moved out of Miari and into a third-tier room salon, she will continue to work until either she kills herself or they throw her away like a used dishrag.

It still amazes me—the naïveté of the women of this country. Especially the wives. What, exactly, do they think their men do between the hours of 8 P.M. and midnight every weeknight? Who do they think keeps these thousands of room salons flush with money? And even the ones that do know—they pretend to be blind to the fact that their husbands pick out a different girl to fuck every week. They pretend so deeply that they actually forget.

I glare at Miho, who is looking so concerned. She will definitely be one of those clueless bats when she gets married.

"Miho's boyfriend is a real chaebol," I say to Nami.

Her eyes widen a little in alarm, and then they lapse back into glaze. She doesn't even ask which company his family owns.

"Why do you think he likes you?" I ask Miho. I am genuinely curious. Miho is pretty but not to the level of perfection you can achieve with surgery, and she has no family or money. But for some reason this boy from one of this country's richest families is dating her. It's a mystery.

"Why, what do you mean by that?" she says. But she smiles to let me know that she is not actually offended.

"I don't know, sometimes I think I know men, and then I think I can't understand them at all," I say.

"Oh, by the way, I told him you are my friend from middle school and that you're a flight attendant," says Miho, looking apologetic. "Can you just say you don't want to talk about work? I don't want you to have to lie too much."

"Why a flight attendant? That's very specific." Although, of course, one couldn't possibly introduce me as a room salon girl. Miho is the only person who knows, apart from the girls I work with and the men who pay for me.

"Well, you have these weird hours and you're so pretty . . ." She trails off. "I couldn't really think of anything else that entails that kind of thing. But now that I think about it, it's kind of an elaborate lie." Miho looks distressed. "I mean, what if he asks you about your flight routes and favorite countries?" she says, working herself up. "He's so well-traveled."

I shrug. "I'm okay with flight attendant," I say. "I'll just change the

----

subject if I don't know the answer to something he asks." There was a time after I left Miari but before I joined Ajax that I briefly toyed with the idea of really becoming a flight attendant. I even enrolled in one of those flight attendant academies at Gangnam Station for two weeks, learning "how to bend the knees, not the hips" and all that crap. But then I found out how much their salaries are—even the ones who go to Middle Eastern airlines and make double the domestic salaries—and I quit immediately. Then I started working at Ajax because, well, that's all I know how to do, really—gaze at men adoringly and drink their liquor.

"Why don't you say that you quit and you're now trying to become an actress?" Nami says and then shuts her mouth quickly, like she did something wrong.

Miho claps her hands. "That's perfect! Why didn't I think of that?" She beams and looks at Nami.

"How about you, Nami, what do you do again?" she asks.

"Oh, that's what I'm trying to do," Nami says and giggles, without missing a beat. "We're both desperate actresses!" I look at her. It's true, she's quicker than she lets on.

"Whatever you want, Miho," I say, rolling my eyes.

"Well, I don't want you to be uncomfortable, you know? So yeah, that would be great—you're trying to become an actress."

"Okay," I say. "I don't care."

WHEN HANBIN FINALLY ARRIVES, it's almost midnight and every table is full. People are not drunk yet, but they are shouting at each other happily.

He's good-looking all right, and much taller than I imagined, and

----

built solidly, with a tan face and clean-cut hair. His clothes are expensive and stylish but not too stylish—a patterned blue Paul Smith shirt, dark jeans, and caramel-colored leather sneakers. I especially like the firm leanness of his body. Miho perks up immediately when she sees him, while Nami slumps even more over her shot glass. I keep my smile cool and distant.

"Hello," I say.

"Hi," he says. "You know, I'm very excited. It's the first time I'm meeting Miho's friends, even after all this time." The owner brings a plastic stool and Hanbin gives it a small kick before sitting down on it. "This is some place," he says, looking around. His energy and upbeat attitude seem incongruous with everyone else in this bar, who all look as if life has beaten them hard this week.

We make quick introductions—just names, nothing else, and he orders another round of soju.

"What did you work on today?" he asks Miho. He listens, engrossed, as she tells him about how she has spent all day painting glass.

I like how engaged he is in her story. I can't remember the last time a man asked me about my day and then actually paid attention to the answer, forget finding it interesting. Nami is also watching the two of them out of the corner of her eye, and I can tell she is hanging on avidly—not to their words, but to how their bodies pivot toward each other as they talk.

"You know, my mom has a really good friend who is an artist and has a glassblowing studio in Paju," he says to Miho. "I've been before—you would really love it. Why don't we go next week and you can meet him and see his work? He's so anxious to impress Mom, he'll be happy to show you around," he says.

"But what would your mother say?" she says, looking dismayed. "I

----

wouldn't want her to think I'm trying to take advantage of your family in any way."

"It's fine, I'll just ask her assistant to arrange everything. It'll be my thing. She knows I really liked it last time I was there."

"Maybe," says Miho in a worried voice. She yawns and the dark circles under her eyes turn darker as she rubs them.

"Look, you're hungry," says Hanbin. "You haven't eaten anything, huh? I can tell." He turns around and motions to the owner, who comes running over. "Hurry up on the food please," he says loudly. The owner bows and runs back to the kitchen and returns shortly with the kimchijeon, which Hanbin cuts up for Miho with his chopsticks. Nami is rapt now, sucking on a dark red lollipop as she keeps staring.

"You don't do things in moderation. You just shut down when you don't eat like this. You can't work if your body shuts down." His voice is chiding and tender as he places more food on her plate. It's clear that he likes taking this role with her.

He turns and says to me, "Don't you think? She's like that Snickers commercial."

"I'm just jealous she can diet without even noticing she's hungry," I say flippantly, although I'm perfectly serious. He laughs and picks up his phone, texting for a minute.

"Sung and Woojin want to go to karaoke," he says to Miho. "They're near here so I'm telling them to meet us at Champion."

Miho nods, still eating with dainty, ferocious bites.

"You guys are coming too, right?" Hanbin says to Nami and me, and we nod. This means free drinking. Little does he know what his bill will be, I think, but he's the type to hand over his credit card without even looking. And Miho doesn't even drink that much. What a waste.

- - - -

AT KARAOKE, Hanbin's friends join us and things get fun real fast. They are both yoohaksaeng—rich kids who studied in America for high school and college. I like yoohaksaeng because they tend to be more experimental with sexual positions because they've watched a lot of American porn. It is apparently very ridiculous and intense but often focuses on women's pleasure, which is measured by how loud she moans.

Nami is acting silly—she's taken off her sweater and her white short-sleeved blouse is showing the tops of her breasts, which bounce and squeeze together when she laughs. Of course, the boys like that a lot and they are deliberately choosing fast dance songs to try to get her to dance. They keep ordering more drinks.

Miho is already sleeping in the corner, cheeks rosy red from her two drinks. I think this is probably why Nami was able to loosen up. She grabs the karaoke mic and enters the hottest girl group song of the year—she's of course memorized the whole routine and she breaks into the dance as she sings. It's funny how her eyes are gleaming as she bounces up and down. She does not look like this when she's singing this song at work, I'm sure.

Around 3 A.M., I want to go home and sleep. Hanbin is also sleeping on a chair, so I wave goodbye to Nami and the boys and drag Miho into a cab. I sleep until noon the next day and wake up with a headache.

THE WORKWEEK PASSES by in a haze. I don't know why, but lately I keep getting crippling hangovers, which I never had a prob-

----

lem with before. And Bruce has not been by yet this week. Perhaps it is because of his upcoming engagement. Perhaps he is sick of me.

Don't get me wrong. I have no delusions about Bruce particularly. I dated clients before who were richer or nicer than he is and I am not an idiot.

Yes, he has asked for me every time he's been here. Sometimes, depending on his mood, he'll give me considerable sums of money "to go buy something pretty."

But he doesn't give me money out of an especial fondness for me. He doesn't smile at me over candlelight dinners or anything, and mostly we are too drunk by the time we reach a hotel room so we just watch TV in bed and fall asleep together. I think that's what I like the most about him—that I feel comfortable enough to sleep with his arm draped over me.

I WAS HOPING for a few easy nights, but it's my luck to get a string of insane drinkers this week—the type that keep making us girls drink too, instead of just getting shitfaced themselves and having us pour. It isn't only me—some of the other girls are throwing up by 10 P.M. on one especially bad night. The customer who keeps making everyone drink isn't even the one who is paying or getting taken out, which always pisses me off. If you're not the one spending the money or being sucked up to, you need to shut up and be wallpaper. I almost say something cutting when this ugly, skinny guy who is obviously just a tagalong keeps trying to make me drink.

"Why waste the expensive stuff on me?" I say, trying to laugh. He ignores me and says, "Drink! Drink! Drink! Drink!" with feverish eyes.

- - - -

I rearrange my mouth into a smile before taking the shot with a long sigh for his benefit.

WHEN NAMI TEXTS me about drinking the following Saturday, I reply that I don't want to go out because of my headache, but she can come over if she wants.

"Is Miho unni there?" she texts.

"No."

"Is she coming back anytime soon?"

"She left pretty late this morning, so probably not," I write back, a little annoyed.

Despite what I said about not drinking, Nami brings over several bottles of soju, along with a box of fried chicken wings, and says I don't need to drink, the soju is for her. Her eyes keep darting around nervously until I finally snap at her to stop making me jittery.

We rip into the fried chicken in front of the TV, watching another K-pop special. It defies logic, how many new groups debut every week. The girls sashay and jump frenetically onstage in their miniskirts and knee-high socks. Nami gets up and follows some moves, singing along with a chicken wing for a mic. Her eyes look especially crazed today, glinting like marbles as she flops her head from side to side.

"You're dripping chicken oil on the floor," I say. Today's hangover is not the worst of the week, but it still throbs relentlessly.

Nami sits back down when a has-been male singer, so old—in his late thirties—comes on and starts singing a love ballad.

"I should go soon," she says, drinking a shot and looking toward the door.

- - - -

"What? You just got here. What's wrong with you today?"

She fidgets and hems and haws and then I drag it out of her. She has apparently been sleeping with Hanbin. I blink and blink as she tells me the story.

After I had left with Miho that night, Hanbin woke up and they all drank even more. Nami said she blacked out early, but what she could remember was that at some point there was just her and Hanbin in the room and she was on her knees, blowing him. He couldn't finish, however, and insisted on going to a hotel next door, where she had blown him some more and then they'd had violent sex and fallen asleep. In the morning, they'd had sex again and then he had insisted on getting her number before she left. He'd been texting her all week to meet up again, and she'd met him yesterday afternoon and they had gone to a hotel again.

I am silent as she tells me this.

"Is he giving you money?" I ask after a long pause. She shakes her head and looks miserable. I reach over for some soju and take a swig straight from the bottle. "I guess I *am* drinking today."

Nami dumps the chicken bones into the trash and then sits back down across from me and reaches for another bottle. "You know, this is the first time I've slept with someone who isn't a customer," she says hesitantly, after she takes a gulp. "But it's kind of all a dream, like I am watching it happen on TV or something. I mean, I know it's happening but I can't really wake up."

I swirl my glass and hope getting drunk will kill the headache this time. "Do you guys talk and stuff?" I ask. "Or is it just all sex?" I'm curious what he's like in bed, chaebol boy. Miho never talks about it.

"Yeah, a little," she says. "He's really sweet afterward. And he

----

takes me to eat at these really nice restaurants and laughs when I eat a lot." She crinkles her forehead. "He has a lot of things he has to worry about."

"Like what?" I say skeptically. "How to sleep with as many girls as possible without paying them?"

"Yesterday, he told me his father has a demon inside of him," she says.

"A demon? What does that mean?"

"I don't know—Hanbin oppa kept repeating that, and saying he needs to be exorcised by a mudang. And that his mother has been banished to a basement room of his house." Nami looks down at the floor.

"He's known you for two seconds and he is telling you this? That's so weird." Especially since Miho had told me that Hanbin doesn't talk about his father, ever. But then again, all rich kids are weird in their own ways. One guy who was a regular when I was at Miari was always flaunting his money, and once he laid money out on the bed and had me bury my face in it while he fucked me from behind. He had seen it in some movie. That made me think he was probably not that rich, but then again, he did come a few times a week so he could not have been poor.

"You better not be asking me for advice," I say finally with a sigh.

"I'm not asking you for advice. I just don't want to go behind your back." Nami opens another bottle and pours another shot for herself, not even offering me one.

"This is you not going behind my back?" I blink. "But now it is one more thing I have to worry about."

Nami looks wounded and we are both silent, but then I pull her toward me and hug her. She smells like almond shampoo and cheap perfume. "Did he say anything about Miho?" I ask.

- - - -

"No," she says, taking a strand of my hair and twisting it around her finger. "He hasn't mentioned her once."

WHEN SHE LEAVES, taking all her trash with her in the little plastic bag that she brought her chicken in, I feel both agitated and weary. A sickly feeling settles across my shoulders like a heavy cape, and no matter what drama or reality show comes on TV, I find my mind wandering. It's maddening, how I am wasting my day off on a bad mood.

I try to trace the reason for this feeling. It can't be surprise at Hanbin—first of all, I had fully been expecting him to be an asshole like all the other rich boys with Mom's Maseratis and Dad's credit cards. Hadn't I? It was also not like Miho and I were actual friends anyway. We never talked about anything personal—I don't think I'd ever talked to her about my father or my sister. It wasn't like Hanbin was really going to marry her.

The bad mood was probably protectiveness toward Nami, if anything. I couldn't remember a single time she had ever talked to me about a boy—outside of work, of course. Work never counts—it doesn't matter how nice a client is. Nami, for all her childishness, knows that by now.

When I hear Miho unlocking the door to her apartment, I stay quiet on my side, hoping she doesn't come over, but she does. She wanders in and pokes her head into my room as I pretend to be engrossed in my phone.

"What are you doing? Did you eat yet?" she says.

Her hair is in braids wound tightly around her head and there are turquoise paint splotches all over her neck and hands. Her face is guileless and happy, which depresses me.

"Did you not eat all day again?" I say, exasperated.

"You know, I really meant to today—I bought this yogurt and a breakfast roll from that new bakery on the corner of Tehranro, and then I must have left the bag somewhere because when I remembered them this afternoon I couldn't find them anywhere," she says. "It's a mystery."

She comes in, oblivious to my mood, and sits on the bed, fingering the dress I wore last night. "I like this color," she says dreamily, running her hands along the hem. The dress is cheap and tight, but I also like the color—a somber slate. None of the other girls like to wear it and it makes me feel as if I am a person of depth.

"Want to go to the aquarium with me?" Miho says abruptly.

"The aquarium? Why?"

"I need to look at fish."

"For work again, you mean?" I say. Last time, she wanted to look at how duck meat was hung at a Beijing duck restaurant.

She nods. "I'm starting this glass project and it made me think of fish. Hanbin can't go with me because he has some family thing."

I roll my eyes, enraged, but she doesn't see.

"The aquarium on the weekend will be overrun with shrieking children," I say, pleased at coming up with such a perfect excuse not to go. "Hundreds of children in an enclosed dark space." I shudder. "Sounds like a horror movie."

Miho looks irked.

"But you should go," I say hastily. "Feed your brain. And maybe all those children will inspire you too. I've heard that children do that sometimes."

She looks at me. "Do you know that all these ob-gyns and birthing centers and postpartum centers are going out of business because nobody is having children? I heard that on the radio news today."

- - - -

106

"Good riddance," I say. "Why would you want to bring more children into this world so that they can suffer and be stressed their entire lives? And they'll disappoint you and you will want to die. *And* you'll be poor."

"I want four kids," she says, grinning.

That's because you're dating a rich boy, I want to say to her. But really, you should know that he's never going to marry you.

"No surgery will be able to fix your vagina after that," I say instead. "You really want to pee every time you sneeze?"

IT'S TRUE, THOUGH. Other than Miho, no one I know wants to have children. Least of all me. Just the thought of getting pregnant makes my blood pressure shoot up.

When my mother was my age, my sister, Haena, was already six and I was three—a fact that my mother reminds us of every time we see her.

"You don't have to be ready before you have children, you just have them and then they will grow up one way or the other," she pleads to us and to Haena especially, since she thinks Haena is still married. "Who will take care of you when you are old? Look at me, what would my life be without you?"

She doesn't understand that I will never have the capacity to shoulder the responsibility of another life when I am scrambling like a madman in my own. It's why I buy ten boxes of birth control pills at a time from the pharmacy. Miho told me once that in America, they don't sell birth control over the counter and you need a doctor to prescribe it. And to see a doctor, you can't just walk in—you have to schedule an appointment days or even *weeks* in advance. A lot of the

----

things she tells me about America puzzle me because it is so different from how I imagine it to be. I suspect there might have been a lot of miscommunication while she was there. She probably didn't understand much of what anyone said to her. I've heard her speak English before and it didn't sound that fluent.

Miho herself doesn't use the pills because she says they affect her moods and her work too much. That and she's afraid they'll prevent her from being able to get pregnant in the future. I told her I hope that's true—for me, I mean.

I'm lucky, though, I haven't had to have an abortion yet because I'm so punctual with taking my pills. It doesn't matter how drunk I get the night before, or even if I am drinking during the day. I've set a daily alarm on my phone and even if my battery is dead my body remembers. I wake up from sleeping like the dead right before it's time for me to take one.

I know a girl—she was a few years older than me—who worked at Ajax but quit because her sponsor wanted her to. She got a fancy apartment and had two babies. The last I'd heard was that she lost her mind and was shipped off to the mental hospital.

I think of her, and I think of Miho and Nami and Haena, and then I go to my fridge and take out a grape vinegar drink and go to the cupboard for soju. Mixing them together, I start drinking, sitting down on the floor in front of the window that looks out onto the street.

I don't know, I have half a mind to move to Hong Kong or New York like a few of the older girls I used to work with, who told me they found jobs in room salons there. Apparently the standards of beauty are very low in those cities and people walk around with all kinds of ugly faces. "You should come too!" they said, as if it was an adventure instead of forced retirement. They gave me their contact

----

information but they didn't even respond when I wrote asking what their new lives are like.

Who knows? Maybe someone will marry me if I move there. A foreign man who will think I was born beautiful, because he cannot tell the difference.

Wonna

This is the fourth time I've gotten pregnant this year and I already know that this one is not going to make it either.

I have not told my husband yet about this conviction—he would just say, "Thoughts become seeds for bad luck!" or something else inane, and try to change the subject.

It wasn't like I had an ominous dream or anything—I just know. A motherly intuition if you will—or the opposite.

In the waiting room of my doctor, three other pregnant women are shifting uncomfortably because of their swollen bellies. None are "glowing"—they all look puffy and tired. Two of them have dragged their husbands here with them—I don't understand why they subject the men to such a waste of time. I never let my own husband come

----

even though he always says he wants to. "Just concentrate on making more money, please," I say, all polite, and he shuts up like a clam. It's difficult enough to be a midlevel employee with a middling paycheck as it is, without taking time off to go to your wife's obstetrician visit. "I don't understand why you want me to have a baby when we won't be able to pay for childcare," I used to say to him before I started trying so desperately to have one. "I won't be able to afford to work, or *not* work."

My bright husband always has an unfailingly asinine answer for such practical questions—"All we need to do is have one and we'll figure it out! Our parents will help!"

I see him sometimes, with his plain, happy-go-lucky smile, and feel my heart wrenching in such pained dislike that I have to look down so that he won't catch the expression on my face. He is a kind man, if nothing else, and I always have to remind myself that marrying him was my choice. All my adult life, and in my marriage, I am trying not to be cruel because I know that it is only a matter of time before what is in my blood rears its ugly head.

"Ms. Kang Wonna," the nurse calls, and I'm ushered into the doctor's pink office, plastered with black-and-white photos of babies and uterus renderings. The doctor behind the desk is a plump little middle-aged woman with round glasses and permed hair.

"This is your first visit with us? And your chart says you are four weeks pregnant?" she says, fiddling with her glasses as she reads my chart. "How are you feeling?"

I consider the question.

"I have a bad feeling," I say, then stop.

"You are experiencing pain, you mean?" She looks appropriately concerned.

"Not yet," I say. "But I can tell it's coming."

She raises an eyebrow and I try to explain.

"I can feel something bad is going to happen to the baby. It's just a feeling—like a sinking. The doctor I was going to before didn't listen to me, so here I am." I say that last part to warn her to be careful of her words, but I am not sure if she understands me.

She looks back down at my chart.

"I see that you have had three previous pregnancies?"

"Yes."

"And you miscarried them all?"

"Yes."

The doctor taps her chart.

"I understand why you would be apprehensive this time around," she says slowly, "but I want you to know that miscarriages are extremely common so you shouldn't feel like it's just something that happens to you. A lot of women miscarry and it's no one's fault. Of course, if you wish, we can run some tests to make sure all is well but I'd like to ask you some more questions first."

She continues to ask uninteresting questions about my physical and mental state and past and I answer them automatically.

"Given everything you have gone through, do you think you may want to speak to a therapist?" she asks. It's my turn to raise my eyebrow.

"Doesn't that mean I lose my insurance?" I say. "I heard that if you get mental treatment, you get dropped and then no insurance company will touch you after that."

"Oh, I don't think that's true still," she says uncertainly. "But I actually don't know for certain. You'd have to call your insurance, I suppose."

"Yeah, no," I say. Even if I had money to waste, it's not like I'm having suicidal thoughts or anything. I knew I shouldn't have brought up this premonition. I don't know why I expected something different from this doctor.

She looks at the clock. "Why don't we go ahead and do an ultrasound." She turns to the nurse, who guides me to the examining table, where I quickly pull down my underwear and hoist my feet into the stirrups. The doctor rolls a lubricated condom down onto the ultrasound rod thing and gently pushes it into me, probing while we both look at the screen.

"Lights, please." The nurse dims the lights and the doctor keeps searching for something while telling me to relax. After a good five minutes of probing, she pulls out the rod and takes her gloves off one by one.

"Well, it's too early to see anything at all, so why don't you come back next week and we can take another look for the sac and the heartbeat. We'll take some blood today and run some tests. Don't worry in the meantime. Either way, you'll be fine."

"Yes, I know," I say, putting my clothes back on as fast as I can. I don't say anything else to her and stalk out the door, trying not to look at the swollen women in the waiting room.

I KNOW IT'S CRAZY, but I took the entire day off for this doctor's appointment today—Department Head Lee said, "God, what is it *now*?" in his sharpest voice when I told him last week. He kept asking the specific reason, but I held out to the last. "Just a personal day," I said, looking down at his shiny brown shoes, and that's when he proceeded to rap me on the head with a rolled-up sheaf of paper. "As

- - - -

everyone knows, *this* is why women can't advance," he said in a loud voice for the entire department to hear, then told me to get out of his sight.

I'd debated whether to take just a half day but it was the thought of my hour-and-a-half commute that decided it for me. So I am sitting in a bakery café on Garosugil, gloriously alone, biting into a buttery almond croissant and flicking crumbs off a scarf I just bought at the boutique on the corner. I don't know what possessed me to buy this scarf—we are so strapped for money as it is—but it's been a while since I bought anything and it looked so chic on the mannequin in the window. Now that I have it on, I can see that the fabric is cheap and the ends are unraveling already. Like everything else in my life, the impulsive choice—the wrong choice.

When I finally check my phone there are three texts from my husband. "Everything okay?" "Haven't heard from you in a while, is something wrong?" "How are you feeling?"

I text a quick "Sorry, busy at work. Will call later." I should have known he'd find a way to interrupt any happy excursion.

On the walk back to the subway station, I try to close my mind to them, but all I can see are babies in their strollers. Just how many babies are there in this city? Aren't the government and the media always bemoaning how our birth rate is the lowest in the world?

All the strollers look precariously high—the Scandinavian ones that are everywhere these days. I want to yell at the mothers—the babies look like they're going to fall out! Stop texting and strolling!

A little baby peers up at me from his stroller and scowls while his mom is browsing through an accessories rack on the street. He's wrapped in a two-tone embroidered cashmere blanket that I recognize from the European baby clothes blogs—it must have cost more

----

than my monthly salary. I give the mom a hard once-over—she looks haggard, even under a full load of makeup.

I don't want anything to do with boys—I just want a tiny little girl, to dress up in soft, chic beige and pink and gray dresses and bounce in my lap. I wouldn't get one of those top-heavy strollers but a sturdy one with a big basket on the bottom for when I'd go grocery shopping with her to make her baby food. All-organic porridge with a little bit of meat and mushrooms and beans and carrots. No salt or sugar until she's at least two. Definitely no cookies or juice or television.

Sometimes, in the middle of the night, I wake up because I have been dreaming that my baby is sleeping next to me and I have rolled over onto her and she is suffocating. I wake up panting, with sweat coating my back.

I don't tell my husband about this, of course. I tell no one.

WALKING UP the front steps of my office-tel, I almost collide with a hurtling body. When we both take a step back, I see that it is a girl from upstairs. She's one of the Loring Center girls who is always ordering food at all hours of the night, the one who has had some kind of massive surgery on her face recently and still has bandages wrapped around her jaw. She apologizes and bows. "That's okay," I whisper.

She bows one more time and then bounces away down the stairs, her step light and buoyant despite her face. Where is she going, looking like that?

I turn after her and watch as she skips away down the street. She looks so free. They all do—the gaggle of girls upstairs.

- - - -

If I had known I would envy children from an orphanage, I would not have lived in so much terror of my grandmother threatening to drop me off at one.

That girl was actually the reason my husband and I came to live here, in this office-tel. My husband and I, before we were married, had visited several real estate agents in the Yeoksam area close to his work. We had been sitting in front of a neighborhood map with the agent when I heard voices behind me talking about the Loring Center. I stopped breathing as I listened with all my being.

Long ago, my grandmother had taken me to one of the Loring Center branches, which was one neighborhood over from ours. She sat me down on the steps and said to think about what I had done wrong that day and whether I deserved to come home with her, or be dropped off like the other children whose parents did not want them. She pointed to a large box that protruded from the wall and said all she needed to do was ring the bell that hung over the box for someone to come and take me in.

The girls who were sitting behind us at the real estate office were talking about their dorm room at the Loring Center in Cheongju, and how having a new place together would be like living there again. They were so naïve, those girls, that they would discuss such a thing in front of a real estate agent.

But to my surprise, the agent who was talking to them was quoting a price that seemed not only reasonable but cheap, and he was promising that the office-tel was new and clean. When the girls had left to follow him to see the room, I asked our agent about the office-tel they had just talked about. "I couldn't help overhear that conversation," I said.

"But that's not really for married couples," he said, frowning. He

----

had been thinking of more expensive apartments for us when he heard where my husband worked.

"Cheaper is good," I said. "I want to see that office-tel, please."

And so we had installed ourselves at Color House, happy about the cheaper rent. And I got to see these girls come and go—perhaps I would have been one of them, once upon a time.

Then perhaps I would have been as free as they are. I would love to be on my own, living with a roommate, ordering noodles at 2 A.M., waking up deliciously alone, with no one to ask what my plan is for the day.

I wish I could invite one or more of them over, but that would require me to possess an entirely different personality. I wish I could tell them that I empathize with them, that we are the same. I want to tell them I was given up by my mother too.

I SUPPOSE that thinking about my mother makes not being able to have a baby all the more difficult. Getting pregnant is not the issue, it's that these babies keep on dying. I read somewhere that miscarriages are babies self-terminating when they know there will be a problem. It hollows me out, the way that they would rather kill themselves than be born to me.

WHEN I THINK of my mother, I imagine that she is a rich woman—self-made and invincible. I also like to imagine that she is alone and tortured by regret over how she left her baby. Sometimes, if I am in a public space, I look around casually to see if there is a well-dressed woman in expensive sunglasses lurking behind a corner with a hungry expression on her face.

After leaving you, I have never known what it is like to be happy, she says, when she musters up the courage to come talk to me.

When I think of my grandmother, though, I understand my mother for leaving. If I'd had any backbone as a child, I would have run away too.

She is out there somewhere—my mother. Whenever she sees a baby, she is thinking about me.

I HAD NOT even known that all the venomous things my grandmother spewed about my mother abandoning me had been true. I had thought that my mother was with my father overseas as he worked. I did not understand until he came back that my mother had left both of us.

It had been a few weeks after my cousin's accident that my father came for me at my grandmother's house. My grandmother had not spoken to me in those weeks—she had also stopped feeding me— she had stopped being at home altogether during the day because she said she could not bear to be in the same house with me. I made my own rice and ate the dried food that tasted bad uncooked.

But when my father came for me—that was one thing to his credit, that he had packed up and left his life in South America with a local woman when he heard about the accident—my grandmother kicked up a fuss you couldn't believe! She shrieked, she gagged, she threw things and clutched me to her so hard that her nails dug into my neck and I wriggled away and ran to my father, whom I did not even know, calling out, "Father, Father."

When he took me to his new apartment in Seoul, he said that we were both starting over. That we could be happy now.

IT'S PAST 1 A.M. and I'm stooped over the toilet bowl again.

My morning sickness only comes at night, rearing its head after my husband has already gone to sleep. It's mostly in my throat—it feels like I'm going to throw up every few minutes but I never do, then I feel ravenous, but when I go through the list of things to eat in the house, I want to throw up again.

Something not agreeing with you, baby? I want to ask as I gingerly touch my lower stomach. Was it the ice cream? The noodles? They're the only things I can bring myself to eat these days and the reason why my stomach looks like I'm five months pregnant instead of two. I've taken to wearing drapey, shapeless dresses to try to mask my protruding belly—but I'm sure the razor eyes at work will notice before long. My fists clench when I think about what they'll say—and it'll be even worse if I lose this one too. Not that they knew about the other miscarriages—they just gave me hell last time for calling in sick for three days in a row.

Currently, in my New Product Development role, my immediate boss is a thirty-seven-year-old unmarried woman whom I *almost* feel sorry for every time we have team night. The minute dinner starts, the talk always turns to why no one has married her.

"Why don't we go around the table and offer some theories for Miss Chun?" Department Head Lee says once the meat order has been placed by Chief Cho. "Chief Cho, what do you think?"

Then the men take turns dissecting her height (too tall), her education (too threatening), her personality (too strong), her clothes (too dark), and start offering advice about how to attract a man (incorporate cute mannerisms in speech).

Throughout it all, she titters and jokes along with them about her shortcomings. "I know, I really need to tone down my first impression," she says with a pained, toothy smile. All night, she tries desperately to seem like a good sport.

The ones who pay for the ravages of the firing squad are of course us, her underlings. The next day, she will invariably scream at us for "unacceptable work," and make us stay at the office well into the night with her. She's happy at the office—there's no one to go home to. But even if she wasn't such a sour bitch, her complete ineptitude would keep me from feeling sorry for her. The only reason she continues to get promoted is because she stays past 11 P.M. most nights and broadcasts it loudly the next day, with us as witnesses. Management pegs her as "loyal."

I have no desire to stay past midnight every night for a company that treats me like an ant to be crushed by the heel of a shoe. But those who do, the ones with no families, those are the ones that get ahead. The career woman I imagine my mother to be—she is probably one of them too.

I know it's too early for the baby to be kicking—or for me to feel it kicking, anyway—but I could swear that I feel a gentle movement just under my belly button. I place my hand there and listen and wait. For what, I have not a shred of an idea.

"Please stay," I whisper. "Please, please stay."

Miho

I often wonder where I would be today, if my aunt and uncle had not decided they couldn't keep me anymore.

They might have continued to raise me, if my cousin Kyunghee had not been so smart. She was five years older than I was, and from the fifth grade, she had exhibited flaring signs of intelligence that her teachers—even in our forlorn, sleepy school in the middle of the reed fields—were quick to single out and praise. Kyunghee can do long division in her head, Kyunghee can sketch a startling still life from memory, Kyunghee can memorize every king in Korean history. I was proud of her too, my gifted cousin, and my favorite thing to do was take my sketchbook and sit under the big tree outside my aunt and uncle's restaurant and draw while she did her homework beside me, her lip curled in concentration as she worked slowly through her textbook. "Don't get your fingers all dirty," she'd say sometimes when she looked up from her homework, because even back then, I preferred to smudge out all of the edges in my drawings with my fingers. I don't work with pencils much anymore, but when I do, they remind me of her.

Kyunghee did not notice me much. Her brain was always puzzling out things that interested her and she did not care for friends of her own. My aunt and uncle generally left me alone as well. They ran a "taxi food hall" for taxi drivers that served three varieties of hangover stews and simple side dishes. It was probably the cheapest restaurant in our town, on the edge of a patchy field of wildflowers, and we lived in two rooms at the back of the restaurant.

I don't know where it came from—that drive of Kyunghee's. She lived for praise and she was relentless in her studies. While I loafed around and watched the TV that was on for the customers, she would sit in the corner and finish her homework as soon as she got home, and when she did not understand a problem, she would walk to school early and find any teacher or staff person and ask until they showed her the answer. Needless to say, the grown-ups all loved her for this. My aunt and uncle did not know how to help her, but they were grateful to her for being so self-sufficient.

"I don't know who she gets it from," they said, shaking their heads proudly when customers would notice her studying and inevitably remark upon it.

In contrast, I was terrible at school. The only class I liked somewhat was art, but even in art class I struggled with following the very precise directions. I dreaded math, I dreaded Korean, science bewildered me, and sociology I thought was absurd. "This comes from her mother's side of the family," I heard my aunt say often to my uncle. She made no effort to hide her dislike of my mother, who my aunt

----

said had made an alcoholic of my father. My parents had gambled, they drank, they fought, and finally they borrowed money from my aunt and uncle and went off somewhere—together or separately, nobody knew.

They did not hold my parents against me, however, my aunt and uncle. If they'd had a second, slower daughter of their own I think they would have treated her the same way they treated me. Kyunghee was their sun and that was a very natural thing.

When I was in fourth grade, and Kyunghee in the third year of middle school, her teacher came home with Kyunghee and me one day and said that Kyunghee should apply for the accelerated science high school.

"She will almost certainly be accepted if she has just a little direction, a little push," said her teacher, a solemn young woman with harsh bangs and owlish eyes. "She does, however, need to start preparing immediately for the test if you decide to do this."

Preparation meant tutoring, and tutoring meant money and the restaurant had not been doing well for a long time. More and more, I had not been able to watch TV because my aunt and uncle turned it off when there were no customers, to save electricity.

"SO THAT'S WHEN they sent you to an *orphanage*?" Ruby asked incredulously. They were all amazed as they listened to my story. Ruby, Hanbin, their friend Minwoo, and I were at a small, crowded izakaya on St. Marks Place, eating yakitori and drinking shochu. Ruby and Minwoo were fascinated and rapt, while Hanbin was expressionless.

"Well it sounds bad when you say it that way," I said. It was the first time I'd ever told this story to friends. I did have to write a per-

- - - -

sonal essay for my scholarship application, and had to touch on a few of the points in my interview with the committee that ultimately sent me to New York, but this was different. This was like taking a shower in the middle of the room with everyone watching.

"How else would you say it?" Ruby asked.

I DO NOT REMEMBER what they said to me about going to the Loring Center. I don't think I protested. I suppose it must have been difficult for me in the beginning. I do not remember. Or, to be more accurate, I have put a great deal of effort into not remembering. And now, I really do think I was fine.

For my first few months, my aunt and uncle still came to visit me every few weeks. Kyunghee came with them once and looked around and did not say much. She was too busy to come after that. My aunt would bring large containers of food and sometimes ice cream and sometimes they would take me somewhere in the car—mostly to the stationery store, where I was allowed to pick out what I wanted. I usually picked fluorescent gel pens, the ones from Japan that cost over two thousand won each and never developed scabs on the points. I knew they felt bad and I tried to show them all the best parts of the Center—the toddler classroom was bright and neat and the toddlers were cute to look at when they were not crying, and we even had a small, colorful library of English books that Miss Loring had put together herself. Other than in the infant and toddler rooms, there were only girls at the Center. The older boys were sent to other Centers around the country. The older girls—there were four of us in the same age range—had our own large room with our own cubbies and beds and desks and a TV, which we were always fighting about. And Miss Loring had decided to dedicate a

----

room to art when she discovered I liked drawing. It had been a staff meeting room with a long table and plastic chairs, but now there were tin buckets of colored pencils and paints and large sheets of recycled paper stacked on the shelves. While the other girls went to the local public school, Miss Loring arranged for me to attend a small experimental arts school later on, when it became time for me to enter middle school.

"DID YOU MISS HOME?" asked Ruby. "When I first went to boarding school, I couldn't eat for weeks."

"That's because you didn't like the food," said Minwoo as he bit into a delicately grilled chicken wing. "I remember your driver had to bring you Japanese food from Boston every few days."

"Even that was terrible," said Ruby, rolling her eyes. "I hate Boston Asian food. But anyways."

I DON'T THINK I missed "home" much. There wasn't much to miss. During the last few months that I lived there, my aunt had taken to agonizing by herself in the afternoon, when, often, there would be no customers. Her hair covering her face, she would weep over the cutting board as she chopped vegetables, salting the carrots and squash with her tears. Kyunghee avoided coming home at all, burning all-nighters in the study carrel that she rented by the month, while my uncle would often disappear, saying that he was going to drum up some business. The air was thick with stress. I did not realize until recently that my aunt's weepiness could also have stemmed from her condition.

My aunt gave birth in the fall, five months after I had been depos-

----

ited at the Loring Center, to a baby boy that they named Hwan. I did not know she was pregnant until one day she showed up at the Center and her shirt was stretched taut to bursting by her overlarge belly, unmistakably with child. I never met him, my boy cousin, because after he was born they didn't come again. But by then, the Center was home to me. The girls I lived with became my sisters—the ones I covered for and complained to and swapped clothes with.

At the Center, my heart did not feel as if it was being shot with acid the way I felt whenever I saw my aunt and uncle worrying over money, or when Kyunghee tried to help me with my homework and would sigh, exasperated, when I couldn't follow her explanations. No matter how much we fought among ourselves at the Center, we were an impenetrable unit, bristling at any hint of scorn or pity from the other children at school who had parents to go home to. We were brazen and confident in our unity and the teachers did not touch us because they could not predict what the consequences would be if they did. One time, Sujin slapped a girl in her class who said her mother was a beggar, and Miss Loring showed up, dressed purposefully in her floor-length mink coat and matching hat. The sight of Teacher Kil sweating as he tried to speak to her in English (and he was our English teacher!) had us screaming with laughter for days.

The only times I ever felt pain were right after my aunt and uncle's visits, when I would see them walking away toward the bus stop, my aunt waddling as her stomach grew bigger every time I saw her.

She was alarmed, I know, by the disabled people who lived at the Center. There were several boys my age who lived in a separate building from us. Two of them looked all right, but one of them would hit people if he was in a bad mood and the other one could not look at

----

one thing for very long. The other girls and I did not talk to them either—we were cruel with ignorance in those days—but we knew their families who visited, and we knew which tree-canopied benches they liked to sit on outside and what times they would come so that we could avoid them. My aunt and uncle did not say anything when the disabled and their caregivers would cross our path but my aunt would instinctively put her hand on her protruding stomach.

The last time my aunt came, she had to sit and take gulping breaths every few minutes. She said she could feel the baby on her pelvis and that his head was hitting her pelvic bones every time she took a step.

I had not known it would be the last time, but after they left, Miss Loring came to tell me that they had left me an envelope of money, entrusted to her for safekeeping, which they had not done before. When she showed me how much, I was shocked—it was more money than I had ever seen—or heard of—at one time. They must have borrowed it—I knew they had never had this kind of money.

But had I known it was their last visit, I would have been glad. I was grateful I never had to say goodbye to them again.

"I DON'T CARE what your aunt's situation was," said Ruby. "Who *does* that?" We had been eating at the izakaya for almost an hour but no one showed any sign of slowing down. The table was crammed with tiny dishes of grilled meats and vegetables while waiters frantically passed us by with orders from the other tables. As always, I thought of the bill, how much it would be with all of this meat. The tongue in particular was expensive. The endless pours of shochu would also drive up the bill, and I took care not to drink very much.

- - - -

It made me feel less bad when, inevitably, either Hanbin or Minwoo, but usually Hanbin, paid the check. Never once had I heard Ruby offer. When I had offered to chip in early on, when I first met them, Hanbin had just laughed and patted my head while Ruby looked on with amusement.

Ruby's face was flushed and she shook off her camel-colored fur jacket, which slid down the seat and then onto the floor. I bent and picked it up gingerly and draped it back over her chair, my fingers lingering on the softness of the fur.

"So you never saw them again?" she asked, picking at a skewer of chicken hearts. "They never even called you? Do you know where they live now?" She held up the bottle of shochu and shook it, to show that it was empty. Minwoo called a waiter and asked for another bottle, then saw a friend at another table and went to talk to him.

"Maybe we should talk about something else if Miho is uncomfortable," said Hanbin, reaching over to Ruby's cup. It was half full and he picked it up and finished it, putting it down on his side of the table. "And I think you are drinking too fast," he said to her. Looking at him, I thought how big his shoulders were. In his thick, ribbed turtleneck sweater, he looked as if he belonged in some New England catalog against a backdrop of a log house and snow-dusted fir trees. His face was mostly impassive—throughout my story he had not said a word. I noticed just a glint of disapproval, although at whom it was directed was unclear.

"Oh shut up," said Ruby, rudely. "If she was uncomfortable, she wouldn't be telling us in the first place. Don't you want to hear more?" She wasn't even looking at him as she said this.

If anything made me uncomfortable, it was the savage way Ruby talked to Hanbin. I looked down at my plate of food. I hoped they noticed that I wasn't eating very much. I always ate several cups of

----

yogurt or a slab of tofu with soy sauce from the Asian mart before meeting them, to fill myself up.

"Of course I want to hear more," said Hanbin, looking at me. I stared at his hair, glinting under the lamp, to avoid meeting his eyes. "But not if it brings up bad memories. I'm really sorry to hear about all this. It must have been so hard for you." The frown line on his forehead grew deeper.

I mumbled something, embarrassed. I did not want him to feel sorry for me and I regretted telling either of them this. I knew that hearing this story would change the way they treated me. Anxiety, like a dark bat, fluttered in my chest.

"The conclusion of the story is that it all turned out for the best," said Ruby. Her voice was stubborn and triumphant. "She wouldn't be here if she'd stayed with her aunt and uncle."

WHAT RUBY SAID was true. I never would have had a chance to win an art scholarship to America because I did not have any idea such a thing existed. It was the Loring Foundation that had such connections, and it had been Miss Loring who made us practice English every week, saying that we would need it someday. She was also the one who left a specific budget for art supplies when she died abruptly, leaving all of her own money to the Center. All I needed to do was ask, and I was given the money to buy plaster and paint and paper and chisels and knives. Then came the big scandal a few years back about all the chaebol scholarships being granted exclusively to the children of politicians and prosecutors that the chaebol families wanted to keep in their pockets. Suddenly, the foundations had to scramble to find actual children in need to give their scholarships to, and an orphan from an orphanage was at the top of the list. And as

----

the oldest and largest foundation, the Loring Center was at the top of the list of orphanages. When I met the members of the scholarship committee who were in charge of the exchange program at SVA, they were practically swooning with excitement as they introduced themselves. "We've read all about you!" they said. "We are *elated* to have someone like you receive the benefits of this program." My story was the stuff of program brochures, of donor newsletters and feel-good newspaper profiles.

When I graduated and came back to Korea, I never tried to find my aunt and uncle. I would think of them sometimes with pale curiosity, of what they would say if they saw me now, if they would ask me to repay their money. I often wondered where Kyunghee had gone to college, whether she had made it to a SKY university, as had been her goal. She wanted to become a doctor, she said. But I think that's because it was the only job we knew of at the time that made any money.

AFTER THE IZAKAYA, we headed to a party at one of Minwoo and Hanbin's friends' apartments in SoHo. The music was loud even as we came out of the elevator at the end of the hall—a rapacious hip-hop beat which did not prepare me for what the apartment looked like inside. A dark hallway opened sharply into a soaring loft, with a ceiling that must have been five meters high. Sofas and chairs were all upholstered in teal velvet, contrasting sharply with an enormous chandelier dripping with red crystals. I was still not used to the interiors of this world—that of the wealthy Koreans in America. The strange, lavish use of colors in this apartment bewildered and overwhelmed me. Even the scent was heavy and unusual—

- - - -

like burnt roots mixed with flowers and spices. I had never smelled anything like it before, but it was expensive, I could divine that immediately.

A blond, uniformed bartender—the only non-Korean at the party—was in the kitchen mixing drinks on the marble-topped island. There were maybe ten other people there, some of them a lot older—in their early thirties at least. As Ruby and Hanbin and Min-woo said hello to their friends, I detached myself and went to find the bathroom—a dark cave of a room lit with ghostly orbs and stubby white designer candles—where I stared at myself in a gilt-framed mirror, washing my hands and worrying about how I was going to get through this evening. I couldn't just stick near Ruby and not talk to anyone else because that would be even more awkward, I decided. I would venture out on my own for a few minutes and then circle back to Ruby and Hanbin later, when everyone was a little more drunk and no one would really pay attention to me.

When I finally emerged from the bathroom, I headed for the kitchen and asked the bartender for a cranberry cocktail.

"And an Old-Fashioned, thanks."

I turned around to find a tall, thin boy in a leather jacket behind me. He had a sharp, triangular face, with sunken cheeks. I thought I recognized him from school.

"Don't you go to SVA?" he asked, staring down at me. He smelled like American soap.

I nodded. "Do you?" I asked.

"Yeah, I'm a sophomore."

"First-year."

The bartender held out our drinks and I took both, handing the boy his glass.

- - - -

131

"How do you know Byung-joon?" he asked, tilting his head toward the living room, from where the lilt of excited voices trailed back to us.

"I don't know anyone here," I said. "Except for the friends I came with, I mean. Is that the person who lives here?"

"Yeah, this is Byung-joon's apartment," he said, taking a swig of his whiskey. "Who are you here with?"

"Ruby and Hanbin and Minwoo? I don't know if you know them."

"Yes, I know them," he said. "I went to middle school with Minwoo and elementary with Hanbin. They're dating again, right? Hanbin and Ruby?"

"Yes," I said. "They're dating again." I stared into my drink and took a sip.

"They're always on and off, those two," he said, smiling, as if it was a joke between us. With that smile, his face suddenly looked warm—like that of an elegant vampire that had drunk his nightly fill.

"So, where did you go to high school?" he asked. My heart sank. It was probably the most common question I received when I met new Korean study-abroad kids in the city. There were only a handful of possible answers in their circles and the answer immediately established background and context for each other. While most of them had gone to boarding school on the East Coast, there were a few who had gone to the foreign-language high schools in Korea. The boarding school kids were much wealthier and spoke better English, while the foreign-language school kids were geekier. The boarding school kids tended to avoid the Korean school kids. I was neither, obviously.

I had two choices—telling them the name of my high school,

----

which included the province I was from, would immediately label me as some gawk-worthy hick. I chose to go with a more vague answer.

"I went to a small arts school in Korea," I said, hoping that would be enough. Not that I really cared what he thought of me, but I had come to dread the moment of the raised eyebrows, if not actual derision. Too late, I remembered that he went to SVA, so of course he would ask the name of the art school.

"Seoul Arts?" he asked knowingly.

"No," I said, and then after a pause, "It was in Cheongju, actually."

"Cheongju? Oh wow," he said. "That's so interesting! I've never met anyone from Cheongju. Apart from, you know, distant relatives or something." He looked at me with great interest. "Cheongju," he said again.

I smiled weakly.

"You don't have, like, an accent or anything," he said. "Actually, I have no idea if people from Cheongju have accents. Sorry, is that rude?" He smiled again and shook off his jacket, and from the redness of his neck I realized he had probably drunk a lot. The flush of his neck contrasted sharply with his white face.

"What's your major?" I asked. Not fine arts, I was guessing.

"Design. But I'm taking a lot of film classes this semester actually. Wondering if I should switch. How did you end up here?"

"Hey, Jae, it's been a long time." The boy and I turned to see Hanbin sliding onto the barstool next to me. He nodded to Jae, who looked a bit surprised, then pleased.

"Hanbin! A really long time. At that poker game in Boston, right? That was the last time I saw you?"

"Yeah, man." Hanbin gestured to the bartender and ordered a whiskey.

"I was just talking to your friend here, who turns out to be at SVA too," said the boy. "I'm Jae Kong by the way."

"I'm Miho," I said.

"You know each other through Ruby?" he guessed. I nodded.

"Yes, Miho's a really good friend of ours," said Hanbin. I may have been imagining it, but his tone sounded like it had a steel edge to it. "She's one of Ruby's best friends, actually."

"Oh wow," said the boy, looking at me again. "Cool, man."

Hanbin started talking to me about a Japanese movie we had seen at Ruby's apartment the previous week. It was odd that he was talking about it—since it hadn't been particularly interesting and he'd fallen asleep almost halfway through. After a few minutes of being ignored, Jae saw someone else he knew and sauntered off.

"I'm sorry if he was bothering you," said Hanbin abruptly, swirling his whiskey. "He's kind of annoying. I think Ruby went to school with him in Korea."

I shook my head. "He wasn't bothering me."

"You know, even before I heard about the orphanage, I knew you were different," he said, not looking at me. "I didn't realize that was why, though. It must have been really hard, going through all that. It makes you think. Like, everyone I know is kind of the same—they've had the same sort of life growing up," he said. "It's different getting to know you, you know what I mean?" He ran his hand through his hair absentmindedly and I thought again how handsome he looked.

"You're so normal too," he added.

I frowned uncertainly. "What does *that* mean?" I asked. He sounded as if he wanted to be congratulated for this observation.

"I don't know, I feel like I would be all kinds of messed up if I'd had to go through what you went through—no offense," he said quickly.

134

I felt a hot embarrassment searing into my stomach and took a quick sip of my drink. But he was talking to me in a more intimate way than he ever had before, and for that I had no choice but to continue in this moment as if it were like any other.

Hanbin looked at me and reached over and touched my shoulder, letting his hand rest for a moment before he gave it a squeeze. I stood there, even after he dropped his arm back to his side.

"What I mean to say is, I'm glad you're here," he said. "And not somewhere else."

THE TRUTH WAS, I did not know if I deserved to be there. The luck of the timing of the chaebol scholarship scandal and my story had opened all my doors. I was unsure about my work.

In the beginning, when I first moved to New York and met Ruby and Hanbin and all of their friends, I had let them see my insecurity, my terror, simply because I had been drowning in a kind of panic in this alien world. They'd never seen anyone so raw before and they must have marveled at me. They cloaked themselves so well with assurance, smug and luminous.

"Thanks, I guess," I replied to Hanbin, in my most bored voice. "I think Ruby is looking for you." I could see her in the corner, gesturing toward us. Hanbin looked at me for a second and then turned and went to her, joining the group that had formed around her. It was not that she was talking—she was sipping her drink and appeared not to be listening to the conversation at all, but she was always the center of the universe. She made the party crackle to life just by standing there with her cherry-stained mouth and fur coat, her eyes glinting in mockery.

Taking my own drink, I turned around and looked for the boy

----

who had been talking to me earlier. There was nothing better to do when you had no one to talk to at a party than appear to be looking for someone, that I knew. I walked around the first floor, listening carefully to the slices of conversations that I could overhear, then walked up to the second floor, where the walls were painted shades of magenta to contrast with the ebony light fixtures. I imagined how satisfying it would be to paint a wall this color and wondered if that was the perfect job for me, and how long it would take to become qualified. I would really enjoy that—slathering walls with deep colors, painting delicate, fantastical murals. I could see New Yorkers paying a lot of money for home murals.

Hearing voices at the end of the hall, I followed the sound until I came to a partially open door. I pushed it further open recklessly.

It was a study that looked like a movie set of a study, with a mahogany desk in front of the window and floor-to-ceiling shelves lined with books. In the center of the room, four or five people were sitting on two olive sofas that faced each other. They were talking and drinking while a toy poodle sniffed around on the carpet.

"Hey! Come over here."

The boy I had been talking to downstairs waved from where he was sitting. The conversation paused as I walked toward them, trying not to look self-conscious as all eyes focused on me.

"Here, let me pull up a chair." He walked to the desk and brought the chair over next to the sofas.

"This is Byung-joon, who lives here," Jae said, nodding to one of the guys on the other sofa, who lifted his chin in a half nod. "This is— Sorry, what was your name again?" he said, turning to me.

"What the . . . ," the girl sitting to his right asked, her question turning into a laugh. She had shoulder-length bleached hair and cat-eye glasses. "You don't even know her name? This is hilarious."

"I was talking to her downstairs," he said in a mock-aggrieved voice. "Ruby brought her, they're best friends."

With that, the mood shifted from mild to naked interest.

"How do you know Ruby?"

"Did you go to school with her?"

"What year are you at SVA?"

I smiled and said something I'd heard Ruby say once when asked a question she didn't want to answer. "Don't worry about it." This made the others laugh and then they stopped asking questions, looking almost sheepish, before turning back to their previous conversation.

"What was your name again?" I asked the boy.

"Jae," he said. "Your elder at SVA, so you need to be more respectful to me," he joked.

I gave a mock deep bow. "Of course, sunbaenim," I said. "I'm Miho. Are you in art school too?" I asked, turning to Byung-joon.

"Who, me?" asked Byung-joon in astonishment. "No, I'm at NYU."

"I was just thinking how striking the colors are in this apartment," I said, my heart beating fast. "So I was wondering if you were an art student, like us."

"No, no," he said, almost disdainfully. "My decorator did everything. She flew everything in from Portugal, including the painter. He was included with the paint."

Byung-joon's phone rang and he answered in English. "Okay, send him up." Then, standing, he announced, "Pizza's here! I ordered Papa John's!"

Everyone whooped and hollered.

"Dude, I haven't had Papa John's since I was in Korea!" "Awesome!" "I'm *starving*!"

I was still learning the appropriate levels of reaction in this world. Things I should not express shock or delight at. Things I should be

----

overjoyed about. I was not supposed to be amazed by the unusual beauty of the apartment, but thick-crust pizza called for riots.

I stayed sitting while most of the others got up and followed Byung-joon, the puppy yipping at his heels as it followed him out. I looked at Jae out of the corner of my eye. If he moved to leave, then I'd follow.

"You're not hungry?" he asked, still sitting, and I shook my head. "Not really—we just came from dinner," I said.

"Me too, but I'm sure I'll get hungry again in a minute."

"Should you go down then?"

"No, he usually orders tons—it won't run out," said Jae, rolling his eyes. "Then he complains about what it does to his low-carb diet. For dinner he made us get sashimi at his favorite sushi place, but then he gets hungry like, two hours later."

I laughed. This was nice, talking to a boy as if it came naturally to me. I wished I could do it better with Hanbin.

"So how do you know Byung-joon?" I asked.

"Oh, we're family friends. Our dads went to the same high school and college. I grew up with him pretty much. What about you? Do you have a lot of friends from Cheongju here?"

"No," I said. I could have added "of course not," but didn't.

"They're back in Korea," I said. "A lot of them moved to Seoul for university."

"That makes sense," he said. "Cheongju's pretty small, right?"

"Yes," I said. "It's pretty small."

IT WAS SO SMALL that it felt like everyone in town knew us: the Loring Center kids. Orphaned, disabled, or delinquent. Our abandonment scared people, as if it might be contagious. Upon meeting

----

any of us for the first time, people were amazed if we had our faculties intact, as so many did not, and shunned us regardless. In our city, the word "Loring" was synonymous with "retarded." "Isn't he Loring?" or "You look so Loring!" By the time we were in high school, the word was so embedded in the local vernacular that many kids didn't even know it wasn't a real English word.

"Can't wait to get out of this shitty backwater hellhole," my friend Sujin used to shriek whenever she'd come home to the Center after getting in trouble with her teachers. I was lucky: the teachers in my arts high school liked me, but Sujin had been branded a mischief-maker at her school, and we no longer had Miss Loring behind us. She was years dead by then and the directors at the Center changed almost yearly.

I never expected Sujin to actually make it on her own, but she left the first chance she could. She carved out a little life in Seoul, sliver by sliver, reporting back to the rest of us that the word "Loring" meant nothing to people there. Two of the other girls also left for Seoul not long after she did, but I was the first to come to America. Without being adopted, I mean.

"YOU WANT SOME more?" asked Jae, pointing to my glass, which was sitting heavy and empty in my hand.

"Yeah," I said.

"Oh, there's plenty here, you don't need to go to the downstairs bar," he said. Getting up, he walked over to one of the shelves behind me, which I now saw was stocked like a bar, with crystal tumblers and decanters filled with amber liquors.

"Unless you want cranberry again," he said, stopping and looking at me.

- - - -

"No, that's okay. Whiskey is good."

"Here," he said, pouring a glass and handing it to me, then turning around to pour one for himself. "There's ice on the table in the bucket."

We started talking about school—which professors he liked and which to avoid—which cafés had the best seats to study in and where to buy art supplies. His voice was nice: it quickened in excitement whenever he talked about things he liked. He was more animated than the other kids I had encountered at SVA—and in his animation he seemed vulnerable, and to me that vulnerability was moving because I had not seen it since I had come to New York.

"And I heard the library pays pretty well for jobs too," he said. "If you're looking for student jobs. Not to assume that you are——" He stopped what he was saying, looking embarrassed. This was endearing, also.

"I actually have a job already," I said. "I'm working in one of the student galleries." I did not add that it was Ruby's gallery and that was how we had met.

"Oh cool!" he said, relieved that he had not offended me. The fact that he was even worried about that made me feel a rush of affection for him.

Before I could think too much or stop myself I leaned over and gave him a kiss on the cheek.

It was just a peck, and then I drew back into my chair—what I'd done had startled both of us. He smiled and then in a gentle fluid motion, he took both of my hands in his and pulled me over to the couch and then started kissing me, his lips cold and wet and spicy from the whiskey.

"You're really pretty," he whispered. "Your hair is unreal—like

----

something out of a painting. I'm glad I started talking to you down-stairs."

I laughed a little for no reason at all and was leaning against him. This was exhilarating, this soft sofa, the books that surrounded us, his warmth through his sweater. My cheeks were warm from the alcohol, and the hip-hop music that had been too loud when I was downstairs seemed low and soothing now. I had no idea where to leap from here, but I was wildly content.

The door opened and Byung-joon came into the room, Hanbin following him. They both stopped when they saw us entwined.

"Hello, what's *this*?" said Byung-joon. "I thought you didn't even know her name."

Stung, I blushed, but Jae just laughed.

"I was just trying to pretend I wasn't interested," he said without missing a beat, as if it were a punch line. Byung-joon laughed a little too, but in a preoccupied way, as if he was already thinking about something else. I glanced at Hanbin, who was staring down at us with frosty eyes.

"We were talking about how Miho is working in a gallery," said Jae. "You should go see it, Byung-joon. Didn't you say you wanted to buy something for your kitchen?"

Byung-joon looked pained. "Yes, but I have very specific stuff in mind, so I think I'm just going listen to my decorator," he said.

I was mortified that Hanbin would think I was trying to talk myself up somehow.

"I work in Ruby's gallery," I said, not looking at Hanbin. "She has beautiful selections, even if it is a student gallery."

"Oh, Ruby's gallery?" Byung-joon looked discountenanced. "I did hear that she started one . . . she only uses student works?"

"For now," said Hanbin. He was looking at books, running his finger along the shelf. "It's practice for her."

"Of course," said Byung-joon. "Well, then I should definitely go help a friend out. And see the new artists who will be the next big thing!" He guffawed. "Not that Ruby needs any help," he amended, glancing at Hanbin.

"It's a fun little project for her," Hanbin said. "Miho can tell you all about it." He still wouldn't look at me, and it was dizzying—how my heart was soaring and skidding and plunging all at once. And my face! I was blushing again. I was glad Hanbin was not looking at me.

"Here," said Jae, pouring some more whiskey into my glass and handing it back to me. "Anyone else want some more?"

Byung-joon said yes and Jae poured him some too.

"Your face is all red," said Hanbin abruptly. Looking up, I saw that he was talking to me from where he stood by the bookshelf. "Like, bright red."

I clapped my hands to my cheeks and was surprised at how hot they felt.

"You should probably stop drinking if you don't want to look so crazy," he said.

"All you need is some Pepcid before you drink," said Jae. "It's a little trick I use because I get super red too. Here, I'll give you some." Taking his wallet from his pocket, he opened it and fished out a sleeve of white pellets, which he held out to me.

"It won't help now—you have to take that before you drink anything," said Hanbin.

I didn't know what Pepcid was—drugs? But I wasn't about to ask. I took the tablets and put them in my purse. "I'll try it next time," I said weakly. "I have to go to the bathroom." I really needed to see what my face looked like—if I looked as crazy as Hanbin said.

- - - -

As I passed Hanbin on the way out of the room, he said in a low voice, "You should go home, Miho. Don't make a fool of yourself. It's embarrassing."

With the door shut behind me, I felt tears welling and I hurried to the bathroom I'd seen down the hallway. Locking the door, I started crying for real until I saw myself in the mirror and stopped, horrified. My face was distorted and ferocious, patterned with red welts. I looked down and closed my eyes.

Remorse, that was all I allowed myself to feel. "How Loring," they would have said if they could see me now, all the girls from the Center. "Stop being so Loring," I could hear them jeer. Because secretly, to each other and to ourselves, even we used that word that way.

Ara

I do not like going back to Cheongju. I feel bad because it is no fault of my parents that their only daughter has not been to see them in three years. I know the other servants of the Big House pity them twice over, for having a mute daughter in the first place, and an ungrateful one at that. She would rather spend holidays alone than travel home like the rest of the country.

Perhaps this is why I feel so at home with Sujin or Miho. Neither is the type that longs for family. Anyone else would fault me for being a bad daughter, or wonder how it is that I do not withdraw to where I came from, bruised by an impatient city.

My parents are old. They should have had a daughter who is filial and generous, one who sends them a percentage of her paycheck and comes home every month with news of promotions and romantic conquests. TV dramas depict such daughters in droves—with their doe-eyed faces that furrow in sorrow when they choose their beloved, destitute parents over their fabulously wealthy suitors because you cannot have both. I have never met such a daughter in real life, but perhaps that's because they're all at home, busy being virtuous. Kyuri, I suppose, comes close, but she has her own share of problems that would kill her mother and sister if they ever found out.

But for Sujin, and for Sujin alone, I am thinking of going home for Lunar New Year and taking her with me. Watching her fall apart yet again this week in front of our bathroom mirror, agitated and despairing, I have been asking myself how I can get her mind off the state of her face. It has actually come a long way but she is unable to get over how it stays stubbornly swollen.

"All the girls in the blogs had their swelling go down so much faster. It's been more than two months! This really isn't normal, is it? I should call Dr. Shim, right? Don't you think so, Ara? And I keep hearing a clicking sound in my jaw when I *walk*. That cannot be normal or they would have told me at the hospital, right?"

It is true that she does seem to have more swelling in her jawline than the girls from the blogs, but the lower part of her face does not protrude like that of a fish anymore—instead her mouth has moved so far inward that she now, in my secret opinion, looks toothless. Although I assure her that she will look better than any of the bloggers in the end—her transformation will be all the more dramatic for being so prolonged—she pushes my notepad away whenever I write this.

It was of course Taein who gave me the idea and the courage to think it over. In his latest SwitchBox message, he said that he was going home to Gwangju before leaving for Crown's world tour. It would be his first homecoming since his debut. He said our roots are

----

what make us who we are and he wouldn't change the hardships in his past for anything, because they are what inform his lyrics and music and even his dancing today. And if he can find it in his heart to go visit his estranged mother and four older brothers, who used to ignore him and then sued him for a share of his Crown earnings, I can go home too. I have to admit that it makes me feel warm all over, to embark on this parallel journey with Taein.

Sujin will protest at first. What about our tradition, she'll say. Every major holiday, we patronize a new bathhouse and spend the entire day roving from themed room to themed room and stone bath to stone bath, and at night we fall asleep in the TV room with snail masks smeared on our faces and oil of Jeju flowers packed into our brittle hair.

Over the years, we've been surprised by the number of people we see at these baths. It is nice to know that we are not the only ones who don't want to go home.

I love our made-up tradition as much as Sujin does, but I read somewhere that it's best to avoid saunas for a month after surgery for risk of infection, and while hers was more than two months ago, I'd rather not have her go. Having strangers stare at her would also be quite catastrophic for her mental state.

So when my mother sends her usual tentative text about my plans for Lunar New Year and how she hopes I will come home because she has something important to discuss with me, I finally respond yes. And add that Sujin will be joining me. *She is recovering from a big surgery and needs a change of scenery,* I write. This is to let my mother know that she should not get her fragile hopes up about this becoming a regular thing. I imagine my mother gaping at my unexpected reply, and how she will rush to the Big House garage to find my father.

While we are home, Sujin will have to focus all her energies on

- - - -

distracting me from getting upset. To overcompensate for my wretched memories, she'll work herself into a frenzy.

The things I do for her.

WE TRAVEL THE DAY of the actual Lunar New Year, as tickets for the other days were sold out long ago. Miho is also with us. She'd heard we were going back to Cheongju and she wanted to come along and visit her teacher's grave at the Loring Center. I'd felt obligated to invite her to stay with us, and she accepted with alacrity despite my halfhearted offer. Kyuri had already left to visit her mother a few days ago, and I was glad I didn't have to invite her too.

It will be extremely uncomfortable, I warned Miho, underlining *extremely* several times. *You will be sleeping on the floor. On a thin blanket, not a sleeping mat. And our hot water runs out by early afternoon, or whenever there are too many hot showers in a row. And our toilet is the kind where you have to squat.*

"That's fine," Miho said serenely, twisting her long, sinuous ponytail around a too-thin wrist. "I only wash my hair twice a week anyway, and plus I heard your parents' house is a huge hanok that's centuries old? I think I remember Sujin mentioning it when we were younger. I *really* want to see it." Her vivid, piquant face brimmed with expectation.

I shook my head.

"Wait, you *don't* live in a hanok complex?" she asked.

I sighed and wondered how I would explain it all to her, the antiquated unreality of my parents' life. And besides, why would I be working my fingers to the bone in a hair salon if I was some heiress of a centuries-old hanok? It is a wonder that Miho has survived so long in this world with so little sense.

FRANCES CHA

I went to find Sujin, who was staring at herself in the bathroom mirror again like a ghost with all her matted hair hanging down over her cheeks, and tapped her on the shoulder.

"Oh, just let me be," she said in a huffy voice. I tapped her again, hard.

Can you go be useful please, I wrote and showed her. *Miho thinks I am from a rich family and I need you to spell out what staying at my house will actually entail.* Not that Sujin has ever stayed over before either, but she had been to my house several times in middle school, before the incident.

"Why on earth would she think that?" Sujin asked, but now with a gleam of mission in her eyes as she rushed past me to put Miho straight. I wanted to add that it was most certainly due to Sujin that Miho possessed this misinformation in the first place.

"Apparently you need to understand some things," I heard her say to Miho in a bossy voice as I went into my room and banged the door shut.

SO HERE WE ARE, Sujin, Miho, and I, sitting together at the back of a rattling "express" bus with our bags piled high. Even downtown Cheongju—let alone the back hills, where my family is from—will not know what to make of the likes of us: a freshly upbeat Sujin, hiding behind supersize black sunglasses and a violently colorful scarf; ethereal Miho cocooned in an emerald-colored faux-fur coat; and apprehensive, mousy me. The only thing cheerful about me is my hair. I dyed it fuchsia ten days ago, in a fit of panic after buying the bus tickets home. The roots are already showing in an intentionally cool way (I hope). Manager Kwon loved the idea of my going pink and offered to do the initial bleach himself—he always pushes us to ex-

----

148

IF I HAD YOUR FACE

periment with colors in our own hair, the more maniacal the better. He says customers are happier entrusting their hair to people with imagination. I know it will fade by next week, but for now it makes me happy, as if I have set off a signal to the world. Already, I have noticed how people react with great caution to someone with fuchsia hair, even if that person is mute.

Mercifully, the bus is half empty—most of the filial legions transited days ago to the provinces—and the driver estimates the travel time to be just under three hours.

Sujin and Miho are bickering about whether Sujin should visit the Loring Center and Miss Loring's grave with Miho or not. Sujin has not been back since she left.

"I don't understand, I thought you liked Miss Loring," says Miho, looking hurt.

"You are *so* delusional," says Sujin, looking at me wildly. "You can ask Ara. Did I like anyone at the Loring Center? Especially the white woman? I can't believe you thought that for a single minute!"

I pat her back and write *She hated everyone* on my notepad. Sujin passes it to Miho.

"But Miss Loring was so nice! She left all of her money to all of us, remember? All of our school supplies, art supplies, our clothes— that was all her. You have to appreciate that?" Miho looks aghast at Sujin, who sticks out her lip, aggrieved.

"She liked *you* because you were talented and pretty," says Sujin. "*I* never used the art room. She only liked kids who were special in some way because it made her feel good about looking after us. Like Yunmi in the grade below us. Miss Loring liked her because she was so beautiful and she could sing. She got her some music scholarship." Sujin shrugged and amended, "It's not that she *disliked* the rest of us, she just . . . Oh, whatever, you wouldn't understand. And besides, I

149

totally admit that I caused a lot of trouble, so it's just natural she didn't like me."

"You just said it's not that she didn't like you," says Miho.

"Oh shut up," says Sujin.

Miho frowns and shifts savagely in her seat, jostling the pile of bags next to her. The topmost bag, which is hers, falls to the floor with a thud.

"*Shit*," hisses Miho, staring at it with a stricken face.

We look at her.

"It was my present for your parents," she says wretchedly, hopping down and pulling it up onto her lap. Unzipping it, she pulls out a large black box, which has the Joye department store logo etched in spidery, designer font.

"What was it?" whispers Sujin.

I had told both of them in vain that they shouldn't buy gifts for my parents—they would be utterly wasted. But they had both ignored me—Sujin had brought a large green tea fresh cream cake from the new bakery in Shinyoung Plaza, where people lined up around the block. "At least *you'll* like it even if your parents don't," Sujin had said when I wrote in exasperation that my parents didn't eat Western desserts and they would have no earthly way of knowing that it had cost her almost 100,000 won. And if they *were* to ever find out how much it cost, their heads would explode and they would think that she was not only criminally wasteful but obscene.

Miho pries open the lid and sighs with happiness—the deep square box is packed with neat rows of absurdly perfect-looking blush roses. The fragrance that arises from them is startling and lovely in the stale bus air. Sujin and I look at each other—I've never seen an arrangement like this before, but it's obvious they are monstrously expensive. And flowers are the worst possible gift to get

----

people like us! Miho should know this and not waste her money! I start sighing again, and Sujin jabs me with her elbow.

"They are beautiful," Sujin says. "That tumble didn't hurt them one bit."

"They're supposed to be able to last a *year,* can you believe it?" says Miho. "Hanbin's mother had the chemical technology patented in Korea last year."

I sigh and smile at her and hope that she got a discount from her boyfriend at least although I highly doubt it. There is really nothing else to do but turn to the window. We are on the highway now and it is unbelievable how much construction is going on even as we speed further and further away from Gangnam. Each building is topped with a gargantuan orange crane reeling large beams and planks through the air. The scale of these new apartment complexes takes my breath away—I cannot imagine them all filling with people and furniture and light. Hundreds, no, thousands of apartments, so far away from the heart of the capital, and yet I will never be able to afford a single one, no matter how much I save all my life. In a way, I will be glad when we are almost home and the scenery will turn into rice fields and farm plots, and I will be reminded of how far I have come, instead of what I cannot reach.

AT THE TAXI line at Cheongju station, we have to wait half an hour for a car because no one likes to work on New Year's Day. I read somewhere that many of the drivers who work on holidays are ex-convicts who cannot go home to their families because of shame. Fortunately there is a bench by the taxi stand and we huddle together for warmth, Sujin and Miho giggling at the hostile looks we are getting from the occasional passersby. "Home sweet home," says Sujin,

----

theatrically. It's true, no one in Gangnam would give us a second glance—green coats and pink hair and all. Just the fact that we are waiting at the stand marks us as "other"—the rest of the disembarking passengers had cars and family members waiting on the curb with eager smiles.

After three years of being away, it's hard to believe that this dinky two-story building the size of a chain grocery store back in Seoul is one of the main transit hubs here. When I was young, it had seemed to me that the rest of the world was compressed into this bus station, the people with the quicker steps and large travel bags heading for darkly glamorous lives.

A lone taxi loops around the deserted street and we load ourselves in with sighs of relief while Sujin gives the driver the address.

"There's a big hanok estate around there, right?" says the driver, taking another look at us in the rearview mirror. "I heard they film a lot of TV shows there. That actor Lee Hoonki came a few months ago, my buddy drove him there once. You girls live in the area?"

"No, no," says Sujin. "We just somehow are staying there for a few days because we know some people."

There is a silence, and then Sujin abruptly starts chatting up the driver again, which is unusual for her. I wonder if she is remembering what I am remembering—that we are going to pass The Arch on the way to my house.

MAYBE IF I THINK about it hard enough, I will arrive at the conclusion that I didn't come home for three years because I didn't want to walk past the site of my injury. You see, there is only one road to the Big House and there is no way to avoid it.

I am sure most people don't even register the little stone arch

----

when they walk or drive past it—it is faded and so far off the dirt path that it is a wonder it was ever built. I must be the only person that attaches any significance to it whatsoever. When we were in middle school, that was where the bad kids liked to hang out after dark—every crevice was crammed with cigarette butts and gum wrappers and broken lighters. In the years following my accident, I never saw anyone linger there. Rumors about bloodstains and bad luck had made the rounds at the local schools.

UNTIL I LOST my voice, my parents had been saving money to buy a small apartment in the city, which they had been assured would double in value in the following decade. One of the other house-keepers in the Big House had a son who was a real estate agent with connections on the local zoning council, who tipped him off to gov-ernment developments.

So, it was not only I who lost my way in life that day, but my par-ents. That's why I left. I cannot bear to see my parents still living in the little annex on the Big House estate, when they should be going home every night to a gleaming new apartment now worth four times what they would have paid, thanks to the new train station. According to social media posts by old classmates, the formerly de-caying district reverberates with fresh life and money. Instead, that money was counted out to specialist after specialist who told me what I already knew—that I had lost my voice and was unlikely to ever speak again.

I think the hardest part was seeing my parents so terrified on my behalf. I do not know what kind of life they thought I had been head-ing toward, given that I had never stood out academically in any way and had no flaming career ambitions, but my mother in particular

- - - -

became catatonic with grief and had to be hospitalized herself at one point.

It was only recently that I understood they were now worried that no normal man would marry me. The idea that I would never experience motherhood was so distressing that it unleashed a separate wave of guilt for their not having given me siblings. "We thought we were too old," said my mother, twisting her hands. "We were selfish, and now you will have no one when we die."

OFTEN WHEN I am in a place that is crowded and loud, I look around at all the people who are talking and I think about how much of their being is concentrated in their voices, and how I am living a fraction of that life. And then I play a useless game with myself—would it have been preferable to have lost my hearing or sight instead? The sickening self-pity sharpens when I actually listen to what people are talking about.

WHEN OUR TAXI pulls up to the main gate of the Big House, I have to tell the driver to keep going.

"Isn't this the front door?" he says, confused. Sujin has to tell him there's another entrance around the corner and Miho presses her nose against the window to get a better look as we whisk past.

It's not as if my family is forced to use the back entrance—my parents use the front gate several times a day as they go about their jobs—but the back way is the shortest way to our little annex and I'd rather not see anyone from the Big House right now. The black car is parked out front—the bulky Equus, which must be fifteen years old but still as glossy as a mirror, thanks to my father.

My father, or Changee, as he is known by everyone in the neighborhood, has been the Big House chauffeur since he came back from the army in his early twenties. He was the master's manservant's youngest son, and he married my mother, the maid's daughter; they had me very late in life. My father is a quiet man and he did not inherit any of his own father's interest in weaponry. I heard Jun, the youngest son of the Big House, talking about my notorious grandfather to some school friends once. They were examining the enormous wooden staff displayed in his father's meditation room.

"Seo-sshi made that—he was my grandfather's 'slave of the body,'" Jun was saying. "They say he killed several men with it."

"Can he make us one? Is he still around?" asked one of his friends, and I leaned closer from where I had been cleaning the windows of the living room to try to catch a glimpse of them.

"Well, we have Changee, who's the son of Seo-sshi, but he's just a driver and I don't think he knows how to make weapons. But maybe I'll tell him to go learn and make me one," he said. I had been about to muster up the nerve to tell them what I knew about that staff— how it had been used in a fight against a local gang in the market, and how a foreign man had offered a great deal of money for it. But when I heard what Jun said, I threw the wet rag I had been cleaning with on the floor, which was as rebellious a gesture as I could make. Vowing never to set foot in that house again, I stormed off to the annex, only to be told by my mother to run some rice cakes over to Big House kitchen because Jun had brought company over.

WHEN MY MOTHER and father were married, my mother moved into a small annex that had been hastily built at the far end of the estate as a wedding gift, away from the other servants' quarters. Be-

----

cause it was the only structure on the estate that was not traditional hanok architecture, it was also easily the smallest and ugliest building in the complex—a concrete, oblong box with a blue roof that had two small rooms and a kitchen. My grandfather's stern portrait had presided over my room all my life. It was in that room now that both Sujin and Miho would be staying with me.

A few days ago, I had texted my mother to ask if we could borrow more sleeping mats from the Big House. "That cannot possibly be asked," she had responded. "How can you even think of such a thing?"

I had closed my eyes in exasperation when she texted back. There were entire wings that were lying empty and unused, and certainly dozens of luxurious, thick, embroidered sleeping mats. Lady Chang had petted me when I was younger—she would say yes if asked. But my friends and I would be sleeping on thin blankets instead.

AS WE SLIP past the back entrance, Miho comes to a dramatic stop in the middle of the path, surveying the grounds. "This is *so* beautiful," she says in the dreamy voice that is starting to irritate me now. "How old is it? It must be centuries old, right?"

I shrug. It is at least a hundred years old, that I know. The Big Family is obsessed with their lineage.

"You never asked?" marvels Miho. Her eyes are hungry as they travel across the lotus pond, the pagoda, pruned pine gardens, and in the distance, the Big House itself, with its elaborately crafted woodwork and the sloping, gabled roof. Enormous stone frogs stand guard in front of each building's entrance. The grass has been cut to perfection by my father—that is another one of his duties around the house.

"It's not *her* family—why should she care?" snaps Sujin, and I grin at her.

- - - -

"If I lived here, I would never leave," says Miho, still staring.

Perhaps unsurprisingly, she keeps it up even when we finally reach the annex. Setting her bags down in the dim living room, she says it's so cool to see where I grew up and how lucky I was to have my own room as a child.

My parents are not here, of course, even though I did text them what bus we were taking. It doesn't matter that it's a holiday—holidays are the busiest times, with all the extra cooking and cleaning and shopping and rituals.

I try to see it through Miho's and Sujin's eyes, and it is as painful as I predicted. The edges of the living room wallpaper have turned a shade of yellow, and in the far corner a triangular flypaper is studded with insect bodies—a few still flickering with life. I also hope Miho doesn't notice my parents' matching "Adidis" slippers in the foyer.

Miho smiles at me and asks where the bathroom is. I point to the right and walk to the kitchen, where Sujin has already poured herself some barley tea from a jug in the fridge and is eating a rice cake from a plate my mother left on the table.

"It's kind of eerie how it's stayed exactly the same," Sujin says, gesturing around her. "I feel like I'm in middle school again. Your mother made these, right? You used to bring them to school." Sujin pushes the plate toward me but I shake my head. Even as a child, I could see only how much work and cleanup they involved, and I did not like to eat them.

WE GO FIND my mother in the kitchen of the Big House. She is making dumplings with Mrs. Youngja and Mrs. Sukhyang at the round table. Waving their flour-coated hands, Mrs. Youngja and Mrs. Sukhyang yell in excitement when they see me.

"Look who it is! Ara! Pink hair! Oh my goodness! And you gained some weight!"

"No, she hasn't, she's lost weight!"

Mrs. Youngja and Mrs. Sukhyang immediately start squabbling while my mother waves me closer. When she soundlessly wraps me in an emotional hug, my heart gives a guilty jump as I take in how lined her face has become. Her skin looks powdery and thin, and uneven silver streaks her hair. Can she have aged this much in what seems so short a time?

I write a New Year greeting and show her. I also write out Sujin's and Miho's names and beckon them to come say hello.

They enter shyly, then bow. Elders make them uneasy.

"It's been a long time," says my mother to Sujin. I am relieved that there is no sorrow or reproach lining her voice. She sounds too ex-hausted to mind the girl she once disapproved of for leading her daughter astray.

"It's so wonderful to be back here again!" says Sujin loudly.

I am waiting for my mother to comment on Sujin's face—she looks like a completely different person after all, but my mother doesn't say a thing.

"You've been here before?" asks Mrs. Youngja, as she rummages in the refrigerator to find us some snacks. "Are you a school friend of Ara's?" Mrs. Youngja is a relatively new addition to the staff—she started working at the Big House when I was in high school. Mrs. Sukhyang is a good decade older than my mother, but she looks about the same age, probably due to the harsh blue-black shade of her hair.

"She is a middle school friend of Ara's," my mother answers. And then she says something that flabbergasts me. "You know, one of those children from the orphanage."

My throat constricting, I look at Sujin and Miho sharply, and so do Mrs. Youngja and Mrs. Sukhyang. The girls haven't heard that reference, or that tone, in a long time.

"I grew up there too," says Miho steadily. The women cluck in sympathy—"motherless poor things" is the prevailing sentiment. But we all know that the minute we leave the kitchen, that sympathy will be undercut by something else. I'm sorry, I telegraph to Sujin, who blinks rapidly to say it's fine and I'm not to worry about it.

"Come, come, you need to eat after such a long journey," says Mrs. Sukhyang. She opens the lid of one of the pots on the stove and carefully drops in the dumplings.

"They live in Gangnam, you know," Mrs. Youngja says knowingly to Mrs. Sukhyang. Without holiday traffic, it is barely two hours away by bus, but I know that neither of them has been anywhere near where we live now. All of their children live in the Cheongju area; some of them further out in Daejeon.

My mother brings kimchi and dumpling sauce to the table and indicates for us to sit down. Miho says thank you softly and Sujin echoes her.

"She has gotten much prettier," says Mrs. Youngja to my mother.

"Such style," says Mrs. Sukhyang.

"It's Gangnam style," they chortle together.

"When are you girls leaving?" asks Mrs. Youngja.

"The day after tomorrow," says Sujin.

"What? That's so soon! Well, there isn't any time, then," says Mrs. Sukhyang. "You better ask Ara quick."

"Ask her what?" Sujin says. The women look at her and I know what they are thinking—how forward, such bad manners, must be the orphanage. My skin tingles but Sujin winks at me.

My mother looks pained but seems to make up her mind. It can't

----

be all that serious if she is going to tell me in front of a kitchen full of people.

"How is the salon job going?" she asks me slowly.

"It's going *great*," pipes Sujin. "Ara can cut my hair with her eyes closed now. She has so many regulars that they have to call at least a week in advance for an appointment. So many rich ladies who all want her to give them digital perms. They *love* talking to her. They say she is very soothing."

"Is that right?" asks my mother, smiling with pride. I am about to shrug, but Sujin jabs me under the table, so I grimace and nod instead.

What did you want to talk to me about? I write.

My mother takes the notepad and holds it closer to see, and then takes a breath. "Now that you are home, I just want you to set aside some time," she says. "You're getting older, and so many of your friends are marrying."

What are you talking about? I write furiously. *No one is getting married. Don't you ever see the news? It's a national problem.*

She waits for me to finish writing, and then reads what I wrote.

"Well, here everyone is getting married. You know Hyehwa? From the bakery?"

Hyehwa had been my year in high school. Sujin and I both nod.

"She's getting married next month! I see her every week when we get our bread. Maybe you can stop by and tell her congratulations in person while you are here."

I had thought that my parents would have given up by now on their mute, wayward, idol-obsessed daughter. Hyehwa had always been a goody two-shoes in school. Maybe Sujin pushed her around a few times, I don't remember. I glance at Sujin, but she is looking very innocent as she spoons more broth from her bowl.

"Moon the hairdresser is looking for an assistant," says my mother abruptly. "Do you remember him?"

Of course I knew him—shaggy Mr. Moon, who had a beard and a raspy voice. I'd swept floors for him for a summer in high school and babysat his son sometimes. He had given me free hair tint samples that I had passed to Sujin.

They must be doing well if he needs an assistant, I write. His wife and her twin sister also worked in the salon, I remember. But my mother couldn't possibly be thinking that I would come work for Mr. Moon's tiny little shop back home.

"His wife left," she says. "Her sister too. They went back to Daejeon."

Well that is sad, I write.

"His son really liked you," she says.

The beady-eyed Moon baby definitely had not liked me. He had shrieked his head off whenever I took him for a walk in the stroller.

"We were talking about you, and he remembers you warmly," says my mother. The other two women are watching me with owlish eyes. "He asks about you quite often."

"He is a good man, that Moon," says Mrs. Sukhyang, nodding. "He was too good for that tramp of a wife of his."

Sujin and I exchange amused glances, but Miho leans forward.

"How old is he?" she asks.

"Oh, in his prime," says Mrs. Youngja. "I saw him helping the herbal medicine doctor move in enormous medicine cabinets the other day. Moon was just carrying them on his bare shoulders as if they were small sacks of rice!"

"I wonder if he would be able to match her Gangnam salary though," Miho says gravely, not looking at me.

"Salary?" sputters Mrs. Sukhyang. "It's not about the *money*." She

- - - -

stops, posed. "It's about what kind of man would appreciate pink hair!" she says triumphantly.

"You have to be practical, Ara," says my mother, staring at me. "He would like to meet you while you are here."

"I bet he would," says Sujin darkly. "She's ten years younger than his already young wife!"

"Why did she leave?" asks Miho.

"I never liked her," says Mrs. Sukhyang emphatically. "When they first opened, she gave me a horrendous haircut that Moon had to fix afterward. And I think she was *drunk*." No one else speaks.

"Just meet him once," says my mother, pleading. "Just once. Is it too much for a mother to ask for? A chance at a normal life for her daughter? In Gangnam, people are not normal—they do not lead normal lives. Here, you would be cared for. It would be comfortable. But just one *conversation*—that is all I am asking."

I close my eyes and take a breath. I can feel Sujin's distressed, near-hysterical energy—as distractions go, this is proving extremely successful. For Sujin's sake I close my eyes as if I am in pain, when actually, I think this is all hysterically funny. Mr. Moon! And the Moon baby!

"We will work on her, don't worry," says Miho in a reassuring voice. "You can be sure we'll talk about it all night."

I AM IN DESPAIR as we walk out of the kitchen, my mother having sent us to the basement to bring up some urns of white kimchi.

"Wow," murmurs Miho behind me as we noiselessly pass the main hallway to the stairs. I do not know what she is so oohing about—it is just a very old house with very old Western furniture that doesn't match the traditional Korean architecture at all. It's not like one of

----

those beautifully curated hanok guesthouses with mother-of-pearl inlaid furniture and embroidered silk screens.

In the basement there are rows and rows of urns. I head to the white kimchi corner and pick the smallest jar. To my left, Miho is opening one of the biggest jars, and the spicy, pungent aroma wafts up through the dim hall. "Smells amazing," she says, while Sujin slaps her hand and slides the lid back on.

Why did you tell my mother you will try to persuade me? I write and show her.

"Why *wouldn't* you see him?" says Miho.

"What are you saying, you crazy girl?" says Sujin.

"Look, not even counting the fact that it would make your elderly mom happy and shut her up by taking up ten minutes of your time, but why *wouldn't* you go see what an alternate life is like?" Miho lifts the lid of another urn, and this time, she dips a finger in and licks it. She turns to look at me and shrugs.

"If I were you I would look at every single option and then see what is the best, and that way you will have more conviction about whatever you choose," she says.

I shake my head. Perhaps that works for her, but I don't need to go see Mr. Moon to know what my life would be like here. It does not even matter how nice he is, or whether he would make a good husband. To me it is about what is written in people's eyes when they look at me here. It would just be another entry on the long list of the lowly life of the Big House servants' daughter, mute and second wife. I would rather die alone in the middle of the city listening to Taein's voice every day on my phone.

What makes me sad is that my mother thinks this is the best my life can be.

"Well," says Sujin. "Miho kind of has a point."

- - - -

I glare at her.

"It would make your mom so happy if we go around and see him, and it would be funny!"

I shake my head with violence.

"Oh, come on," says Sujin. "There's nothing to do here anyway."

You could revisit the Loring Center with Miho, I write.

"And why would I do that?" she says, her eyes glinting.

IT IS NEW YEAR'S DAY, he is probably not at his stupid shop, I write and show Sujin before we start walking over to the bike shed. None of us have brought any gloves and our fingers are going to freeze off if we bike into town.

"Well then, we can go get some coffee at the bakery and say congrats to Hyehwa," Sujin says. "Make her give us a discount." She smiles evilly.

We round the corner and Sujin leads the way through one of the inner gates. She has a good memory, that one. We have only gone bike riding a few times and that was years and years ago. My father still keeps all the bikes in the shed clean and oiled, although I doubt anyone uses them, now that all the children of the Big House have left the nest.

In front of the bike shed, we run into a man on the path wearing a thick black down coat. It is the youngest son, Jun, who looks at us with a startled smile, hands in his coat pockets. I haven't seen him in years, ever since he went for his mandatory military service. I had heard from my mother that he is a nuclear scientist now, working at a government think tank. He is the only one of the children who is still unmarried.

"Hello," he says. "Who are you?" His voice is friendly and inter-

----

ested as he looks at us but mostly at Miho. She does look very out of place here, in her emerald green coat and her flowing hair, which she has fashioned into a high ponytail for the bike ride.

The girls fall back a little and I bow, catching his eye. "Oh, it's Ara!" he says in surprise. "Are these your friends?" His tone takes on the jolly, avuncular tone of the Big Family that I mind so much. I nod.

"Hello," pipes up Sujin. "We're visiting Ara's parents for New Year's."

"Ah, I see," he says, running his fingers through his hair. "New friends from Seoul."

"Happy New Year," says Sujin, not contradicting him. She had met him several times in our past life.

"Happy New Year," he says.

Bowing again, I make the first move to walk past him and into the shed, and the girls follow. As I pick my old bike and search for others that Sujin and Miho can ride, I look up, and he is still standing at the end of the path, looking back at us before he catches my eye. He waves and I turn away, pretending not to see him.

WHEN I WAS in school, I used to live for glimpses of Jun. Those were the years I helped my mother in the Big House after school, so that I could go sit on his chair and sometimes even his bed when my mother wasn't looking. If my life was a drama, he would have fallen in love with me and battled his parents for a happy ending with the housekeeper's daughter.

But here we are, my friends and I, streaming into town on rusty, creaking bikes, going to peek at a lonely old man who has failed at love, who has a son and already thinks in terms of concessions.

All for a joke, of course.

- - - -

I would care if I hadn't already stopped caring about anything years ago, the day I lost my voice.

IT TAKES US almost twenty minutes to get to town because Miho is precarious on a bike, plus she keeps stopping to stare at the trees even though Sujin and I yell at her that it's cold and to please take a photo on her phone and stare at it later. "But the colors don't show up properly in a photo," she protests.

The bakery is on the same street as the Moon hair salon, but the girls insist on heading to the salon first. There are no cars because everyone is still eating and making merry at home with their families.

"We won't go in or anything," Miho says between pants as she pedals harder. "So stop worrying so much, Ara! I just want to have an image of what he looks like."

Sujin only laughs and sticks her tongue out in my general direction.

It seems to me that it is particularly cruel of Miho to insist on this when her boyfriend, Hanbin, is not only Mr. Handsome and Rich but also our age and childless. If I didn't know her, I would think that she wants to see Moon just to make fun of me. But she is so genuinely curious about so many things that I have to believe her. She will often strike up conversations with strangers on the subway, to their surprise and distrust, and comes away baffled by their hostility. "In New York, you can talk to anyone about anything at any time and have a conversation so long you'll fall a little bit in love with that person, and then never see them again," she told me. It now feels strange to her that in Korea, if you try to strike up a conversation with someone

- - - -

you have not been introduced to, people look at you as they would at a large rat, but if even the flimsiest of introductions is made by the most peripheral of acquaintances, they fuss over you like a long-lost sibling.

We pull up with our bikes across the street from the salon, which is as small as I remember it—just three fake leather swivel seats in a glass box of a store, with a sign outside that reads MOON HAIR & STYLE in English and OPEN on the door. The only reason I even agreed to get on this bike was because I had been so sure it would be closed for the holiday. Who is getting haircuts today anyway? Isn't it bad luck to cut your hair on New Year's?

He is inside sweeping, his back toward us. Hair is all over the floor. I remember cleaning those floors for him, trying to do it as quickly as I could so that the next customer could sit down. During that summer I was working here, when the salon had only been open for a few months, there had been long waits for a haircut by Mr. Moon, especially after he gave the grocery store owner a drastic haircut that miraculously transformed her face, and subsequently her personality. He never bothered with his own hair, which is still shaggy and wild, and now even from across the street I can see that it is unwashed and graying.

"He seems to need a haircut," says Sujin. "Maybe you could go in there and give him one."

Miho starts giggling. I make a face and take out my notepad and am fishing for my pen when I hear Sujin say, "Uh-oh."

When I look up, Mr. Moon is standing on the doorstep with the door open, waving at us to come toward him. His usually expressionless face looks keen.

"He means us, right?" says Sujin, looking around to check.

- - - -

"Look how excited he is to see you!" whispers Miho.

Stifling more giggles, Miho hops off her bike and starts rolling it across the street, and Sujin does the same. Furious, I follow them.

"It's been a long time," he says slowly, his gaze on me. "Are you home for the holiday? These must be your friends." He nods to Sujin and Miho.

"Happy New Year!" says Sujin, bowing. "Ara used to give me all the hair dye you gave her when she worked here. I went to school with her."

"Ah, that friend," says Mr. Moon with recognition. "She asked for violet coating once, I think."

"That's right!" says Sujin. "It was summer break."

"I like the pink," says Mr. Moon, nodding toward me. "That must have taken a long time." I give him a weak smile.

"Ara works in a really big salon in Gangnam now," says Sujin.

"I heard from her mother," he says. "That's really impressive."

"Are you spending the New Year here in the salon?" asks Miho. I frown at her but she pretends not to see me.

"Yes, well," he says. "Nothing much else to do, I'm afraid. And I actually had a few customers come in this morning. Busy people, you know, who don't have the time otherwise."

I reach over and tap Sujin on the shoulder and jerk my head in the direction of the bakery.

"Oh, we were on our way to say hi to our friend at the bakery who's getting married," says Sujin. Clearly I have been tortured enough. She hops back on her bicycle. "Good seeing you!"

I am about to hop onto my own seat when Mr. Moon says, "Actually, I have something for you, Ara. Could you come in for a second?"

"We'll be in the bakery, Ara!" says Miho, and they push off to-

----

gether, the traitors. I put the brake down on my bike and slowly follow him up the steps and into the salon again.

Inside, the world is muted and smells of hairspray and wax and
hair oil. It is the familiar smell that abruptly wakes me up—I hadn't
realized until now that I had been in an almost dreamlike state.
Coming back home, seeing Jun, biking through barren streets had
not felt real.

In the back of the salon, Mr. Moon opens a drawer in a wooden
dresser and shuffles through a pile of notebooks. Up close, I see that
he is much older—he looks tired and has gained some weight in the
face. His skin is darker and more leathery than it used to be, but his
eyes had taken on an alarmingly emotional light when he looked at
me. I pick up a finishing spray and pretend to look at it, then set it
back down.

"I was cleaning out all the drawers and I found this the other day,"
he says, handing it to me. "I think it's yours?"

It's a bright blue notebook of mine from high school, from my
ethics and morality class. I must have left it behind one of the eve-
nings I was working here. I flip through it and wonder at my neat
handwriting. "Public Order and Social Ethics," "Rules of Modern Society," "Philosophy of Morality." It had been an easy class and I had
been surprised to have been ranked in the top ten across the entire
grade—in all three years of high school that had been the only subject I had found effortless. Perhaps it was years of heightened noon-
chi—my skill of reading people was rarely wrong—but the answers
in the multiple-choice tests had seemed to me clear to the point of
idiocy.

I give a little smile and bow of thank you, and roll up the notebook to put in my bag. As I turn to leave Mr. Moon clears his throat.

"I'm glad to hear that you are doing well in Seoul," he says. His

- - - -

tone indicates that he wants to say something else. I sigh inwardly and send a mental distress signal to Sujin.

"You probably have everything you need in terms of supplies, huh?" he says, waving awkwardly around the shop. "Otherwise I would give you something . . . some finishing oil, hair packs . . ."

I shake my head.

"Well then," he says. He takes a breath and faces me. "You know, I always thought I would live in Seoul. It's a funny thing. You don't realize how set you get in your ways as you grow older."

I wait to hear what he is trying to say.

"I'm glad you are living your life in this adventurous way that I never got to. It makes me feel so proud when I hear about you. It's a strange thing. I imagine it will be that way with my son one day, but people say never to expect much from children so I don't know. I suppose I feel this way because I had a hand in your life, and that these adventures have been possible because of me."

He coughs self-consciously and I feel very confused. Wiping his hands on his pants, he continues.

"I know, I have come to the realization these days that I am a foolish man. Not having a kid to hurry home to, and not having his cries and tantrums and needs filling up every waking moment of my life—it leaves a lot of time for thinking and remembering conversations that should have happened, but did not. And I want to rid my life of any regret. If I were to die tomorrow, I want to have said everything I should have to the people I know."

He proceeds to tell me that he was the person who had called the police that night—that night of my injury. He had been walking to the Big House that day because Lady Chang had come into the shop for the first time and had left her scarf there. He couldn't bear to

----

170

think of Lady Chang worrying about the fate of her expensive scarf at the hands of his customers and he did not have her phone number, so he'd put it carefully into a shopping bag and set off for the Big House after his last customer of the evening.

In the twilight he had enjoyed the walk very much until he began hearing the unmistakable sounds of violence. His first reaction had been fear—he had turned around and started walking quickly away, but almost instantly he had come back to his senses and realized that the screams were those of young girls. He imagined the worst and he had to step up. He called the police from his phone and gave them the location and a description of what he was hearing, and as soon as he hung up, he crept toward the arch.

He saw me first, he says. He recognized me from my trips to the salon with my mother. In fact, she had been the one who had introduced him to Lady Chang, who continued to this day to be a loyal customer.

He saw me and what was happening to me and he began running toward us. It looked—he said—as if the girl was going to kill me. She appeared entirely crazed and was brutally smashing something against my head and showing no signs of stopping. He started yelling "Police! Police!" and other things he could not remember. In an instant, all the students, including me, had disappeared so fast that he had been dumbfounded. He'd taken a few halfhearted steps in the direction I had gone, but then had heard sirens and decided to stay to talk to the police so that they would not see him running and mistake him for a villain in the scenario. And sure enough, the police had seemed suspicious of his involvement, but luckily his clothes were free of bloodstains and a great deal of blood had been spilled that night. They asked if he had recognized anyone and he

----

said that it had been one of his younger customers but he did not know my name, which was true. At the time, he had also not known that I lived at the Big House.

"It has recently come to my attention—actually, yesterday, when one of the women who work with your mother had her hair permed—that my inquiring about you and how you are doing in Seoul has been misconstrued as something resembling romantic attention, especially since, well, as I am sure you know, the situation with my wife," he says quietly, looking at the floor. "It has made me quite miserable to think that people were thinking that about me, but I did not know how to set things right. This is why I was so astonished to find you and your friends looking straight at me through the window just now, because I had been pondering how to rectify matters."

His phone rings and he fishes it out of his pocket. "Lawyer Ko" lights up the screen and he silences it, grimacing, before his eyes return to me. He takes a deep breath.

"No matter how dark things get for me, the memory that I saved a life—that my life has mattered—has been something I can cling to," he says with a catch in his voice. "It is, perhaps, the only lifeline that I possess. And I am so grateful that I can tell you this. What your life means to your parents—you will realize it one day, when you have your own children."

LATER, WHEN SUJIN and Miho finally emerge from the bakery carrying paper bags of free bread and cakes that Hyehwa has clearly piled upon them, I am sitting on the curb looking up at the cloudless wintry sky and wondering if I am a happier person than I was twenty minutes ago, when I did not know what I know now.

"Hey! So did he propose?" asks Sujin, as she breaks off a piece of choux cream pie and feeds it to me. It is cold and sweet and I immediately hold out my hand for more.

"I can't believe someone our age is getting married," says Miho, looking back at the bakery, where I see a trim Hyehwa organizing cake slices through the cloudy glass window. "Do you want to go in there and say hello?" she asks. I shake my head.

"I'm sorry, but getting married in your twenties is just ridiculous," says Sujin in an exaggerated hushed voice. "What a fool."

They quarrel over whether we will all head to the Loring Center now together, or if Sujin will just return to the Big House by herself.

"You think Ara wants to be here? Now we're doing what *you* don't want to do, and you better just suck it up," says Miho, reaching out and giving Sujin a little poke. Loading the bags full of bread onto the handlebars, Sujin exhales a sigh of resignation and says the bread and cakes better be going to the children and not a loaf to the teachers. And with that, the three of us hop on our creaking, frozen bicycles and start off toward the Loring Center, each of us grasping at our own shifting versions of the past.

Kyuri

Bruce has not been to the room salon for almost three weeks now. And the last two times he was here he sat me alongside fat, foreign investors, clearly to punish me. I still have a bad taste in my mouth from finding out about his engagement, but Madam has been commenting on his absence and I need her to shut her face. I have tried texting him, but he doesn't even respond. The bastard.

I don't know what possesses me, but when the last Sunday of the month rolls around, I tell Sujin that I am going to treat her to dinner at Seul-kuk, at the Reign Hotel, to celebrate the holiday. Independence Movement Day has been looming for weeks—I have been staring at the calendar, waiting for the days to pass.

It takes a few attempts to convince her to go, because you can still see the stitches on her puffy eyelids and the lower half of her face

----

174

looks blown up, like a sad, old balloon. I say she looks pretty and no one will even notice.

"I still can't chew that well," she says slowly, shaking her head. "My teeth are not aligned. And I still feel so self-conscious on the street even with a mask."

"They have the best jajangmyeon—the noodles are going to be so soft," I say instead. "And there's soup. So many different kinds of soup. Shark fin soup. Have you ever had *real* shark fin soup?"

"They don't sell that anymore. And I would never eat the fin of a poor shark," says Sujin. "And isn't Seul-kuk the most expensive Chinese restaurant in the entire country? One of my clients from the nail salon was talking about that place—a bowl of jajangmyeon is almost forty thousand won there! Kyuri, you can't be serious. You're usually so careful with money!" Her eyes are round in her swollen face.

"Look, I want to see if it's as good as they say on TV, okay? Are you coming or not?"

When we show up at the Reign Hotel a little before seven and take the elevator to the second floor—Sujin having taken an hour to get dressed, even with my help and my accessories—the restaurant is full and the host asks us to wait in the hall. And so we do, settling ourselves in the red silk chairs by the entrance, my head whipping around whenever I hear the ping of an elevator.

"What's wrong with you?" hisses Sujin, but then I see a group arriving that must be them. A family of four, very dressed up, faces taut. The mother, fussy-looking in a lime green knit two-piece with a parrot-shaped sparkling brooch on the lapel, is clucking like a hen and picking lint off the father's suit as he brushes her away. The brother looks pleasant and tall, the girl is wearing a conservative blush-colored long-sleeved dress and carrying a matching tweed Chanel bag from two seasons ago. She's pretty, in a washed-out way,

----

but completely flat-chested—and looks much younger than I would have guessed. Bruce constantly tells me how much he adores my breasts. "I fantasize about them at the office," he says. "I get delirious thinking about tickling your nipples until they get hard."

And then, right behind them, the other elevator opens and Bruce stalks out, his parents and two spindly, chiffon-clad sisters in tow. A strand of hair hangs over his eyes and I want to brush it back.

Bruce's mother is terribly thin and dressed in what almost looks like deep mourning, in head-to-toe heavy black silk. Enormous diamonds sparkle at her ears and wrists and throat.

"Why, hello," cry the mothers, "so nice to finally meet you!"

The men shake hands gruffly and there is a disgusting orgy of bowing and compliments all around. Bruce is smiling widely with his hands in his pockets, as if he hadn't been dreading this moment for months.

"Looks like a sangyeonrae," whispers Sujin into my ear. "They look straight out of a drama! Can you believe the jewelry? It must be real, right?"

"Shall we go in?" they murmur and start filing past us, none of them giving us a glance. Bruce and his girlfriend are at the back, whispering and smiling together. Then he sees me.

For a second, he stops walking. I am looking at him with my head tilted, my fingers clutching the first Chanel bag that he bought me—a dark red caviar jumbo flap with leather rosettes and gold hardware. It's a thing of beauty, this bag. My most cherished possession. He blinks in bewilderment and confusion, but almost immediately, his face hardens to stone. The girlfriend looks up at him with a question and he puts his arm around her and steers her past us, into the low din of the restaurant.

"Excuse me, your table is ready now if you'll follow me," says a voice in my ear and I jump a little. Sujin flutters ahead with the supercilious host and I follow in a dream. As we begin the meal, the waiter keeps recommending the damn set menu. I resign myself to spending twice the exorbitant rate I'd already budgeted in my head. At least Sujin enjoys herself—she spoons up every drop of every sauce on both our plates. "Do you realize how much that slice of abalone costs? What do you mean you can't eat it? You are being so ridiculous, Kyuri!"

Halfway through our meal I get a text.

"Your life is over, you psycho bitch."

It's from Bruce, of course. From the next room, a lifetime and a universe away.

A FEW YEARS AGO, I had a friend who left the room salon we both worked at when she got engaged. She had been set up on a blind date by her mother's friend and it had worked out and suddenly she was to be married. I don't know how she paid off her debts to the shop.

We drank together often and she was so happy about her new life. She showed me the bridal furniture she was getting for the apartment she was going to live in with her husband. We sighed over how pretty the lace was on the bedroom set, how darling her little ivory dining table looked next to her accent wall.

One day, I called her and her phone had been disconnected. She had changed her number because she no longer wanted to get phone calls from me and the other girls.

I understood, of course. I had thought, naïvely, that I would be

- - - -

there at the wedding, holding her veil and sprinkling handfuls of rice and rose petals down the aisle. But I was happy for her to escape this life, and I did not blame her.

She called me a few months after her wedding from a blocked number. She sounded upbeat but distant. "I am always amazed by how busy I am!" she said, launching immediately into her narrative. "It's crazy how much time goes into grocery shopping and cleaning and cooking and the logistics of running a house. And I have to look after my in-laws. They are retired so they need a lot of care. They expect it of me."

She did not ask me a single question. At the end of that brief conversation she said that she was sorry she had changed her number and that she wished me luck. Then she hung up and she did not call me again.

I'VE HAD FRIENDS before who were taken in by men who wanted them to become their seconds. These girls would then leave the shop, making a big fuss about how they would invite the rest of us over to their new apartments when they were all set up. Of course there was no mention of love or anything, but what would always make me angry was the embers of hope glowing in their eyes that they could not hide. The men had told them things that fanned it. Sometimes it was a year or even two years later, but they all came back. Every single one.

They'd played house in a nice apartment, sometimes even a beautiful apartment, and practiced monogamy and invited us girls over and watched TV and waited around a lot. Their reasons for coming back were somewhat varied—sometimes they couldn't stand the

----

watchfulness of the neighbors, who they claimed knew they were mistresses and were afraid they'd bring the apartment prices down. Sometimes they got pregnant and had abortions. Sometimes the wives found out and they had hot coffee thrown in their faces and threats to have their uteri ripped out.

Most of the time, though, the men grew tired of it all first. And when the girls came back, they were older and usually fatter and they had to go on extreme diets and take pills and all that or the madams would shame them ceaselessly. And their hope-filled glimmers would be crushed to powder.

But back to Bruce—I don't know what came over me that Sunday at the Reign Hotel. I have always thought of hope as a natural folly of youth that should be discarded as soon as possible.

It is inexplicable to me, and I did not know I was capable of surprising myself. Perhaps I liked him more than I realized. I should have known that I could not afford to.

MADAM SLAPS ME when she finds out. It is Monday, the day after, and I am fixing my makeup in the dark, cramped waiting room. She comes running as fast as she can in her tight lace minidress and high heels. She is on the phone but frantically looking for someone. You, she mouths, pointing a bony finger at me. You, come.

Snapping my compact shut, I get up and follow her into an empty room. In the quiet darkness, I can hear a tinny, otherworldly voice yelling on the other end of Madam's phone.

I will ruin you. *Do you understand what I can do to you? WHO I AM? WHO I KNOW? You will never be able to work again!* To my horror, I recognize the crackling, hysterical voice. It is Bruce.

Madam tries to placate him at first, but he does not listen and keeps screaming. Her body has gone rigid and she keeps clenching and unclenching her free hand—the painted talons folding and unfolding.

"She is here right now and I will kill her myself," she seethes into the phone. "Let us handle it. Please, just think about it for a few days before doing anything hotheaded, *please*. I am *so* sorry."

When she hangs up, she slaps me so hard I fall to the floor. I was already crying from terror and she is so angry that she picks up a whiskey glass from a set on the table and throws it against the wall. It shatters around me like fireworks.

"You fucking cunt," she screams. "Are you out of your mind? What have you done?"

At the sound of the breaking glass, the door swings open and girls swarm in as Madam yells for someone to bring her an empty bottle. If not for Yedam and Seohyeon holding her back, she would be smashing a bottle against my head. I heard she did that once, to a girl who slapped a customer. The girl had already been in a great deal of debt to her when it happened, and she had had to get more than fifty stitches in her scalp. The customer had been about to sue the shop but stopped, mollified, when he heard about the girl's injuries.

The manager comes running in and tells Madam that things will be fine, that Bruce is just angry now and it will pass, and isn't Kyuri the shop's ace? So many men asking for her every night and Madam doesn't want to lose all that business, does she?

Breathing hard, Madam stands in the middle of the room, not looking at anyone. The only sound I hear is some quiet, stilted sobbing, and I realize that it is coming from me. Then she turns on her heel and stalks out without another word and the girls help me up

- - - -

and hug me. They are asking what happened, why is Madam so mad? They want to know so that they won't repeat my mistake, whatever I did.

I tell them that one of my regulars is angry with me and leave it at that.

FOR A WEEK I hold my breath and live as if I am swimming in a dream. At work, in the rooms, I am bubbly, I am witty, I am effervescent to the point of frenzy. A few of my customers ask me why I am so high. "Did something exciting happen? Share the good news!" they say when I can't keep still and bounce around, drunk out of my mind. They think I am even greater fun than usual.

"You are why I come here, Kyuri," they say, slapping their thighs appreciatively and calling the waiter to order more drinks. I sing, I dance, I do splits and my tight, rented dress rips and they scream with laughter. "This is not what I expected from a ten percent joint," say some of the new customers who are here with the regulars, but they say it in an entertained and not disapproving way.

All the while I am praying that Bruce's fury is cooling. The manager has already told me that Madam added a charge for her broken glass and cleaning bill to my debts to her.

"Just so you know, she might charge a few other things to you too, just to relieve her anger. I would let it go if I were you," he says nervously, pulling at the cuffs of his sleeves. He is new and very nice, unlike the other managers. He looks like a teenager with overgrown bangs—although he must be in his late thirties at least. His skin is terrible, and I want to recommend some face masks to him because he is so nice. I am sure it won't last long, though, his niceness. Money will turn him soon enough. When he warns me, I say nothing, just

----

pick at my nails, which need repolishing. I have been neglecting them shamefully.

ON FRIDAY, one of Bruce's friends—the pudgy lawyer—comes in with his clients and co-workers. When I hear this from Sejeong, who has just come into the room I am working in, I excuse myself and hurry over to his.

"Oh, no, no, no," he says in alarm, his plump face flushing when I walk in and sit down next to him. "Not you."

"Why?" I say gaily, tossing back my hair as my heart starts to pound. "Aren't you glad to see me? I missed you so much!"

"I heard what happened," he says in a low voice. "Our group of friends—we all know." He leans forward and whispers, "I didn't want to come here, but my client insisted, okay? And I could have told my client the story too and he definitely would have gone some-where else, but my girlfriend's place happens to be close to here and I want to stop by before I have to go home."

I look at him unhappily. I've only had a few drinks in my first two rooms, but my heart is already starting to feel as if it's being squeezed.

"I don't know that what I did was so wrong," I say. I know I shouldn't talk about it, especially here and now, but I just can't help myself.

He looks at me in disbelief. "This is exactly what's so terrible about it," he says. "Are you serious? Are you insane? Someone actually has to explain this to you? I don't even know where to begin. Do you even understand how humiliated his family would have been because of you? At the *Reign* Hotel? Are you kidding me?"

His raised voice draws attention and the room falls silent. The other girls quickly try to start up conversations again, but a lean man

----

with silvery hair addresses him sharply. "What is the matter?" he says, looking displeased. "Why is the mood in the room turning this way?" He is clearly the client.

The chubby lawyer looks panicked. "I'm sorry, sir," he says, swallowing. "Er, this girl, she was secretly trying to throw away her drink, so I was getting angry."

I am caught off guard, but I quickly bow my head in the client's direction. "I'm so sorry, sir," I say. "I was drinking too quickly so I just wanted to rest a bit but I should not have."

My stomach is clenched so hard it hurts, but I hurriedly take up my glass and gulp the whiskey down. "It seems particularly smooth tonight!" I say with a big smile. "You ordered the expensive stuff!"

The client laughs and says he likes my style. He points to my cup, and I hurry to fill it again. Taking a quick deep breath, I drink another shot. It burns down my throat. "I like good drinkers," he booms. "I like this place. No one tries to back out of the party. I'm sure you were mistaken, Shim-byun. The girls here—their livers are made of iron."

"Of course, sir, I love this place too!" says the lawyer hastily. "Kyuri here is one of the prettiest girls in the shop. We were just teasing each other. She has a great sense of humor."

"Oh really?" says the client. "You're funny too? Why don't you come over here, then?" He pats the seat next to him and nods curtly to Miyeon, the girl sitting next to him, to switch.

"What an honor!" I say, bouncing up instantly. The room tilts sharply around me but I ignore it.

"I'm warning you, if you try to secretly throw away a drink on my watch, there will be big trouble," he says as I perch next to him. "I'm spending good money here and I can't stand that kind of thing."

"Of course not, sir. I wouldn't dream of it! And honestly, I was

----

waiting for someone to pour me some more, but I didn't want to make you men seem like weak drinkers next to me," I say. I am babbling, really, and have little idea of what I am saying, but he pours me some more and we drink and then we drink and drink some more and I do not remember anything after that.

The next morning, I throw up so much in bed that Miho is wakened by the noise and runs to the convenience store to buy me some hangover powder and Pocari Sweat and has to spend the rest of the morning washing my sheets for me. I am seeing rivers of stars and cannot get up, and while Miho is hanging the sheets up to dry, I fall asleep again on the floor of my room, clutching my coverless pillow to my chest.

When I finally wake up again, it is almost dinnertime. There is clanging coming from the kitchen, and when I limp out of my room I see Sujin heating up some hangover stew on the stove.

"Miho had to leave for the studio so she called me over," she says when she sees me. "I went to that hangover stew place you like near the puppy spa. I love that place so much—today you could see all the puppies in the hinoki baths with mini-towels wrapped around their heads like little old women!" She cracks up, stirring the bubbling stew with a plastic spoon.

When I don't answer, she squints and points to the dining chair, and I sink into it. "How much did you drink last night?" she asks tentatively.

I can barely shrug and I gingerly lower my head into my hands.

She ladles the stew into a bowl and brings it over to me with a spoon and chopsticks and some kimchi.

I peek at her as she starts ladling some more into a bowl for herself, humming cheerfully.

I know Sujin is not an idiot. She just seems simple because she

----

reverts so naturally to a positive state. That would be essential for surviving in my industry, though I don't think anyone can truly come out unscathed.

One would think seeing me like this would be more than fair warning to steer clear.

But I know what she would think even if I told her what was happening—she would think it's my fault for making terrible choices. "I told you Seul-kuk was a bad idea," she'd say. She does not know what this work does to you—how you cannot hold on to your old perspective. You will not be able to save your money because there will never be enough of it. You will keep doing things you never expected to do. You will be affected in ways you could never imagine.

I know, because that is what has happened to me. I never would have thought I would end up like this, with no money to speak of, a body that is breaking down, and an imminent expiration date.

I start eating in silence as she joins me at the table.

THE POLICE COME on a Tuesday. We are getting ready for what is always our busiest evening, with reservations for every room. Until then, Madam has been happy—something close to a smile hovering on her toad-like face as she flits in and out of rooms, checking over the girls, telling them to go change their dresses if she doesn't like the way they fit, ignoring me when she crosses my path.

There are two policemen. We have not had any warning because they walked right downstairs without waiting for the door manager to call. From upstairs we just hear a strangled yelp of "Police!" but it's too late—they are already here and suddenly the girls are scampering into the changing rooms, terrified and breathless. Usually, they come after letting salons know days in advance and the "sweeps" are

----

a formality—a joke more than anything. But a raid without warning—if anything serious happens, the girls take the blame. It's never the Madam or the actual owner of the room salon, who is always some shadowy fuck who's busy pretending like he's high society, his wife sucking up to richer people, trying to pretend like their money isn't dirty. It has always been that way and it will always be. Us girls, we have been trained for years: "Say that you were the one who wanted to sleep with the customer. You just wanted some money. Got it?" So the girl gets jailed and fined for prostitution, and vilified in society as someone who does this for easy money. The girls who die in the process—the ones who are beaten to death or the ones who kill themselves—they don't even make the news.

I am the only one that lingers behind in the hallway. I want to know what the cops are saying. There is a middle-aged one, who is bored and annoyed, and a rookie, who is standing with his mouth agape. He looks like he is in middle school, this young cop.

"Listen, I don't like having to come here either, but this is a matter of someone official reporting prostitution in this establishment, so what are we supposed to do, eh?" the older policeman is barking at Madam. He flaps sheets of paper on the front desk. "Here, it says the charge—attempted prostitution and fraud. This gentleman claims you billed him millions of won. I was sent here by my boss, who says this came from one of his boss's bosses. I don't even know who his bosses *are*. That's how high up this is. Do you understand me?"

Madam is distraught. "This is a complete misunderstanding," she says, her voice quivering in what she is hoping they will read as fear, but what I know is anger. She is trying to appeal to their sense of chivalry. It's too bad that she is ugly as sin.

They must have planned it this way, because it can't be worse tim-

----

ing. It is 6:30 P.M. now and the first customers will be arriving soon. If they see the police here, the entire night's business will be lost and men might stay away for good. And I have no doubt that Madam will put this all on my tab. My debt will run to several tens of millions of won before the night is over. I feel like I am about to faint.

I can see Madam calculating all this too as her head swerves frantically in the direction of the wall clock, and then back to the policemen.

Pulling myself together, I take a breath and step forward.

"Is this a report filed by Choi Jang-chan?" I say. It's Bruce's real name.

"Yes," says the older cop angrily. "Who are you?"

"I'm his girlfriend," I say, clearing my throat nervously. "We had a fight and this is his way of getting back at me."

They look at each other and then give me an up and down stare. There is a wary silence. "Is that true? This is just some lovers' spat?" says the older one, finally. He has a look on his face that says, *These rich men—they're all the same.* He is now incensed.

"I know his name, don't I?" I say. "I have texts that show we are very close. I don't know what he is saying about me to the police, but he is very angry with me right now because I went somewhere he didn't want me to. It's a long story that is embarrassing to tell. Look, I'll come to the police station and give my statement, but please don't let our personal fight interfere with business here. This is not the shop's fault, it's my fault." I bow deeply to Madam. "I'm so sorry about this," I say. "I have no words." I bow again and cower, but inside I am feeling stronger, almost euphoric.

Madam opens and closes her mouth several times. She is deciding which course of action to take. So is the older policeman, who is surveying me with disgust. The younger one is speechless.

- - - -

"Lovers' quarrels!" says Madam finally. "Rich people these days are too much! Just because they get angry doesn't mean they can make accusations about a business when people's livelihoods depend on it! And what about your busy jobs too? I'm sure you have better things to do than run around after a rich man's girlfriend simply because he knows your superiors. That's just not right."

Trust her to prick a man's pride and self-righteousness for a nudge in her desired direction.

"Ridiculous," mutters the older policeman bitterly. We are all watching him now, to see what he will say. Madam looks at the clock again, and I know she is experiencing several mini heart attacks. The manager will have to start making calls to clients with reservations soon, to tell them not to come.

"All right, you," he says, pointing to me. "Come with us right now. Don't think you're going to change your clothes or anything. I've wasted enough time as it is coming down here."

There is a muted collective sigh of relief from the hallway, where the girls and waiters are hiding behind partially closed doors, eavesdropping.

As I scurry toward the stairs after the police, our manager runs up, pushing his suit jacket into my arms, and I smile in gratitude toward him. In the police car, I put it on and feel the pockets, in which there is some cash and a small bag of nuts, thank goodness. It's going to be a long night.

WHEN I WAS working in Miari, I saw and experienced things that I always assumed would be the rock bottom of my life. I lived and worked among people who were either so evil or so lost that they did not have a single thought in their heads. When I got there, I vowed to

----

get out as fast as I could, and when I did they told me I was a ruthless, toxic bitch, that they couldn't believe how ungrateful I was to leave them behind when they had done so much for me. They tallied things they actually viewed as favors—"I gave you time off each week to go to the bathhouse," "I bought you those expensive shoes," "I helped you decorate your 'room,'" "I took you to the doctor when you were sick."

Speaking of those hoity-toity doctors and pharmacists who run their clinics in districts like Miari and profit off the working girls and their sicknesses—they are no better than the gutter trash who come around selling lubricants and "handmade" dresses to the girls to wear in our glass showrooms that light up red in the night.

They are no better than the managers and the pimps and the politicians and the policemen and the public who vilify only the girls. "This was your choice," they say. They are gutter trash, every last one of them.

AT THE STATION, they make me wait for hours before taking my statement, to punish me. They do not know how grateful I am to be here rather than drinking in the shop. By the time I am allowed to leave, it is late and there are already a handful of drunk people on the streets, leaning on lampposts at the crosswalks, waiting for the lights to change.

I know I should be hungry, but all I can feel is a headache coming on again. I have to do something before it comes at me full force, which will be in a matter of hours, and then I won't be able to walk straight. I find a chair outside a convenience store and fish out my phone from the manager's silky suit jacket.

I have several texts. One is from the manager, who says that I

----

shouldn't worry because business has not been affected at all. Madam won't be able to say otherwise because there were so many witnesses who can vouch that it was a busy night.

He also writes that I should not come back to the shop after the police. "Go home and rest," he texts with a winky emoji and a sweating face emoji.

There are a few texts from the girls—the younger ones who look up to me—asking if I am all right.

I text them all smiley faces. I don't have the capacity to respond further. And I don't have much time before the headache will hit. I have to find a pharmacy.

I start composing a new text message.

"Hi, it's me," I type. It is to Bruce.

I know I probably won't have a chance to say this to you in person because you don't want to talk to me.

I know I made a huge mistake, going to the restaurant the way I did. I understand that now.

I missed you. And I wanted to see what kind of girl you would spend the rest of your life with. I wanted to see your family too. It was just pure curiosity on my part. I had no ill intentions toward you, I swear.

I know this will be hard for you to believe, but that is really all I wanted to do. I just wanted to see you having dinner with the girl you are going to marry.

I wasn't going to talk to you there. It was just the closest I could come to something like that—to being somewhere like that with you. And I didn't make a scene, did I? If I wanted to, I could have.

You were so good to me that it hurt me to hear you were getting married. And you didn't even tell me directly because you didn't

----

*think it was necessary. Perhaps I should have continued to act as if
nothing was different. But I have feelings. You should know that.*

*Everyone is so angry with me, and I'm going to take on a suicidal
amount of debt at the shop because of what happened. I had some
idea of what the consequences would be but I still went to see you and
her. That is how much I was in love with you. You do know that,
right?*

*I just want to say that I am sorry. I know I will never see you
again. I hope you can forgive me.*

MY HEADACHE HAS arrived with a vengeance and it is unfurling
throughout my body. I am shaking as I finish composing the text and
press send. I am kneading my temples as hard as I can, but it does not
make a dent in the pain. People walking by look at me in alarm because I am lurching back and forth in this chair. I stand up and look
around for a pharmacy, even though I know that five, six painkillers
will not be enough to help and the doctor warned me about taking
any more than three at a time. "That kind of dosage is for people who
have just given birth," he warned. What about people who will never
be able to give birth? I wanted to ask.

I find a pharmacy and I stumble in and ask for the strongest dose
of painkillers they can give me. As I reach into the suit pocket for the
cash, I feel my phone buzzing and I draw it out.

It is a text from Bruce.

All right, it says. *Now fuck off.*

ALMOST WEEPING with relief, I hand over cash and walk out of
the pharmacy without waiting for the change.

- - - -

As the door closes behind me, I hear the pharmacist call, "Are you sure you are okay, miss?" His gentle voice falls like a patter of rain. I raise my hand and nod as I pry the pills from the thick packaging.

I'm okay. I have survived the day, again. All I need now is for these stupid fucking pills to work.

Miho

When it comes to love, I am not quite the fool that my room-mate, Kyuri, believes me to be. Lately, she has been look-ing at me with great pity, alternating with scorn, and I know that she is contemplating my impending heartbreak. She considers it entirely my fault, for setting my heart up to be broken in the first place, with reckless disregard for the prime years of my man-attracting life.

It is her job to know men of course, and she thinks she can sum up Hanbin, my boyfriend, and how he will leave me. She believes girls should operate like Venus flytraps—opening only for prey that can actually be caught.

Of course, Kyuri cannot help thinking like this, as her own life

----

193

remains deliberately stripped of love. When I ask her if she ever wants to get married, she snorts. "Not meant to be," she says, blinking her mink-like eyelashes and wondering out loud at my rudeness for even raising the subject to her. But Kyuri is still the one out of all of us—even including the impressionable Sujin who lives in front of the TV—who cries the most when one of the characters has to leave the other for martyr-like reasons.

Kyuri also suffers from persecution mania. This is entirely my own and secret opinion. She sees herself as the victim—of men, of the room salon industry, of Korean society, of the government. She never questions her own judgment, or how she creates and wallows in these situations. But that is another story.

One day, years after we stop living together, I will embark on a Kyuri series. I know that with absolute certainty. I cannot start now, when I am in the midst of my Ruby series, nor while I am still living with Kyuri. I need time and distance between us. But this is why I relish living with Kyuri *now*. I am spoon-feeding the muse that lives in a well deep inside of my brain—hearing Kyuri's stories, watching her drink to oblivion every weekend, obsessing over her face and her body and her clothes and her bags. I take photos of her and her things whenever I can. I will need them to remember her by. The other girls too, I have glimmers of them lurking in the outer regions of my mind; Sujin's terrifying transformation, and dear, silent Ara and her antediluvian upbringing. It will take a few years, though, before I can commit them to paper or form.

AS FOR HANBIN, I don't need Kyuri or Hanbin's mother to know that he will not be my salvation.

- - - -

SOMETIMES, WHEN HE is holding me and I feel like I am liquid in his arms, I wonder if anything else in my life will seem real after this. It is as if I traveled beyond the earth and reached out and touched a burning star, and it is both unendurable and terrifying.

I AM GLAD, then, that I will never love someone again in this way. I would not survive a second time. In America, one of my professors said once that the best art comes from an unbearable life—if you live through it, that is.

WHEN I WENT to Hanbin about a month after Ruby killed herself, he told me he had been afraid. Afraid to sleep, because she lived in his dreams. Afraid to talk to anyone, in case they were judging him. When he finally ventured outside, people looked at him with a mixture of horror and blame and pity and thirst, and he had never known such combinations of expressions were possible on a human face.

He had asked if there had been a note for him, or any note at all. Her father's people had told Hanbin that if she had stayed away from the likes of him, this wouldn't have happened.

He looked so small then, it was as if his spine had curled inward, like a snake about to go to sleep.

His tortured face broke my heart, and for the first time I was blinded with rage at Ruby, for doing this to him—to us—with her

----

reckless and destructive selfishness. To myself, I repeated what others had been saying about her. That anyone with her privileges had no right to be unhappy.

So I went to Hanbin and drew him down with me and lay beside him on his bed, which smelled like sweat and tears and musk and sorrow, and I comforted him with my body, and when we were entwined it seemed like the most natural thing in the world.

Afterward, it was as if I had been suffocating all my life and only then was I able to breathe.

AT MY STUDIO, I am working on yet another Ruby sculpture when the director of the department comes barging in and interrupts me. I hate it when he does this and I have hung a DO NOT DISTURB sign on the door, but it is in English and perhaps it does not register with him.

"Everything going well?" he asks, beaming. It is clear from the self-satisfied expression on his face that he has some news, and it is likely to be good news. He circles the sculpture and me several times and clears his throat loudly. Perhaps he is disturbed by it, although it is positively demure by the standards of our department. The undergraduates' work, especially, makes my eyes widen. It makes me want to ask about their parents. It's part of my PR story that I have had a difficult childhood, but these undergraduates with rich parents who can send them to these schools without scholarships and have their children pursue art careers in this country— they are the ones who have apparently known unbounded depths of despair and hatred.

The director had liked the last piece I did—the installation with the boat. He had me take so many photographs in front of the sculpture that I joked I should have made room for myself on the boat, and to my horror he said that would be a brilliant new series and I should include myself in anything I do from now on. "I would be happy to take the photograph myself—it would be a collaboration!" he said, enraptured.

This latest sculpture is a departure for me, because I am using acrylic on wood, and also incorporating fabric. In this one, Ruby is a kumiho in human form, a terrifying girl carrying a basket of jewels, her bead of powers hidden among them, her shoulders covered with a hooded cape made of out of fox fur, which melds into her body and turns into a fox's hind legs. Her nine tails spread thickly out on the ground behind her. She has been feasting on meat—human flesh—and blood drips down her chin. I am working on her mouth, how to get her pointed white teeth to show while the rest of her mouth is filled with blood. When I fall into daydreaming, I dream wistfully about having enough money to fill her wicker basket with actual jewels. Practically speaking, I could probably sell the sculpture faster that way, if the jewels were priced in. To the Middle East perhaps. Ruby would have had contacts there. China for sure, but Ruby detested the fuerdai.

The director clears his throat. Reluctantly, I step away from my sculpture and walk over to my paint-splattered sink to wash my hands. As I am drying them on my apron, I ask how the preparations are coming along for the upcoming anniversary exhibition. It is the fiftieth anniversary of the university this year, and they have started landscaping the campus for the festivities. The construction has been driving me to the brink of lunacy.

"Guess what! There is some amazing news!" he says. "Congressman Yang is coming." He cannot contain his glee and his body gives a little spasm of delight. He looks just like a character in a comic book.

Which has possibilities. I start thinking of a tableau with a little man with a clock face. To torture him I could have him drown in a tank of water.

"Do you understand what that means?" He looks at me with an injured expression when I do not respond with joy and incredulity.

"Is he going to speak at graduation?" I ask faintly, glancing back at my work.

He looks at me.

"Look, Miss Miho," he says after a drawn-out pause. "I know you think this conversation is irrelevant to you, but I assure you that this could not be further from the truth."

I have annoyed him. I am repentant—he has made it possible for me to have a space and a position and money—scant as the amount may be. I walk over to my stylish little fifties-style fridge, which Hanbin bought me as a congratulations-for-getting-a-studio present, and pull out two orange fiber drinks and hand one to the director. I love these drinks because of their color. Orange is a shade that is so often ridiculed in the world. But I love these glass bottles filled with sunrise-colored liquids in my beautiful Italian fridge with vintage lettering, which is undoubtedly the most expensive thing I own.

"I'm sorry," I say. "It takes a minute to pull myself out of my work. I'm all yours. Please enlighten me."

I sit down on a stool and face him, trying to mimic the expression Kyuri has taught me for lulling a man into thinking he has your full attention. It is all about opening the eyes wide and pulling your ears back, with only the hint of a smile lurking in the corners of your mouth.

He clears his throat.

"The reason why these politicians are important is because they can channel funds, or they can influence chaebol to set funds aside,

- - - -

and you get to keep creating work that can make our school famous. Understand?"

I nod. This is, indeed, important.

"Anyway, I am hard at work trying to organize this luncheon for potential patrons and politicians, and I came here to tell you that you will attend. I have made a booking at the Hotel of the Artists for next Monday at noon. So make sure . . ." He stops. I am waiting expectantly.

"Well, you know. Just be a good representative for this entire school," he finishes lamely. He wants to drive home the crushing responsibility that rests on my shoulders.

"Is Miss Mari coming?" I ask. She is the other recipient of the fellowship. She creates digital installations depicting brain waves or something like that.

"No," says the director. "Miss Mari is not . . . Let's just say her work represents her better than she herself can."

I smile sweetly and say I am honored. Mari, who is a good ten years older than me, is a bit of a wild card. She is near forty, divorced and overweight, which renders her entirely invisible in the eyes of Korean men of every generation. While I have been greatly entertained by her company the few times I have spoken with her at these mandatory events, she chooses her words according to shock value, and the director is clearly balking at the thought of placing her in the vicinity of a potential donor.

"You are the department's mascot, don't forget," says the director, beaming once more now that I have said the right things in the right way. "We are featuring you on the poster for the exhibition! The photographer will be coming around in the next week or so. She will coordinate beforehand about what to wear, and hair and makeup." I bow deeply and he stalks out, appeased.

It is an easy thing, keeping elders happy. All you have to do is smile wide and say hello and thank you and goodbye with deep earnestness.

This is something many of my generation—and my chosen vocation—do not understand.

IN THE EVENING, I meet Hanbin for dinner and I tell him about my upcoming parade in front of a line of donors.

"That's amazing!" he says with delight, his tanned, handsome face breaking into a smile. Happiness, like a warm blanket, settles around my shoulders. We are eating grilled eel in the foodie street in front of school, because he says we both need energy recharging.

He is doubly happy for me because, in the past year, he has offered several times to introduce me to gallerists that he knows through his mother, and I have constantly refused. These offers do not come lightly from him, I know, because my accepting a favor like that would mean his family would then owe these people a favor, and his mother would hear of it and she would be, at the very least, wild with fury. I am trying to do this all on my own, and I know that is the way to actually keep him. He could buy all the art of all the graduate students in my department combined for half of what he paid for his car last year. It goes without saying that he could buy out all of my art in my upcoming solo show in May at the university's gallery.

He is expertly grilling the pieces of eel and keeps placing them on my plate. I have not been able to tell him until now that I do not like eel because he already thinks I'm too picky.

Hoe, for instance. When I was growing up, we never had hoe, and every time he takes me to an expensive hoe restaurant, his eyes light

----

up when the server brings us a beautifully arranged plate of paper-thin slices of raw white fish, topped off with sea cucumber or sea urchin. It takes singular effort to keep the queasiness from printing itself on my face. "The chef saved the best mackerel for us—I called the restaurant last week to tell them we were coming today," he says to me, piling the translucent slivers high on my plate. "And guess what, he has set aside really high-quality pufferfish sashimi too, that he'll be bringing out himself!"

Ruby, I think, suspected this about me. One of the wonderful things she did—without ever acknowledging it—was to stop trying to coax me to eat raw seafood. Or foie gras. Or lamb. Or rabbit. Or any sort of food I had never experienced growing up.

But oddly, even after years of dining alongside these refined palates, my aversions are only getting worse. Give me ramen and tteokbokki and soondae any day. Or no food at all. I am happy with no food.

Usually Hanbin would have gotten angry if I started saying I was full this early, but he does not seem to care today. He is either excited or restless, and I ask him what's going on.

"Not a thing," he says, shaking his head. "Work is crazy. I don't want to talk about it. It's fucking depressing."

Hanbin is working as the bellboy in his family's hotel. It's been a recent trend for hotel families to put their heirs to work in the trenches of their empires. He began as a parking attendant the summer after he graduated from Columbia, and after a few months was reassigned to washing dishes in the kitchen.

His mother pretends to be horrified that her husband is relegating her son to such menial labor, but according to Hanbin she's actually quite tickled. It gives her a fresh new way of bragging about the hotel and her son and how farsighted her husband is to dream up such a grueling CEO-training program.

One would think that the management wouldn't actually make him do any work, but recent chaebol scandals have changed a lot of people's thinking. There are still the sycophants that grovel and fawn, but many are also contemptuously watchful—waiting for the owner families to make a mistake so they can pounce and report it to the police or the press. "Unions!" Hanbin tends to say explosively out of nowhere from time to time.

"At least you don't have to pluck used condoms off the floor and sponge dirty toilet bowls on your knees," I said to him the other week when he was complaining about how terrible his day had been. I was thinking about the stories that Sujin told me about working as a maid in a love motel the first few months she was in Seoul while she was attending a hair and beauty academy. The hotel she worked at charged by the hour, and the turnover was so fast that she lost six kilograms in two weeks because she had no time to eat, and also just because she had no appetite after cleaning all the condoms and multicolored stains every hour. She heartily recommended it as a weight-loss program.

When I said this, Hanbin looked at me without saying a word and I knew that he was shocked. I hastily said I'd just read an article written by a journalist who had gone undercover at a love motel as a cleaner, and then his expression eased somewhat. He laughed and said that his hotel was not like that. He actually believed it too.

RUBY LOVED HOTELS also. She had one of her people forward her all the hotel news—which ones were serving a new afternoon tea, which one had a new executive chef, which one had a new spa package, and she would scoop me up and off we would go.

One time she called me to a hotel presidential suite, where she had her papers spread out all over the conference table. She had ordered three tiers of mini cakes and bonbons with afternoon tea, which she was eating while typing on her laptop.

"What is *this*?" I asked when I walked in. The suite was breathtaking for its size alone. Every surface seemed to be wrapped in marble, and I had to pass through two foyers just to find her.

"Eh, it's super old," she said, rolling her eyes and pointing to the crystal chandelier. "This is straight out of the nineteen forties or something. I told them they need to close the hotel for a few years to renovate. *At least*."

I wandered through room after room, touching the edges of beautiful sofas, gilded frames, satin curtains, and a real fireplace mantel. There was a bright red Steinway grand piano in the living room against a startling floor-to-ceiling view of the city. In the bathrooms, tiny crystal bottles of perfume lined the shelves and clusters of peonies were floating in crystal spheres.

"Do you see the *swan's head*?" Ruby called to me. "Where are we, czarist Russia?"

She was referring to the faucet on the deep soaking tub, from which a slender gilded swan's neck and head emerged, water meant to spout from its beak. I secretly thought it quite lovely, and had run my fingers along the curved neck.

When I walked back to where Ruby was, she was on the phone ordering more room service. "What do you want?" she asked me, covering the mouthpiece.

When I shrugged helplessly, she rolled her eyes again. "Can you send up some grilled scallops—on a bed of mixed greens. Fresh, not frozen. Balsamic sauce on the side? And actually, can you send someone to pick up an Italian sandwich from that sandwich place on the corner—the famous one? I forget the name."

Slamming down the phone, she grinned. "Seafood for me. Sandwich for you. I'm going to write down the time and the temperature of the food when it gets here. This is real work, you know. Presidents don't wait for shit when they're staying here."

"What is going on?" I asked. This was unusual spending, even for her. A presidential suite on a weekday afternoon for no apparent reason?

"Oh, our company just bought this hotel," said Ruby, waving her hand around. "I read it in the news, because no one ever tells me *anything,* so I called Korea and asked them to arrange a stay immediately. And then when I got here, I asked for this suite!" She laughed. "They're going to kill me when they find out, but they won't dare tell my father. They're just going to have to figure out a solution."

I stared at her wide-eyed. "But what if they *do* tell your father and he's furious? Isn't this going to be, like, tens of thousands of dollars or something? Hundreds of thousands?" I really had no idea.

"I kind of *hope* they tell him," said Ruby. "At least he'll know that I am following the company news." And she continued spooning strawberry shortcake into her mouth.

Do you wonder, then, that I can't paint anything other than Ruby? That scene in the suite, I can see as clearly as if it were before me now. I painted it two months ago, as a tea party on a lily pad on a lake, a swan spouting tea into her teacup, with peonies and rubies in her hair. Hundreds of fish heads bobbing on the surface of the lake, turned in her direction.

When she told me that Hanbin was coming over after class, I excused myself to go work on my final project. I did not want to see him impressed by Ruby, what she could command at will. I did not want to think that they would be sleeping together on the bed like a cloud.

- - - -

But now, I think perhaps that's precisely why he likes me—I am a welcome change because with me he can play the role of the provider. There is a limit to how much Korean men are willing to endure female money, especially if they are wealthy themselves.

AFTER THE EEL, I am thinking Hanbin is going to suggest a movie or heading to a hotel room, but he says he is tired and he'll take me home. It must have really been a bad day at work—perhaps another guest yelled at him for being slow with the luggage.

He drops me off in front of my office-tel, and I wave goodbye to his retreating Porsche and walk forlornly up to the apartment. Usually, I am the one who is fending off advances, saying I am too tired for sex today, and no, you cannot see my work or my room.

Inside, I mope about some more, touching the spines of books I have been meaning to start for ages, rummaging through the kitchen cupboards to see if there is any ramen left, staring at my colorless face in the bathroom mirror.

Finally, I start working again in my room—beginning a sketch on a small letter-size sheet of paper. A sea of thrashing eels, above it, floating, a four-poster bed, from which I am looking down. This time it is not Ruby, it is me, and I am naked. I erase lightly and coax one of the eels to become a slender tree. I start adding tiny starlike flowers onto the branches.

I shouldn't be going into such detail with pencil—this is a stupid little sketch—but I can't help myself. I used to do this a lot—sketch out the entire idea first before re-creating it as a larger painting or a sculpture—but I don't usually do it anymore. It vexes me, but relieves me too, working in minutiae, in pencil, thinking about oils. The flowers should be a dusty pink—or would coral work better?

Should there be a butterfly or two? Should they turn back into eels and come into the bed?

I do not realize how much time has passed when I look up and see that Kyuri has come in and she is standing in my doorway staring at me. Her head is hanging to one side the way it does when she is just drunk enough to say the most outrageous things, but not drunk enough to go to sleep anytime soon. I sigh. This probably means I won't get more work done—it's just as well.

"You know what I think when I look at you?" says Kyuri, tilting her head abruptly to the opposite side. I can practically see the fumes of alcohol wafting off her.

"What?" I say. "And hello to you."

"I wish I had a talent that had decided my vocation *for* me," she says. She sounds aggrieved. "So that there never was a choice. Of doing anything else." What she is implying is that I am lucky and she is not.

"Art doesn't feed you," I say, indignantly. "So many people who are a million times more talented than I am can't get a job, or they can't sell their paintings. After this fellowship, who knows what I'm going to do?"

An artist's career is a phantasm, shimmering from one angle, gone from the next. I had been told over and over in New York that I needed to be part of a community, not only for encouragement and inspiration and all of those fine things but for practical job tips. Like the best restaurants to waitress at. Ruby had made me apply for my current fellowship a few months before she killed herself.

I already know that Kyuri almost begrudges me my career—fledgling as it may be—and all of our conversations usually end up running along these lines sooner or later. It is part of what I was saying earlier, her persistence in thinking that she is a victim and others have been born under lucky stars.

"Well, you are so smart to have gotten this far then," she says enviously. "You're so sly, you know. You weasel your way into the best things somehow."

This annoys me so much I feel a rush of blood in my cheeks. Usually I brush off things she says that are much worse. Perhaps it is because I am hungry, or because Hanbin went away so early.

"Why do you have to put it that way?" I say. "Are you trying to pick a fight with me? You don't think I work hard? That I'm not terrified that I am going to lose everything any second?"

"Why are you getting so upset?" she asks, genuinely surprised. "I'm just saying I envy you! That's flattering! Feel lucky!"

Because she is so taken aback, I calm down.

"I'm sorry," I say. "I guess I'm in kind of a bad mood today. It's nothing to do with you."

"Why, because of work?" she asks. "No, it's Hanbin, isn't it!" she says with certainty.

I shake my head, hoping she will go away. I look down at my sketch. But when I look back at Kyuri, she has such a worried expression on her face that, in spite of myself, I am touched. No matter what her wrongful assumptions are, she is, at least, a friend who cares, and I know how rare that is. Which is precisely why I cannot paint a Kyuri series right now.

But when I do start it, I will do it as a gisaeng series. Perhaps I will paint her as a ghost, with red eyes. Her back arched. Syringes plunging into her face and wrists. Wearing a gisaeng hanbok. I need to do research on gisaeng hanbok. What colors they wore to seduce men centuries ago. A ghost gisaeng series. I stare at her, seeing this and more, and she recoils.

"What?" she says. "Why are you looking at me like that? What is it? Is it really about Hanbin? What did he do?"

I shake my head, to clear it, although my other strong impulse is to start sketching it then and there so that I don't lose this. But there is a note in her voice that sets me off.

"I really wish you wouldn't harp on him so much," I say. "I feel like you think he's just the worst for dating me because I don't deserve him or something. It really makes me uncomfortable."

There, I said it. In reality, her talking about Hanbin does not bother me as much as I just made it sound, but today I am prickly.

"You have it so wrong, it's incredible," she says, her voice trembling and ice cold. "Do you know how much of a dilemma I face every day? Whenever I see you, I am trying to ascertain what I think needs more protecting—your future, your idealism, your misplaced faith."

"What are you *talking* about?" I say.

"I'm talking about Hanbin," says Kyuri, spitting out every word. "And I was so conflicted about whether to tell you."

I am wondering if I missed part of the conversation. I tend to do that a lot when I am drawing in my head. "What?"

She glares at me and takes a breath and says "Never mind!" explosively before flouncing to her room. But I am not about to let this go.

"Kyuri. Tell me now. What are you talking about?" I follow her into her room and grab her arm. If this is just mean-spirited hysteria, I do not need it in my life.

She pushes me away from her, and starts changing her clothes without looking at me. In her pajamas, she sits in front of her painted vanity and begins removing her makeup with two pumps of her costly fermented cleansing oil. There is something about this picture—of her in a lace-edged slip, in front of her oval mirror, slowly wiping off the colors of her face in anger—which is riveting. I have a violent urge to run to my room to get my camera, to capture this so I can work with it later.

"Are you sure you want to know?" she asks, turning to me and breaking my trance. Every trace of eyeliner and blush and lipstick has been removed and her skin glistens from the oil.

We look at each other for a long moment.

There is only one thing that this could be, this truth she is dangling in front of me, and in that respect, I already know.

"Just tell me," I whisper.

She tilts her head from side to side. Then she opens her mouth. "He is sleeping with at least one other girl," she says. "I'm sorry, I really am." She cannot meet my gaze. "I mean, isn't it kind of a relief in a way? This way you do not have to wait until he breaks up with you, and you can just label him a typical asshole bastard and be done with him, instead of harboring any kind of delusion that you are going to marry him, and then it will be years more of your life that you cannot afford just down the drain."

She stumbles over these words hurriedly, sounding like one of those evangelists talking to someone on the verge of conversion.

"Oh," I say quietly. It is on the tip of my tongue to say so many things—"How do you know?" "Who is it?" or the futile "That cannot be true." But it is easy to see from her face that she is telling the truth. I have to hold on to something because I feel as if I am about to keel over. I turn around—and totter back to my room like an old lady. I feel as if I am floating above my body—watching myself find my way back to my paintings. In my torment, I cannot process this.

I do not want to know. I do not want to know.

"Miho," says Kyuri. She is behind me, her voice soft and compassionate now. She regrets telling me.

I wave my hand at her without looking behind me, to signal to her to go away.

- - - -

In my room, I take up my little drawing. With a pang I realize that this will be painful for me to look at from now on. It is a pity, because I already loved it. This does not mean I will not be able to work on it, though——I can attack it with more fervor, more anger, and most likely it will be the better for it.

I feel as if I am sleepwalking, and I wander into the bathroom and start running the shower. It occurs to me that I will have a great deal of time from this moment on. Thank goodness I will be able to work.

I take off my clothes and my jewelry——my gold necklace with a palette-shaped pendant was of course from Hanbin, as was my eternity ring of tiny black diamonds.

The glass and the mirror are soon swallowed up in steam and fog. Closing my eyes, I endure the hot water beating down upon my head and body.

What am I to do now? It gnaws at me bleakly, this question. For all that I had thought I protected my heart, knowing this would happen one day, I am not prepared.

I wish I were dead, so that I did not have to feel this pain.

I REMEMBER MY AUNT telling my cousin Kyunghee and me, when we were small, that my grandmother had died of anger. She had choked to death on han——the rage and resentment and despair—— seeing her parents die before her eyes, having served her mother-in-law as a body slave until she aged long before her time. To have a son——my father——that turned out to be a weak fool, led astray by a cunning daughter-in-law——my mother.

My aunt told us that we inherited my grandmother's wrath, that this kind of potent han could not just die off with the passing of an

----

old woman. That we should be careful to curb ourselves, to avoid situations that could lead to altercations.

You do not know what you are capable of, she said with a sigh. We nodded fearfully. She herself regretted certain incidents in her life, my aunt said. And she didn't want us to end up feeling the same.

THE IDEA TO EXTRACT the SD card from Hanbin's dashcam comes from the latest drama that Kyuri is watching. Since she refuses to tell me how she found out about Hanbin, and since I have nothing else to say to her, the television has been blaring nonstop for the past few days and we have settled into a chilly coexistence.

The scene that gives me this brilliant idea unfolds on the screen when I sit down at our tiny table with the ramen I made. In the drama, the chaebol son is in love with the girl who everyone thinks is his sister. The father, who suspects this unpalatable relationship, sneaks into his son's car at night and extracts the SD card from the dashcam. Reviewing the videos confirms his hunch.

The scene with the SD card arrests me, and I swivel my head toward Kyuri to see if it is occurring to her that this is occurring to *me*. She pays me no attention. The way that she is sitting on the floor with her back and neck completely stiff makes me suspect that she must have gotten another treatment. Most likely a session of that bone therapy she is addicted to where they massage the shit out of you for two hours. The one time I went, on her recommendation, I asked for face therapy and they started pressing my jaw so hard I cried for them to stop. When I asked for my money back, they refused, so I gifted the rest of the sessions to Kyuri. That, they allowed.

But the dashcam—this could truly work. Hanbin had installed

----

one that records the inside of the car after he had his laptop stolen by a valet parking attendant.

The trick is to get Hanbin out of his car long enough that I can take out the SD card. After studying videos online, I am pretty sure I can do it fairly quickly, but I will fumble if I am frazzled about getting caught.

I FINALLY DO it on the day that we are meeting his friends for drinks in Itaewon. After he picks me up at the studio, he finds a miraculous street parking spot just a block away from the restaurant. We are walking there when I take a deep breath and say that I just realized I left my phone in his car.

"I'll go get it," I say.

"No, no, let me. It'll take me two seconds." He is already turning back when I add that I think several of my "female items" also must have spilled out of my purse. There is nothing like the mention of menstrual products to send a guy running in the other direction.

And then it is the easiest thing in the world to obtain the evidence.

AT HOME AFTER drinks, I go through the videos on my computer. After scrolling and scrolling, I find it: the one of him having sex with a girl in his car. It is dark and it is difficult to see because the images are blurry, but the rhythm and sounds are unmistakable. I stop the video and close my eyes. Then I crawl under my desk and curl up to see if the sharp stabs I am feeling will go away.

They don't, of course, and my legs are shaking like a dog's.

- - - -

IF I HAD YOUR FACE

I wonder if I will not survive this moment, if I will combust instead. But I want to see the girl's face, to see what it is about her that attracted him to her. I crawl back up to my seat and rewind—there must be a close shot of her in the front seat before they moved to the back. And, yes, here it is, the door opening and a girl getting in. The girl is Nami. Kyuri's friend. The prepubescent idiot with giant breasts. The one who I am quite certain is an escort of some kind as well.

I watch as they ride in silence and then Hanbin parks and they both get out of their front seats and get into the backseat, and then the scene I was just watching unfolds again. They have not said a word to each other, so it is clear that this has happened before—probably many times. It must have started that time when I called him to come drink with us. I had gone home with Kyuri and I had not realized that they had stayed out longer.

I lie on the bed for a long time, unseeing in the dark, and then go back to my computer and watch some more. Then I have to go back to my bed again.

Over the next few days I go through every single recording on the card. My heart splinters every time I hear his voice. I learn from his phone conversations that he is being set up on seon with the daughter of the Ilsun Group, and the wedding date may as well be set.

The seon is to be next month, when she returns home from a culinary program in Paris.

IN A WAY, I think I am now experiencing true freedom for the first time in my life. That is the way to think of this—that this is karma, and also absolution.

- - - -

I HAD BEEN drowning slowly in my guilt, for coveting him when he was Ruby's, for going to him and daring to show him my heart. I had been inhabiting a world not meant for me.

HE WAS ALWAYS offering things. I shrank from accepting because I thought that was the way to show my love for him, to show that I loved him beyond material things and the world he represented, the connections that could launch a career in the time it took to sneeze.

I had not wanted to burden him in any way, and I agonized over how my decisions would look to his family, of whether one fellowship would look more respectable than another.

I never allowed him to see my work because the only work I have been able to create has been of Ruby.

I RELISH the thought of him attending my exhibition, only to find Ruby at every turn—her face, her body, her hatreds and desires, her apathy and disdain, her cherished treasures.

BUT BEFORE he sees her in my work, I will suck everything I can from him. I will be wild and unleashed. I will now take from him what I can. I have not heard Kyuri's philosophies on men all this time for nothing.

I WILL ASK him to buy me jewelry.

I will ask him to buy out my exhibition, so that I can land another from the press on that alone.

I will leak to the women's magazines—the thick bibles of paparazzi photos of the rich and famous—that he is my boyfriend.

I will build myself up so high in such a short time that when he leaves me, I will become a lightning storm, a nuclear apocalypse.

I WILL NOT come out of this with nothing.

Wonna

The baby is tapping again. When she does this my heart lurches and I stop in the middle of whatever I am doing and I put my hands on my belly to feel her.

I do not know what this is—it only started earlier this week. I cannot tell if this is what they call "kicking" or if she has the hiccups.

Whatever it is, I am so grateful that a gush of hope springs deep inside me and it is everything I can do to not break down completely in public. I want to share this with someone—anyone. I want to clutch the lady who is sitting next to me on the subway and tell her. I want her to know a little world is erupting inside of me. My baby is trying to talk to me. She is trying to live.

FOR THE PAST three months, I have been playing a little game with myself. I call it a game but it is more a series of negotiations. With whom, I do not know, because I do not believe in God.

The game goes like this. If my baby lives for another week, I will do this. Or I will give another thing up. Last week, I promised to never smoke a cigarette again even after I give birth—although I do not like to think that far ahead for fear that I will be punished for doing so. I don't even smoke that much but I was running out of stuff to relinquish. The previous week, I promised I would never take fat pills again, even if I feel sick looking at my reflection. And the week before that, I vowed to never drink again to the point of blacking out.

I almost told my husband about this game but I caught myself in time. He would not think it exemplary or empowered or motherly, which is how it makes me feel.

During my last visit, the doctor told me now that I have crossed into the second trimester, the odds of a miscarriage are only 2, perhaps 3 percent, so I shouldn't worry so much anymore. I told her that to the 2 percent, the experience is 100 percent and I still know something will go wrong with the pregnancy, I just don't know when. She looked at me strangely and I regretted speaking. She has a face like a stone tower.

MY HUSBAND is in China again this week for work. This means at night, I can stretch my body across the whole bed and the sheets feel

----

twice as delicious against my skin. I can roll toward either side of the bed and toss and turn to my heart's content.

If there was a marriage handbook of do's and don'ts, the first chapter should be titled "Buy a King-Size Bed."

With a queen bed, my husband always falls asleep first and I end up glaring balefully at him as he shifts way past the halfway line. His arm or leg ends up plopping on my body and I cannot fall asleep, so I stare at the ceiling in hatred, then I jab his back and he rolls over to his side, but it is only a matter of time before he rolls back to me. And now that I am pregnant, with the first series of negotiations about my baby with the unnamed deities, I gave up my sleeping pills too. I should have stretched out my bargaining—giving up the dosages by 1 milligram a week perhaps. Since I was starting with 10 milligrams a night, it would have given me an extra ten weeks of sleeping aid. But I gave it up completely during the second week or so, and now, if I fall asleep around 3 or 4 A.M., I consider the night saved.

In the beginning of the pregnancy, it used to infuriate me when I couldn't fall asleep because of him. I would shake his shoulders roughly and say, "You are keeping me awake." He would apologize and lie straight on his side, almost falling off the edge because he was so far over, but inevitably he would fall asleep again and roll over to my side and it would be the start of another cycle of chafing.

What changed was that I started reading blogs that said insomnia is inevitable and permanent—once you get pregnant, you will never sleep again anyway. Even when the baby is sleeping you will still not be able to sleep and you will lose your mind.

That was when I decided to try to think that it was not my husband's fault. It is my fault for bringing the queen bed into the marriage in the first place. My father was so amazed that I was getting

----

married at all, let alone to a normal man with a job, that he must have sold something in order to buy it for us. If he was spending money he didn't have anyway, I should have made him spring for a king. But the mattress salesperson did not even attempt an upsell, and said that this bed would be the wisest investment newlyweds could make. They should hang salespeople who tell such lies.

BEFORE MY HUSBAND left for his trip, we got into a fight. "There's a baby fair at SETEC this weekend," he said. I was cooking kalguksu for dinner after work while he was clearing and setting the table. "Don't you want to go look at some clothes and bottles and strollers and stuff? I know it'll take more than a few shopping trips to test gear and figure out what we need. My father said he'll give us some money. He's getting his retirement settlement next month."

I whirled around and fixed him with a stare of disbelief. "You are jinxing this," I said. "Don't talk about her! Don't even *think* about her!"

His brow furrowed slightly.

"Wonna, this is ridiculous," he said. "We're already halfway into the pregnancy. You really need to tell your boss soon. And by the way, you are the one making assumptions. You shouldn't assume it's a girl. I'm starting to get worried about your disappointment if it turns out to be a boy. I hope you will love him just as much if it is."

"Oh shut up," I snapped. "I bet you are *hoping* for a boy!"

It was the first time I had spoken to him that way. Laced with venom the way that my grandmother used to talk. I knew I had hurt him because he then did a rare thing—he didn't talk to me for the rest of the night and even the next morning. I think he expected that I would apologize, because I would catch him casting hurt looks at me throughout the night, but he underestimated me. I took no notice and he took his bowl of kalguksu into the bedroom and ate it sitting at my vanity while staring at his phone. I had to wipe away the droplets of soup splatter later that night after he had gone to sleep.

THESE DAYS, the only time I feel vestiges of fondness for him is at work, whenever and wherever the inevitable husband bashing starts. It used to happen on occasions where there were only female co-workers about—at lunch, or coffee, or while waiting for meetings to start—but these days it's beginning to trickle into regular work conversations even when the men are present.

"This is really the last straw," Bora sunbae would say. "He came home at 3 A.M. last night and woke up Seung-yeon and this morning he asked me to make some hangover stew. And when I said that I have to, you know, *go to work,* he said he was going to ask his mom to make some next time so that he can freeze it and have it on hand. Can you believe it? My mother-in-law already thinks I'm such a neglectful wife and mother."

And then Joo-eun sunbae would chime in. "That is nothing. Do you know how many times my mother-in-law has been in my house this year when we are not at home? Just because they bought us the apartment, my mother-in-law thinks it's *her* house. Whenever she knows we're away, she 'pops by' to put her son's favorite food in the fridge and of course she's snooping all over the place! She asked me accusingly if I am using birth control the other day because she must have seen it in the bathroom in my *bedroom.* I can't even change the locks because that would cause an epic shitstorm that would probably leave me out on the street!"

And I would sit and nod in consternation and sympathy and think warmer thoughts about my husband with his conveniently dead mother.

But if I had known what our long-term housing prospects would be, I might have traded in a dead mother for a live one with cash. Before my husband and I married, I had a vague feeling of reassurance that, oh, this man has a steady job in a top ten conglomerate so our income is accounted for. We'd save up and buy an apartment in a few years—wasn't that what everyone did?

I didn't realize that his monthly salary was only three million won. Or to be more accurate, I did not know that three million won was so worthless. The longer we are married, the more our bankbook seems to shrivel every time I take it out of the drawer.

I know that buying an apartment is a dream in the sky. But each month, I have been scrimping every penny, scouring for opportunities to have someone treat us for meals. In addition to toilet paper, I've started taking home the sponges and dish soap from the office kitchen. I wish there was some way I could resell office supplies. Our cupboard has a stockpile of very nice pens.

HE'S RIGHT ABOUT one thing, though, as much as I hate to admit it. I do have to tell work soon if I am to apply for maternity leave. I am hoping for more than a year, although I have heard that if it goes more than a year, it becomes unpaid. But these are just rumors that I have to verify. Our HR department is notorious for leaks, however, and if my immediate boss finds out that I told HR before I told her . . . my knees actually buckle to think of this.

I have been worrying about how to tell her ever since I began to

----

think there was a chance that this baby might make it. How does one talk to a bitter, unmarried, workaholic female boss about such a thing? I am scared that she will say it is ridiculous to have paid maternity leave, especially since we can all assume that she will never get one. "No. No. No. Why should you be paid for not working, when everyone else works twice as hard as you? So that you can play with a baby at home? Women like you are the reason companies do not want to hire women. And that sets back women everywhere. If you were a man, how many days off would you take after having a baby? That's right, none." And then she will do what she can to demote me when I do come back to work, somehow in the name of feminism. If I ever try to leave at a decent hour—say, before dinnertime—she will concentrate her fury and aim it at me like a blowtorch. I know her tactics. I know her caustic, embittered mind. If she wasn't such a raging bitch, I would feel sorry for her. Instead, my hate is a heavy rock sitting in the middle of my chest. Every day, it sinks a little lower toward my stomach.

My only resort is to pump Bora sunbae for information. She only recently joined our department, so I do not know much about her, but she has a son who is somewhere around three or four years old. I wonder if her boss in her former department was nicer than Miss Chun and whether she felt such fear about broaching the topic of maternity leave. I resolve to ask her about it at lunch, when one can glean such tantalizing tidbits about private lives.

AT 11:55 A.M., everyone on the floor stands up simultaneously and makes for the elevator, where we press the down button and let four full elevators come and go before we finally get to the lobby,

----

twenty minutes later. It is the same every day and every day I wonder why I do not go twenty minutes before everyone else and say that I will come back twenty minutes earlier too. I'm sure everyone thinks the same thing I do. But no one does it except Department Head Lee.

When we make it to the lobby, I realize my mistake. Our team is going to Sun Tuna today for lunch. Not only is it sashimi, but it is tuna, the worst kind for pregnancy. I should have stayed in and eaten the cup of ramen at my desk. I kick myself mentally, but then I remember that I vowed to give up convenience store food six weeks ago. I would pretend an emergency phone call and extricate myself, but Chief Cho is buying lunch as a thank-you for coming to his wedding and it has taken three months of scheduling and rescheduling to get our entire team here. It would look terrible if I left now. It would be one less person to pay for, so he would probably secretly be happy, but he would still fake-fume about it for weeks. It is not worth it.

Through some strategic maneuvering, I am seated at the end of the table across from Bora sunbae, hoping no one will notice that I am not eating the tuna. I make a show of heartily eating the banchan and asking the server for more.

"So, is it wonderful? Married life?" Someone throws out the question as a courtesy.

Chief Cho preens. "Of course, it's nice to come home to a hot homemade dinner every evening. I highly recommend it so far."

"You better get started if you want children," pipes up Mr. Geum. "It's so hard to run around with the kids when you're older. Your back hurts."

Then someone at the other end of the table starts to talk about

----

how old they feel and all the aches and pains they are experiencing these days and the conversation threatens to veer away from children. So I say hurriedly, "Are *you* planning on having more kids, Bora sunbae?"

She has a mouthful of tuna, so she almost chokes when she shakes her head vehemently.

"Are you kidding?" she asks loudly, so that everyone's attention turns to her. "I am so *done* after one child."

Chief Cho, who is older than Bora by at least three years, clucks. "Well, you know what they say. It's hard when they're young but they are your greatest assets when you are older. I personally want three." He beams. "And all you young people, you better get cracking. Don't wait like me. I regret it already."

I see Miss Chun at the far end, stabbing her tuna with her chopsticks.

"A child is like a sinkhole for money," says Bora. "The more money you throw in there, the bigger the hole gets."

Everyone laughs. It is safe to assume from Bora's wry tone that she is joking. She can talk about money like this only because she has a lot of it. Her husband is a lawyer whose father is a famous doctor of Korean medicine in Shinchon.

"Why?" I ask, willing my voice to sound lightly curious. "Why does a child require so much money?" I know that strollers cost more than one would think, and then once your children enter elementary school, you need to start paying for after-school classes and tutoring, which builds up exponentially, and then there is of course college tuition, but why a three-year-old would require a lot of money is beyond my imagination. Perhaps she is projecting those future costs? Or buying her baby ginseng extracts and silver spoon sets? The state

----

pays for nursery school and I heard that they give you cash in monthly installments for having a baby at all, because they need the population to grow.

Bora sunbae looks at me and laughs. "I mean, it's no wonder no one is having babies these days. I don't blame them. Let me just recount this past month, OK? Let's see—he's at school, which, I applied for the free state-run daycare but of course he didn't get in, so we decided to go with an English daycare, which is 1.2 million a month." She does not hear my sharp intake of breath here, and continues. "School is from 9 A.M. to 3 P.M., which means my ajumma has to come in the morning at eight and stay until I get home at night. So I have to pay the ajumma two million won a month. Then, clothes. I don't know why, but kids need a lot of freaking clothes. I feel like I have to go buy some every week. And every time I take him grocery shopping, we have to buy a toy or else he throws a screaming fit in the middle of the store and I want to die of shame. And books! Do you know how much books cost? They sell children's books in sets of thirty or fifty. And I had to buy that fox robot that reads books out loud because everyone in his class has one." She rattles on and I am listening to her in a murky dream.

I know that most of the things on her list are frivolities. There will be no extra toys or reading robots or book sets of fifty for my child. But I'm also not naïve enough to think that I won't want them when the time comes. It will wring my heart that I can't buy things for my daughter.

The conversation switches to vacations because Bora sunbae is talking about how she "had to" book the kids' suite and the children's activities package at a hotel in Jeju. I give up on asking her about maternity leave as she clearly exists on a different planet, where it does not matter. She probably didn't even ask for paid leave.

- - - -

WE ARE BACK in the office when at around 3 P.M. Miss Chun calls me to the meeting room. She does not specify what report to bring, or what update I am to give her, so I gather everything I am working on to have whatever she needs.

She is sitting at the end of the table, looking grimly down at a sheaf of papers. She loves calling people in here because she can pretend that this is her office and that her desk isn't the same size as ours out on the floor. I bow and sit down two seats away from her, fumbling with my reports.

"Hold on," she says without looking at me. She flips through the rest of the papers for a good five minutes, and all I can do is stare at the first pages of my reports and wonder when I wrote them because I do not remember writing these words at all.

"So," she says. "Miss Wonna."

"Yes?"

"I'm not going to beat around the bush here. Are you pregnant?"

I am so shocked that I actually gasp. My hands fly to my stomach.

"How did you know?" I say.

"I have eyes," she snaps. "And a brain. And your reports have been the worst I've ever seen, and that's saying something because they were never very good."

I stare down at them and nod. "I'm sorry," I whisper. I don't know if I am apologizing for the pregnancy or the reports.

"When are you due?" Her voice is crisp. I can feel her eyes boring holes into my skull.

"September ninth."

"And have you talked to HR?"

"No . . ."

"Good."

I look up in fear. She settles back in her chair and sighs.

"I am going to tell you this now very clearly," she says in a weary voice. "I cannot spare you because there is a companywide hiring freeze on top of a giant round of layoffs coming our way. Honestly, if there wasn't a hiring freeze, I would have fired you a long time ago, but now I have to make do with you because if I lose even you, I can't replace you and that is more work for the rest of us. Do you understand?"

I nod silently.

"We have four new projects coming up in the second quarter of next year. If we don't deliver on them, this entire department will be gone. My boss has told me that this project is a test to determine whether to keep us or not. Now, if the department goes, I will stay because of my position. I will just be moved to another department. Everyone under me, however, will be laid off. So I don't think it'll be quite fair for you to take a long maternity leave when your colleagues will all be working to save their livelihoods, do you? Especially when we don't have the head count to add anyone else?"

She is looking at me and looking through me at the same time. I wonder why she did not tell me to close the door. My first instinct, always, is to be secretive. The fact that she is talking about cosmic events in my life in such a matter-of-fact way has me gasping for air again. But she is waiting for a reply.

"Yes," I say.

"Yes, what?"

I plead with my eyes. Just tell me what you want me to say.

She blinks and sighs again.

"I think the most we can spare you for is three months. Let me rephrase that. We cannot spare you at all, but if you absolutely must take maternity leave, then I will leave it to your conscience. In light of this information, I trust that you would not apply for more than that. Or let me put it this way. If we do not perform well and the entire department goes, then you will have as long a maternity leave as you desire." Her sarcasm slices the air.

"You know, in America, they have three weeks of maternity leave. Or something like that. Anyway, I am sorry the situation is what it is." She frowns darkly, and when I don't say anything, she waves her hand at me to leave. I stand up and bow deeply.

AT MY DESK for the rest of the afternoon, all I can do is stare at my screen and do mental calculations. If I have to return to work after three months, then we will have to hire an ajumma until my daughter can enter a state-run daycare, when she turns one. Perhaps I could find a cheap one for around 1.5 million won. It would only be for nine months, I tell myself. Bora probably overpays for a good one. Maybe her ajumma even speaks English.

If this job goes away, I will not be able to find another one. That I know for a fact. No one will hire me, because even this job I got through my husband's father's connections when he was still working. There will be no use looking for another job. And if I don't have a job, we will not be able to pay for rent and food, let alone a baby and an apartment, on my husband's three-million-won salary. I start hyperventilating.

"Are you all right?" Miss Jung is in the bathroom fixing her lipstick when I walk in and slump over the sink.

"I think I have to take the rest of the day off," I say. "I am not feeling that well."

I am giving up nine months of maternity leave. Surely Miss Chun won't say anything about leaving a few hours earlier today. I pack up my things and go home without even calling HR about taking a half day.

BABY MUST HAVE FELT a jolt because she is tapping again. I am smiling and tapping back at her as I walk slowly up to my apartment. When I open the door, my husband is standing in the hallway, wearing his navy suit and looking so scared that my own surprised yelp dies on my lips.

"I thought you were coming back on Saturday," I say, breathing hard. "You scared me!"

He doesn't answer, but just stands there looking so nervous I become confused.

"Um, what are you doing?" I say.

"I'm not feeling well so I came home early," he says, putting his hands into his pockets.

"Oh," I say. "Are you sick?" I motion for him to move aside and let me enter.

"My stomach," he says. "Just not feeling great."

I go to put my bag down in the bedroom and then realize that his suitcase is not there. Usually when he comes back from a trip, the house looks like the aftermath of a hurricane, with dirty socks and underwear strewn all over the place. I wander back and see that it is not in the living room either, and he is still standing where he was a few seconds ago.

- - - -

229

"Where's your suitcase?" I ask.

He is at the kitchen table clearing away a half-eaten bowl of jjam-bong. He dumps the remainder of the bright orange stew into the sink.

"Your stomach hurts and you're eating spicy stew?" I say. He still has his back turned to me at the sink. "Why didn't you tell me you were flying back early?" Not that I actually care. I'm just confused because he's usually overcommunicative about things like this.

He turns around slowly, drying his hands on the washcloth, while I start wiping down the table for flecks of soup.

"And you know you left your dress shoes here? Did you have to go buy some for the meetings? Didn't you say they dress superformally there?" I ask, rinsing the washcloth in the sink next to him.

"Yes, I need those dress shoes," he says, clearing his throat loudly. "That's why I'm here, actually. I need them for an interview this af-ternoon. You're home early." He trails off.

"An interview?" I ask. "What kind of interview?" For a promo-tion? I want to ask in hope, but I force myself not to.

"It's for this job at BPN Group," he says.

"Why on earth would you interview there?" I ask. BPN is a third-tier conglomerate.

He stares at me again and then takes a deep breath. "I can't do this anymore," he says.

"Do *what*?" I ask.

"Listen, Wonna, why don't you sit down?" he says. He guides me to the kitchen table and pours me some water from the refrigerator. After pouring himself another glass he starts to explain.

That he has not been on a business trip the past two times he said he was. That he actually lost his job two months ago. That he has

----

been staying with his father when he pretended to leave so that he could apply for jobs and interviews. That he did not want to worry me in my condition, but perhaps it was for the best that I found out because he felt terrible about keeping a secret from me like this. That he was looking for a job that offered free daycare at work the way his old job had.

"But what about—what about when you put on a suit every morning and go to work?" I say, stupefied.

He tells me then that he had been dressing as if he was going to work, and then he would just come back home for the rest of the day.

It was true, he had been home before me almost every night. I had not given it much thought—I'd believed him when he said his company was trying to promote family time.

"I didn't want to worry you," he says. His eyes and voice are plaintive, but he has taken a step back. He has always been afraid of me; we both realize that now with surprise.

And he stares at me and I at him and we are both listening to the sound of our heavy breathing. Outside our door, footsteps patter up the stairs.

"Don't be upset," he says, waiting to see what I will do next. "It isn't good for the baby."

• • •

I HAVE TO admit that I have no idea what your younger years will look like, other than some very vivid visions of me holding a beribboned, swaddled you in my arms. In these visions, the curtains are drawn but light is seeping through them—it must be your nap time, and I must be trying to put you to sleep in my arms. You are squirming and perturbed, but your gaze is locked on mine and I know just how to soothe you. In my visions the concept of time is hazy, and soon, or perhaps it is hours later, you are quiet and still and slumbering.

You will have things I did not when I was growing up—like cherished photographs and birthday cakes and days spent at the beach.

What I daydream about most is an older version of you. You are a young woman, perhaps the age of those girls who live above me—not that much younger than I am now. But unlike them and unlike me, *you* have a perpetual smile lurking at the corners of your mouth because you've had a happy childhood.

In my daydream, you are coming to visit—you are practically flying to see me because you have some good news and you want to tell me in person because we are so close, you and I, and you want to see my face shimmer with joy. You ring the bell, your foot tapping impatiently, and when I open the door, there you are, in your splendid, regal confidence, wielding your happiness like a scepter. And your news will spill from your mouth, your words running over each other because it is something you have worked hard for and you are so proud to tell me how you have achieved this.

And I will pull you inside, saying come in and sit down and tell me more slowly and fully, and I will cry because the process of raising you will have made me sentimental, and I will wrap my arms around you and marvel at how beautiful you are, how tall and strong and shining. And all of my memories of you will dance in front of my eyes as I thirstily listen to all that you have to say, laughing and holding my hands and leaning on my shoulder, or perhaps putting your head in my lap the way you would do as a child.

And then it is time for you to leave me again, to go back to your

----

own life, humming with aspiration. You don't have to worry about me—I will be the happiest I have ever been, even as my heart breaks a little to let go of you.

Still, I know you will always come back to me. And that will be the only wish I'll have ever known.

Ara

It is only when I jolt awake that I realize I must have fallen asleep at my desk again, watching old videos of Taein on his final reality show, *Slow Life, Happy Life*. He's been lying low ever since his scandal with Candy broke, so I haven't been able to indulge in my favorite routine of binge-watching all his latest TV appearances at once at the end of the week. Instead I have to resort to watching reruns for the eightieth time. This is all Candy's fault and I usually fall asleep fantasizing about her getting blacklisted from every network in the country.

My neck and lower back hurt from my uncomfortable sleeping position. I'm cold—spring is finally here but the temperature still dips at night. I get up, and as I am stretching, I hear an odd sound that seems to come from very far away. I stop stretching and listen.

And there it is again. It is muffled screaming, mixed with some terrified crying. I open my door and step out to the living room, wondering if it is Sujin.

The lights are on in the kitchen and Sujin's door is open but her room is dark, which means she must have come home and gone out again. The clock above the TV reads 3:22 A.M.

And there it is again. That sound. It's definitely a woman screaming. I put my ear against the front door and I can hear it through the door. It is coming from outside. Now it is quiet again. When I peer through the eyehole, I see nothing.

I text into the group chat of the girls who live on our floor— Kyuri, Sujin, and Miho.

"Anyone up/home? Anyone else hear that screaming? I don't think it's our floor but it woke me up."

I wait and stare at my phone. They must be sleeping or out. Kyuri is perhaps with Sujin. Miho might be at the studio? Do I call the police? But how would I be able to tell them the information? Do police take texts? I do not know. I am typing into my search bar "how to text the police" when my phone buzzes.

"I'm on my way home." It's Miho in the group chat. "Should I call the police?"

"Maybe that married couple downstairs is having a fight?" I text.

"No, I saw the husband leave today," texts Miho. "He got into a taxi with giant suitcases."

"How far are you, Miho?" I text.

"About 20 minutes away? I'm on the subway."

Twenty minutes is too long. Someone might be dying.

"Can you call the police then?" I text. "I'm going to go see what it is."

Immediately Miho starts texting furiously.

"Just wait for the police. Hold on. I'm calling now. If you're going to go, wait for me at least!!!"

"It's ok, don't worry," I text. "I'll take a weapon."

"NO!!!!"

It's sweet of her, being worried about me. I'm surprised since she's heard about all the other fights I used to get into when I was young. The problem is, we have no good weapons in the house. Not for a situation like this. I long for my grandfather's long wooden staff, sitting useless back at the Big House. For a second, I plot ways to steal it the next time I go to Cheongju. Not that I would have any idea how to wield it, but I vow to learn.

I'm not sure if a kitchen knife would be a good idea because I have never used one before and it might just distract me in the moment. I put the electric kettle on boil and scan the house again. This is unacceptable. I make a mental note to order weapons. I snatch up a pair of scissors and put it in my pants pocket—they're probably easier to maneuver than a knife—and once the light on the kettle goes off I take the steaming pot and quietly open my front door.

It occurs to me, as I am standing in the hallway waiting to hear a scream, that I have never been in a fight with a male before. I have witnessed them—the boy gangs would routinely have vicious fights when I was in middle school and high school—and the girls would sometimes watch from a distance. The sheer speed and strength—the sound of baseball bats hitting somebody's head—the popping sound that a fist would make on a jaw—never failed to shock me. The first few times, most of the girls cried, even Noh Hyun-jin, who was famous for once having taken six ferocious slaps in the face in a row from our PE teacher without breaking down. I decide that if there is a man downstairs and he is trying to rape or kill someone, the only thing I have going for me is the element of surprise.

I can look both frail and vulnerable—that is what Sujin always says.

Now that I'm in the hallway, it becomes clear that the screams—they are intermittent—are coming from downstairs. The married couple is right beneath us, and I think there is a girl who lives by herself in the other apartment. I walk softly down the stairs and listen right outside the front door of apartment 302.

It's this one. And I can hear more moaning now. Mumblings. Something about a baby? I press my ear closer and I hear only a woman's voice and at first I think she is addressing someone but then it occurs to me that she is just talking to herself. And then she screams in pain so loudly that I jump in fright and almost drop the kettle.

"Who's there?" a woman's voice calls out suddenly, her voice full of fear. I tap on the door, hoping that the taps sound gentle and innocuous.

"Who is it?" she calls again, right before she moans again. There is some shuffling and groaning, and I hear a scraping at the door right in front of me. She is probably looking through the peephole so I back up a little so she can see me more clearly and smile and wave with my free hand.

The door unlocks and opens slowly and she pokes her head out.

"Who is it?" she says. It's the married lady. She looks frightful—her eyes are bloodshot, and her pale face contorted and streaked with tears. She opens the door a bit more and sees that I am holding a water kettle.

"What is it?" she says. "Don't you live upstairs?"

I nod and then I point to my throat and shake my head.

"Huh?" She looks more confused, then she doubles over and lets out a tortured moan.

Setting the kettle down on the floor outside her door, I take her by the shoulders and we go inside her apartment. She is in too much pain and she barely makes it to the living room, where she keels over onto a sofa.

I pat her on the arm and then run out and open the front door again and bring in the hot water. Then I go to her kitchen and look for a mug and pour some for her.

She is writhing on the sofa, clutching her stomach. Tears course down her cheeks. Kneeling in front of her, I run my hands up and down her arms. Then I fish out my phone from my pocket.

"I heard some strange sounds so I came to see if there was something wrong. Do you need me to call an ambulance?" I type into my phone, and then I show her.

Wiping her tears, she takes the phone and reads it. "You can't speak?" she asks, her brows furrowing in surprise. She is exaggerating her words the way most people do when they first find out.

I nod.

She sits up then and grabs my wrist, surprising me.

"Were you born that way?" she asks, with strange desperation. People often ask me this, but she sounds as if there is more to her query than just fleeting curiosity. I blink rapidly and shake my head after a moment.

She sighs and lies back down on the sofa. I wait for a follow-up question about how it happened but it does not come.

"Do you need to go to the emergency room?" I type out again.

She reads it and closes her eyes in pain.

"I don't know," she says, rocking back and forth. "I guess I should but I don't know." She starts crying again. "This doesn't make any sense but I want to wait a little. It's still so early that if there is something wrong I'm sure they'll just kill her to take her out of me."

I gather that she is pregnant and she is talking about her baby.

"I heard that if something is wrong then they will save the mother over the baby and I don't want that to happen. If my baby is going to die then I'll just die with her."

I look down at her and I understand. I nod and bring her some tissues from a box on her kitchen table and she blows her nose. I kneel next to her and start stroking her hair, which is wet from sweat. Even the tensest of my clients tend to relax when I do this, so I hope it helps if only just a little.

I glance around the apartment curiously. It is only slightly bigger than ours and it does not look at all like an apartment for a married couple. Not that I have ever been to a young married person's house, now that I think about it, but the ones I have seen on TV have frilly lace curtains on the windows and blown-up wedding photographs and matching blue and pink mugs and slippers and stuff.

But this apartment, there are no photographs or paintings or frills—it is as stark and muted and neutral as a hospital waiting room. No books or plants either. The only thing that is personal at all is a small bookshelf of CDs in the corner. What a curious woman she must be, not to have a single decoration in her house. Even at the salon, where we each have the little acreage of one chair in front of a mirror, everyone is trying to decorate the hell out of the thirty centimeters of shelf space in front of the mirrors. And she's having a baby! Not a single baby thing anywhere, although I did hear that people do not like buying things early for fear of bad luck . . . Tempting the gods with assumptions of happiness.

My phone starts buzzing, making us both jump. It's Miho calling. She must be very frazzled, to be calling me. "Ara, it's me. Check your texts!! Text me back!!" she says when I pick up, then she hangs up.

- - - -

I open the texts and see that she has texted me a bunch. "Where are you??? Are you ok???? I just knocked on your door and you are not here!!"

I text her back. "Downstairs in 302. Lady in a lot of pain. I'm fine!"

Perhaps ten seconds later, I hear a knock on the door.

"Who's that?" says the woman weakly, and I run to the door and open it.

Miho looks relieved when she sees me. Her long hair is in two flowing braids and she has paint on her hands and arms as usual.

"You scared me!" Miho says in a chiding voice. "You can't do that! Just text and go silent!"

I crinkle my face in apology.

"I called the police," says Miho. I shake my head. "Call them back? Tell them not to come?" she asks, and I nod.

"Who is it?" calls the woman from the living room, and Miho walks in with me.

"Hello, are you okay?" Miho asks gently when she sees the woman lying down. "My friend Ara here texted that she heard screaming and then she didn't text back so I got nervous."

The woman sits up slowly, gingerly touching her stomach.

"I was in a lot of pain," she says. "My husband . . . is not here." She says this hesitantly, then rubs her stomach in a circular motion. "I actually think I am feeling better. It still hurts but less now. I'm pregnant." She says the last part a bit defiantly.

"Do you need to call your doctor?" Miho asks. The woman shakes her head and looks at me. I touch Miho on the arm and shake my head.

"Well, at least you are feeling better," says Miho. "That's good! I'm Miho, by the way. This is Ara. We live upstairs."

- - - -

"Yes, I am sorry," the woman says. "It's very late and I disturbed you. I am surprised the whole office-tel is not pounding on my door."

"Oh, don't worry," says Miho. "Ara is just special. She hears things more acutely than most people. I'm sure everyone else is asleep."

"When is your husband coming back?" I type.

She looks at my text and shakes her head once. And then Miho jabs me in the back to tell me to stop asking.

I go to the kitchen table to check on the hot water I have poured into the mug. It's a drinkable temperature now, so I bring it to the woman and she sips.

"Thank you so much for bringing hot water. It's very thoughtful." She holds the mug with both hands and then places it on her belly.

I smile weakly. It's just as well that she doesn't know I thought she was being raped and I was going to fling the boiling water in her rapist's face.

"It's so late. I feel quite terrible for keeping you up. Please return home and go to sleep. I feel so much better, really." To illustrate her point, she stands up and smiles tremulously.

Miho and I look at the clock, which now reads 4:05 A.M. We both shrug. Miho keeps her own hours and can sleep in as late as she likes.

I have to be at work by 9:30. I haven't had a dedicated assistant since Cherry never came back after that night; I've been laying low and haven't asked for another one yet.

I take the woman's hands in mine and squeeze them. They are bony and soft at the same time.

"Thank you," she says, her eyes cast down to the floor in embarrassment. Miho murmurs good night to her and we leave together, closing the door softly behind us.

THE NEXT DAY at work, I am thinking about the lady. I can't stop thinking about her desperate eyes—how, even despite her pain, she was unwilling to go to the emergency room because they might take the baby out of her.

I cannot imagine feeling that way. I cannot imagine having a child and you have to watch out for him or her and every moment of every day will be devoted to the child with no life of your own. I wonder how that transition happens and what it feels like when that instinct kicks in.

One of my customers said to me once that the problem with a lot of my generation in this country is that we do not live for tomorrow. He was a professor of sociology and had been quizzing the assistants about their life choices, which obviously made them uncomfortable. They would not be working at a salon if they could answer such questions positively, I wanted to say. But of course he and everyone else knew that already, and he was simply being cruel by bringing it up.

"You have to grow up with parents whose lives become better as time goes by, so you learn that you must invest effort for life to improve. But if you grow up around people whose situations become worse as time goes on, then you think that you have to just live for today. And when I ask young people, What about the future? What will you do when the future comes and you have spent everything already? they say they will just die. And that is why Korea has the highest suicide rate in the world."

He said this in a lecturing way, as if to chide everyone who worked in the salon.

I wanted to ask if his own children were brilliant and filial and successful, because no one is actually like that.

Sometimes, it is a good thing that I cannot speak.

KYURI TEXTS ME around dinnertime.

"Our manager says there's a chance Taein will come to Ajax tonight! Madam is not going to be here because she's getting her annual health checkup tomorrow so she has to fast and not drink starting 5 P.M. today. This is perfect. Any chance you can get off work and come here by 9 or so? His manager is definitely coming with *someone* from Taein's company and I am betting that it's really him. And even if it isn't, you can meet his manager at least."

I stare and stare at this text and I can't breathe and I have to sit down and the assistants scatter like roaches when they see my face. Perhaps Cherry told them things about me after all.

It is finally here. The time that I get to meet Taein. I have fantasized about this a thousand times, and each time, he is taken with me and wants to talk to me alone and he takes me to his apartment, where we listen to music all night lying on the floor of his room, like he did in that reality show *My Lonely Room*. I bolt up from my chair and stare at the mirror. I have to go. I know that Kyuri would never have texted me if this was not a real opportunity.

I must transform myself, that is immediately clear. I will have to borrow something to wear from one of the girls. I run through all of their dresses in my head. I once saw Miho wearing some kind of dark green dress that I loved. I will have to ask her about it right now.

I hurry to the front desk and ask how many clients I have left today, and fortunately they tell me it is only two. Mrs. Park Mi-soon

----

and Mr. Lim Myung-sang. I type on my phone that I have an emergency and have to go home, and ask Miss Kim if she can call and ask if they would prefer to reschedule or to just go with whoever is available. Mrs. Park is scheduled for her perm, which she gets only once every three months, but this cannot be helped. And Mr. Lim is just his regular monthly haircut. Miss Kim nods and asks what's wrong, but I shake my head and fly to the locker room, where I change into my regular clothes. As I leave, I catch Miss Kim's eye and motion for her to text me, and she nods and waves me off.

WHEN I GET back to the office-tel, nobody is home and Miho is not answering my text about the dress. I punch in the numbers for the lock to Miho and Kyuri's apartment, and once I'm in I rifle through their closets.

I find the green dress not in Miho's closet but in Kyuri's, and I write in to the group chat. "Borrowing dark green dress from Kyuri's closet, whoever's it is!! Thanks!! Makeup and shoes too!!"

Kyuri's tools do not make Kyuri's face, however, and I emerge from her room looking a bit too pale and wide-eyed for my liking. Eyeliner was never my strong point. At least my hair will look perfect. After putting on the dress, which is a bit tight on me, I curl my hair into waves. Unfortunately, Kyuri's shoes are all too big for me so I have to wear my own, and the only remotely passable ones are some nude heels I bought a few summers ago that hurt my toes. The forecasts all say that there is a chance of showers in the evening, and I take an umbrella because I don't want to ruin the dress.

By the time I catch a cab, it is already past 9 P.M., and I am almost crying with anxiety as we sit in traffic for nearly ten minutes. Kyuri

----

texts me to say that Taein just arrived. She says she'll come up to get me when I arrive.

My heart is bursting as the cab finally pulls up and I see Kyuri waving at me by an entrance where several men in suits are loitering.

"You came!" she squeals, and I can smell the alcohol on her breath. She's drunk already and giggling as she squeezes my hand. We teeter down the stairs together. "So, he's here with his two friends and his manager and then the CEO of his agency is coming later too. And Sujin! Sujin is in another room right now but she'll be coming in soon!"

We walk down a dark hallway where girls and waiters are going in and out of rooms. As doors open and close we hear snippets of laughter or low voices or singing. Finally Kyuri stops and opens the door and pushes me in gently.

Inside, it is dark, with a long rectangular marble table in the middle of the room and a bathroom in the corner. Four men are sitting around the table drinking, and on the far right, it's really Taein.

It seems strange that there are not more people here, that everyone isn't staring at him rapturously. I am *not* hallucinating—his skin is glowing, his face is smaller than I expected—his perfect face, which I stare at every night on the screen, is so close to mine I could reach out and cup it with my hands.

"Come on, Ara," says Kyuri, and she pushes me in until we reach the table and then plops me down next to Taein.

I bow and blush bright red up to my roots.

"You left so fast I was going to get offended, Kyuri," says one of the guys, who is wearing a striped T-shirt and looks around Taein's age.

A guy on the other side says, "Yeah, I didn't realize you were *that*

----

popular, that you can't sit here for ten minutes straight." He has a round face and bad skin and his expression is unkind. "This place is getting too cocky."

"I went to get my friend, who is a huge Taein fan!" says Kyuri merrily. "Not to another room, silly."

"Ugh, seriously, a fan?" says the guy in the striped shirt. "He hates fans."

"No I don't," says Taein quickly, reaching over and mock-punching him on the shoulder. He turns and gives me a wide smile, but I can tell he is on his guard now.

"So what's your name?" says Taein's giant hulk of a manager, turning toward me. His wide face is marked by splotchy acne, and I recognize him too, from all the reality TV shows. He's been with Crown since before their debut. All the stories that have ever been told about him—usually on radio rather than TV—come immediately to mind. He used to hoard food in his room and pretend he didn't have any when the kids were going hungry after practicing all day and had used up the ten-thousand-won food budget for the day. And one time, he forgot to pick them up from the airport because he was too drunk and they actually had to take a taxi home with their own money (when they were not making any money yet).

I wonder how they can stand to be around him now, after all that heart suffering he put them through when they were struggling and poor.

"Her name is Ara," says Kyuri. "She is mute."

"What?" There are yelps from around the table and I flush more.

"I've never met a mute!" says one of the friends. "Wow, this room salon gets more and more interesting every time I come here. How is she supposed to talk to me when she's *mute*?"

"Body language, you idiot," says the tall one, cracking himself up. "She must be fluent in several dialects."

For all the times I imagined meeting Taein, I wonder at myself, why I didn't prepare more for this. Hot tears are building up in my eyes when the door opens and Sujin walks in.

"They told me you were in here!" she says gaily to Kyuri. "Hello, everyone!"

The men cast a glance over her and ignore her. Then she sees me and Taein.

"Ara?" Sujin says when she sees me. "Oh my God!" Instantly, she understands what is happening and hurries to sit down next to me. She pinches me and starts squealing.

"What the fuck," I hear the tall guy mutter. Then he presses the buzzer on the table and a waiter pops in. "Call the madam," he says. Everyone is quiet suddenly, and Kyuri seems agitated.

It only takes a minute for the manager, dressed in all black, to open the door and slide in quietly. "Hello," he says, bowing deeply. "Is something the matter? How can I fix it?"

The tall guy motions to him. "I said, call the *madam*. Not you. I don't know you."

"She is actually not in today but I am sure I can help you. Shall I clear the room?" The manager looks at Kyuri, and I can see that he is trying hard to protect her and, by extension, us. He likes her, it is clear. We are all holding our breath.

"How many times do I have to fucking tell you to call the madam? She has a phone, doesn't she? In fact, I have her number myself. I'll call her now."

To our horror, he fishes his phone out of his pocket and scrolls and dials.

Kyuri mutters "shit" under her breath. Sujin stands and pulls me up by the wrist, and we slowly make our way toward the door.

This is it. Taein did not even talk to me. I did not get to type anything to him. I glance desperately back at him as I walk out the door, and he is joking with his friends, not even noticing me leave.

As the door closes, I hear the friend yelling on the phone. "What's up with the quality control! I thought this was a ten percent! Not a house of amateurs and freaks! How much money have I spent here over the years to be treated like this!"

I am walking fast in spite of my heels, trying to keep up with Sujin and Kyuri. "You both better go," Kyuri says softly as she stops abruptly in front of another door. "I'll see you at home." She opens the door and slips inside. Sujin takes my hand, and we both start walking fast again. I know how she feels and she knows how I feel and soon we are both running.

THE DAY THAT I lost my voice, it was like this too. I was running with Sujin and she was holding my hand leading me out. She was the one who had brought me there in the first place—under the arch by the dirt road after dark, where she said we were going to get initiated into the bad kids' gang, so that we would be the leaders of the school the following year. I had not wanted to go because I was not sure I wanted to be labeled a bad kid, since that meant all of the teachers would hate us and single us out and beat us if they ever saw anything out of line. An iljin boy in the year above us had had one of his eardrums burst after he was hit by the vice principal.

We did not know that the other schools had all heard about our initiation night and had come for vengeance for past years of lost fights. They brought wooden boards and some of them had beer bottles that they smashed on the pavement to turn them into weapons. They surrounded us and we did not know they were actually going to use the broken bottles on us until one of the sunbaes screamed "Run!" and then all the world collapsed into chaos. I never saw the face of the girl who hit me, but Sujin later told me that the girl had a bat.

When we were back on the grounds of the Big House, Sujin woke up my parents before calling an ambulance. I do not remember much from that night, but I do remember Sujin's fingernails, blood and skin under them from where she had scratched the face of the girl who attacked me. When the shouts of "Police!" began, the girl had become distracted, and that was when Sujin slashed her before frantically pulling me away. I could not see straight because of the pain exploding in my head.

"I'm sorry, I'm sorry," she was screaming. That is the memory that is the most difficult to bear from that night. The sound of her choking with anguish for me.

Kyuri

It is the first time in three long and subdued weeks that I've actually felt like going out after work, so when Sujin texted earlier that she would be done around the same time as me today, I told her to come meet me at my favorite samgyeopsal place. She's been in the bathroom for twenty minutes now and I have been grilling and eating and drinking by myself. I can feel people at the other tables feeling sorry for me.

It's 1 A.M. on a Thursday night, so of course the place is packed and the staff are charging around with distressed faces, but I don't care—I hail down a young waiter and make him grill for me while I go find Sujin. In the bathroom, she is prodding her face with a crystal-flecked fingertip in front of the mirror.

"What are you *doing*?" I snap.

"Oh, sorry, sorry," she says, flustered. "I had all this food stuck in my mouth and I was scooping it out and then I thought maybe I got some sensation back in the right part of my chin, but I think I was wrong. Coming!"

Back at the table, she retrieves the tongs from the perspiring waiter and starts flipping the pork belly, setting the pieces that are cooked onto my plate. As I watch her pick up the scissors and start cutting her own pieces into tiny slivers, I feel my chest softening. Of course I remember what it's like—how difficult every meal is—the food getting stuck, the slow chewing, the clicking of the jaw, the numbness and discomfort.

"You get used to it," I say to her, again. After my own surgeries I had to work hard to stop myself from stretching my neck like a crane and constantly poking my chin because I couldn't feel it. Sensation never came back, but that's what hand mirrors and selfie modes were for—to check if food or drink were dribbling down my chin. Wordlessly, I reach into my own bag and hand over my favorite mirror—it is small and round and has a border of lace.

"Oh, it's okay," she says, tilting her head and breaking into a smile. With most of her swelling down, beauty has emerged dramatically from her face this past week. I am amazed, as I always am, at how suddenly it blooms when it finally happens.

I can see the men at adjacent tables sneaking looks at her and then at me. She's taken my advice and sought out my lash place, and they've worked decadent magic on her newly symmetrical eyes. Even her nose looks cuter; a common side benefit from jaw surgery. With a smaller face, untouched features like the forehead and nose tend to look prettier in tandem.

I wish Sujin had been this pretty three weeks ago, that night of the Taein incident. Perhaps she'd have gotten hired at Ajax and we'd

----

all be partying together with Crown now, in some secret private room at some blazing new club. Instead she's working as one of those freelance girls who get carted around in a bus to room salons that are short on girls for the night. And even that was a favor I'd called in to an old friend of mine from my Gangseo days.

"ARE YOU *ACTUALLY* INSANE?" Madam had said, when I had gone to apologize to her a few days after that disastrous night. It was early afternoon and she was sitting at a table in one of the rooms at the salon, writing numbers into a little black book and using her phone as a calculator.

It was Miho who had been adamant about going to apologize in person no matter what. "Just go. It will do so much, trust me. Older people, that's all they want—for others to say they are sorry and make a gesture first." I had been planning to just stay home forever, my debts be damned. "The worst that can happen is that things stay the same," Miho said. She had stopped moping around over that boyfriend of hers, and her smug air of proactive martyrdom was becoming unbearable. Despite her shrill conviction, I still hadn't gone in for a few days until the manager oppa had texted me to say that Madam had said nothing when he mentioned my name. *If you come in now, it'll be like nothing happened,* he texted.

"I am truly, terribly sorry," I said over and over, bowing as deeply as my waist would allow. "I have no words."

Looking back down at her phone, Madam did not acknowledge me. She made me wait there for a good half hour while she balanced her books and made some calls, but I did not move either. I was comfortable prostrate. I pictured her brain whirring inside her large skull as she calculated the optimal way to humiliate me just to the brink of breaking point.

When she finally addressed me, she sounded exasperated but resigned. "Look," she said, slamming her little book shut and making me flinch. "It's no secret that this industry is not what it used to be and everything is hard. Everyone is having a hard time. I am having a hard time, and you bet you'll be having a hard time too, although none of you idiots can think that far ahead, I know."

Her pathetic, ugly face looked old then, and pinched. I thought of all the money she was saving by staying this ugly. Her eyes were not warm, but they had never been, even on my most popular days. "Run along now and make some money like an ace," she said, dismissing me with a faint wave. And so I was released, into air.

DISCREETLY SPITTING OUT some meat into a napkin, Sujin says, "I think you need to find a different kind of job."

I chortle into my shot glass. "You have spent all this time and money and pain to try to get into a room salon, and now you are telling *me* to leave a ten percent?" I say. "And what should I do then? Go clean toilets?" I ask playfully. It is not a question that I have ever seriously considered. Everywhere I look, there are only jobs that I cannot possibly ever land. I know this, because even though I try to avoid the news, headlines about unemployment are flashing all around the city. Just yesterday, I was stuck in traffic and had to stare at the giant TV at the Sinsa Station crossing with the announcer with giant subtitles talking about some ten-year-high and how people are going to start killing other people out of sheer boredom or whatever. Do those unemployment numbers include all the people who own buildings

----

and don't go to work? Every single skyscraper and shopping mall in this city has owners who live at hotel gyms and department stores and never worked a day in their lives. The most regular commute they have is probably to a room salon.

"But I don't think your madam is good to you," Sujin says, which makes me laugh harder. She shakes her head at me in exasperation. "I mean, I know I know, but what I mean is that you seem really stressed out these days. Much more so than I've ever seen you before." The waiter brings another bottle and Sujin fills my glass.

"And what about *you*?" I say. "Is this making you rethink this job too?"

"No, but it's different for me," she says. "I am too busy enjoying being pretty right now." She glances quickly around us, to see if anyone heard her, and blushes when she sees a man staring brazenly. "And plus, I don't really get stressed. Or if I do, I know how to not think about it. Ara can tell you. You learn pretty early on in an orphanage, or else you sink completely. If I've made it this far, I'm set. And this, right now, is really the turning point of my life." She looks at me with earnest eyes. I can tell she is on the verge of tearing up.

"I don't know," I say hurriedly. "Miho doesn't seem like she's handling her stress that well."

"Miho?" says Sujin, sufficiently distracted. "She'll be fine. You don't need to worry. She is just meticulously planning revenge, that's all. We are very solution oriented."

I look at Sujin with amusement. "Revenge for what?" I say, wondering if Miho has told her. Sujin was being quite entertaining today, with her purported deep insights. The thing is, my current situation is not stressful. She should have seen me during my Miari days.

"She just said she found out he was cheating," she says, reaching

----

for a burnt slice of pork belly. "But she should have known better than to expect otherwise. I told her that he would, the first time I heard they were together."

"Have you met him?" I ask, my eyebrow raised.

"No, but I don't need to," she says. "Nobody that handsome and rich is that nice."

"I guess so," I say with a sigh. Suddenly I feel exceedingly tired and I think of Nami. I haven't spoken to her since the day she came over. She had texted me a few times and then stopped when I didn't respond. Light leaked out of me whenever I thought about her.

"I have been compiling some ideas for Miho," Sujin says matter-of-factly. "I just have to check a few things first, like which reporters will actually believe what I say, and which ones might pay and which ones accept anonymous submissions. Miho has to be patient, because it is her destiny to become famous. All of us at the orphanage always said so."

We clink glasses again and drink. I indicate that she has some sauce on her chin and she wipes it off. Then she takes her phone and starts searching through her photo gallery.

"All of us asked her for a drawing to keep because we knew she would be famous one day. Look, this is what she was drawing back in high school." She slides her phone over to me. The screen shows a detailed pencil drawing of a family walking in a procession in a field of flowers. The father is in the front, then the mother, and then an older daughter holding several books to her chest. Trailing behind is a short figure wearing a girls' hanbok but topped with the head of a giant frog staring out with mad, bulbous eyes and a flickering tongue.

"Um, I wouldn't want that in my possession," I say, handing the phone back to her. "You *asked* if you could have that? How awful."

"That was her toad series," says Sujin. "She drew a lot of toad people in wells but this one is cheerful, with all those flowers. No dead people!" She smiles down at the photo.

I always knew they were both cracked.

"I thought going to New York would be good for her, which is why I kicked up such a fuss to the Loring Center, but I suppose that's how she met Hanbin and now she is unhappy. . . ." Sujin trails off. I ask her what she means.

"I was an assistant at the hair salon when I first came to Seoul, and one day I overheard a customer bragging to one of the stylists that her daughter was applying for this art scholarship to New York. I listened as hard as I could and looked it up afterward and I called the Loring Center to make them apply for Miho." Sujin shakes her head. "The adults there never think ahead about our future—to be fair, they're busy putting out fires, with girls like me—but that's why those of us out here are constantly looking for information for the younger ones. That's how I got that salon job too, an unni from the Center called me. I mean, the job was gruesome, but at least it got me here!"

Sujin grins at me, as if she is revealing a finale with a grand twist.

"ANYWAYS, I WAS at Cinderella Clinic this morning for my checkup and I heard that Manager Koo left," says Sujin on the walk home.

"What?" I'm surprised. Manager Koo has been with them since Dr. Shim first opened Cinderella Clinic. I couldn't imagine what he would do without her, since she was the one who was always bringing in new patients and convincing old ones to get the latest surgeries. Her signature move was to indicate her face and body with a little flourish and whisper, "I've had simply *everything* done, so you can ask me anything—anything at all and I will be completely honest with you." She was marvelously compelling, to say the least.

"Yeah, I heard she moved to NVme, that new enormous hospital right off Sinsa Station," says Sujin. "Cinderella Clinic seems to be in shock because everyone was scrambling when I got there. I guess she didn't even find a replacement or train them or whatever because I saw the youngest assistant doing a consultation!"

NVme makes sense—it's the huge new place that everyone is checking out because of an onslaught of recent publicity. I read somewhere that it's the largest plastic surgery hospital in the world. The photos had shown a marble-covered twenty-story building with a spa in the basement and luxury hotel rooms on the top floors for the foreigners who came to Korea on the plastic surgery packages.

"Anyway, I told Dr. Shim that you'd be perfect for the manager job and he seemed to agree," says Sujin.

"You *what?*" I stop walking and stare at her.

"At least, I *think* he agreed." She looks stumped for a second, then brightens again.

"Okay, you need to tell me *exactly* what you said and what he said. Sujin! Are you crazy? Now I can't go there again!"

An image of Dr. Shim's stoic, intelligent face floats into my drink-muddled mind and I am aghast.

At the office-tel, I pull Sujin into my apartment. Miho isn't home yet—she has started going to the studio at night again, fire in her eyes. All I ask is that she doesn't bring her creepy canvases home. I don't want to see any renderings of Nami's head dangling from a stick or whatever disturbed release she's working on.

"Go on," I snap at Sujin.

She walks over to the kitchen and starts pouring some water into a glass. "Okay, okay, I'm sorry I said those things to Dr. Shim, but I

----

was thinking about you and how good you would be at that job and how your madam is so mean, and it would be something different for you, you know? The worst that can happen is they say no," she says. "All I said was that you were thinking about a job switch and how good you would be at it—after all, you introduced me and several other girls, didn't you? And Dr. Shim nodded, like this." She does a decent imitation of him looking brainy and nodding impassively.

I feel color rising in my cheeks as I contemplate what Sujin is saying. Me in a pink blazer, a steel name pin on my lapel, smiling at worried women who want to be looked at with warm eyes. I can't help thinking I do not know how to handle women. But then again, I do not really know how to handle men, either. I think of all the debt I have piling up.

"Just go meet Dr. Shim and see what he says," says Sujin, yawning now. She stands up to leave.

"I'm sure they have a thousand résumés pouring in," I say lightly. "Probably ten thousand. I don't have a résumé."

"Yeah, but you are a walking advertisement for their clinic," she says. "How many surgeries and procedures have you had done there? How many of their patients would apply for this job? I bet you are the only one. Think about it."

As Sujin turns to go, we hear the beeps of Miho's door code being punched in and the sound of her front door opening.

"Hello," Miho says, her head tilting when she sees us. Sujin and I both gasp. Miho's wild, flowing hair has been cut to her shoulders and she looks like an entirely different person. She looks younger. No, older. No, younger. Chic. Radiant. Shocking.

"I know, I know, how cliché can I get?" Miho says, laughing when she sees our expressions. "I actually cried when Ara cut it off. Ara almost cried too. I was the one who had to convince her for a good

----

twenty minutes that I really wanted to cut it. After all her hints that I needed to!"

She swishes her short hair back and forth. It has been ironed completely straight and she looks like a model blown up on the exterior of a luxury mall. "My department head might actually kill me," she says. "Oh well."

"It looks incredible!" says Sujin. She walks over and starts touching strands of it. "Does it feel so liberating?"

Miho nods, but her lip wobbles. "I really regretted it for an hour or two and then completely forgot about it as I was working until I saw my face in a mirror. And then I cried again. But I think I'm okay now. And Ara gave my hair to some charity so that makes me feel a bit better."

"Ara is so talented," I say. "Looking at you makes *me* feel lighter."

"I have a photoshoot next week for a newspaper article about rising artists," says Miho, fingering her ends self-consciously. "I told Ara I might just dye it blue tomorrow. Electric blue. I've always wanted electric blue hair, like Powerade."

"Whoa, whoa. Take it one step at a time," I say. "Give yourself a week at least to think about it. I wouldn't recommend doing such drastic things all at once because you might regret it."

Sujin pokes me from behind.

"See?" she says. "You would be such a natural for that job. That's exactly what Manager Koo said to me during my first consultation. Then she sneakily recommended a dozen more things I should do."

YEARS AGO, back when I was still conflicted about whether to proceed with my surgeries, I went to a well-known fortune-teller who told me that shaving my jaw would take away all the luck that follows in old age. But when she took down my name and date and time of birth and calculated my saju and my future, her face changed. She said that my later years held only terrible luck, so I should try everything I could to alter my fate.

Grimacing in pity, she told me that because of the shape of my nose, all the money that would flow into my life would flow right out again. And she told me that I had the weakest luck in love—that it would be best to marry late, if at all. She said I had the same saju as a famous historical commander, who went to war knowing he had nothing to lose because he knew the fortune of his later years, and he died with honor and glory.

It is easy to leap if you have no choice.

ON SATURDAY MORNING, I find myself sitting in the waiting room of Cinderella Clinic, skittish with nerves for the first time in all my visits here. I place a hand on my right knee to try to stop it from shaking, but it's taken on a savage life of its own.

Usually when I'm here, I pass the time judging the other patients, with their oversized sunglasses and overinjected noses, typing furiously on their phones with both thumbs. *Make sure Yo-han isn't late for his Lego lesson. Did you hear that Daesu got into XX school?* Or something scathing to their husbands, I am sure, although I cannot imagine what texting a husband is like. *Honey, I made your favorite doenjang stew so please come home for dinner for once in your life.* Or, *those lipstick marks on your shirt collar wouldn't come off so I cut it up into ribbons while you were snoring, have a nice day!*

Today, however, I focus on the staff behind the desks. Three of the four pink-blazered assistants I know well but the fourth must be

----

new. She looks young and cautious, and keeps darting glances at the other assistants typing on either side of her. I give her a hard once-over. What made them pick her? She looks stupidly timid and not pretty at all—she has not had much surgery—just her eyes and maybe filler as far as I can tell. Her hair is pulled back into a tight ponytail and her hairline is an embarrassment of uneven, patchy fuzz. I touch my own hair out of habit. Even if I haven't been to the salon in two weeks, my nightly hair masks have ensured that my ends are silky as seaweed.

The other assistants have been here for years, since I have started coming here. They are nice enough, with syrupy sweet voices and brutal efficiency in getting you to pay up front. They have a very particular way of making you feel as if you are lucky to be a patient here, while also giving the impression that they are secretly looking down on you, so that you end up spending a lot of money to force their respect.

Hoping that they will glance up from their screens, I try to infuse admiration into my face. My cheek muscles hurt from all this beaming.

My phone buzzes and I check my phone. It's the manager oppa. *Good morning! Hope you are having a nice day so far. What are you up to?* He has sent a coffee coupon and a winking bunny emoji.

I smile in spite of myself. At first, I did not even notice his niceties—so many little things he would do for me here and there. But now there is no mistaking that he likes me. It is cute and not yet annoying.

Just a makeup lesson, I text him, because even if he is nice, he is a man and he is in Madam's pay. Besides, probably nothing will come of this anyway.

THE RECEPTIONIST CALLS out a name and the woman sitting on my left gathers her things and stands. As she walks into the consultation room I hear her asking about what's on sale this month. I've been coming here long enough to know that the sales don't mean much because you can haggle about anything, but that doesn't stop me from leaning over to the brochure rack and picking up the latest flyer.

"Get Ready for Summer!" A girl in a scarlet bikini is posing by a pool and the sale prices are listed below. Only the "petite" procedures— the noninvasive ones—are featured. I'm sorely tempted by the "Strapless Package," which includes Botox for the back of the shoulders, "fat kill" injections for the underarms, and a choice between Healite II LED therapy or cryotherapy. I tried Healite several times last summer and I liked the results. Going down the list, I am reminded I need more armpit whitening and lip edge injections because the little curls on either side of my lips have begun to droop. I blink and make myself snap out of it—today, I need to focus. From my bag, I retrieve the slim notebook that the married lady gave me from her office, and I check the talking notes that I went over with the girls last night. I have written down the list of girls I have referred here. This includes Miho and Ara because they made appointments earlier this week too so that they could come drop my name and bolster my chances. Ara in particular was very intrigued by all her options after her consultation but said she might start with something small, perhaps just a filler shot for her nose.

My phone buzzes. It's the manager oppa again.

My friend is opening a nap café in Gangnam Station. Do you want to go check it out with me when you're done?

A few seconds later it buzzes again.

Just realized that might sound creepy—just to say hi to my friend I mean, not to actually sleep there! And they have only twin beds, I think! No co-sleeping allowed!

I laugh because he is such an innocent still, somehow, but then I hear one of the assistants call my name. Fumbling with my phone, I stand up quickly and follow her into the consultation room—one that I have been in many times. Turning my phone to silent, I quickly send a thumbs-up emoji to the manager oppa and check my reflection on my phone camera before straightening my posture.

"Dr. Shim will be in shortly," she says in a singsong voice and steps out, closing the door behind her.

I know I will not get this job—nothing in this life is this easy. But as long as I am trying, doesn't that mean something? I think of the fortune-teller, and the girls and the notes from their online interview research that they pored over with me yesterday. I think of my mother, and how I would be able to have her actually see where I work, because it would be a real place, and how happy it would make her. And for some reason, the manager oppa's face also swims into my mind before I quickly banish it. I skim my notes again and my leg shakes even harder.

A few long minutes later, I hear Dr. Shim's voice and heavy footsteps in the hallway. The door handle turns as if in slow motion as he walks in.

Facing him, I smile as widely as my banging heart will allow.

ON MY WAY home later that night, I pick up Ara and Sujin from SeverLand, the new esports entertainment park from Berserk Games, Bruce's Internet game company. To be honest, the only reason I

- - - -

bother to stop by is to buy the rum drink they sell at the fantasy café there. Bruce used to bring me some when he found out I liked rum. They sell it in containers that look like dragons' eggs. In the café, I stare at the rows of glowing eggs and decide not to buy any after all.

I find the two of them gaming furiously in a corner of the PC bang and Sujin gestures that they will get off in ten more minutes. Ara does not even look up. I take in the sea of intense, focused faces, all of whom are putting money into Bruce's pocket every minute they spend at their game pods, and take to wandering around the labyrinthine park as I wait for them, bemused. It's a strange place that manages to be both childlike and violent, with cryptlike doors, intricate murals of battle scenes, and stained-glass windows depicting pixies and dragons and warrior women with ludicrous breasts. I think about how much money each intricate detail must have cost. I remember Bruce brought an artist to Ajax once to discuss which scenes he wanted depicted in the park. The artist didn't say much, just drank a great deal and grunted with his eyes half-closed to everything Bruce said.

The manager oppa told me today that Bruce has been back to Ajax a few times. Everyone is under strict instructions to never let him see me.

SUJIN AND I have to help carry posters of scenes from the game home because Ara went crazy at the gift shop. She has been redecorating her room. "She ripped up all the Taein photos," Sujin whispered to me when I was gasping over the merch prices. I had to persuade Ara not to buy a full cosplay costume of a water pixie from the game.

The air is thick tonight and I wonder if there has been talk of rain. The girls want to hear details about the interview but there isn't much to tell. Dr. Shim's face was impassive as usual and I told them it had been just for practice and they said they would let me know. I do not want them to see that I care so much.

When we reach the office-tel, the married lady Wonna is sitting on the front steps, her hands resting on her stomach.

I don't know if I should tell her how frightening she looks, sitting there on the steps in the shadows like some unearthly wraith, staring out at the street with dull eyes. But I needn't worry—people walk on by, oblivious in their gaiety. Saturday nights are always busy on our street—all the bars are ablaze with light and people are euphorically drunk as they fight over what to do next.

"I was wondering when you would be getting home—I saw that your lights were off and I couldn't sleep," she calls out when she sees us, her face suddenly flaring with warmth. Ara runs up and sits down next to her and starts showing her the posters that she just bought. The married lady is nice enough to act interested, and Sujin joins in, explaining each of the characters.

Sitting down on the cool steps next to Sujin, I bow and say hello and the lady does the same to me. Ara has been keeping us informed of all the latest developments about the married lady and her baby, even though I am not all that interested, to be honest. Apparently, the lady was in a frenzy, decorating the house. *Babies these days have the craziest stuff,* Ara had texted us from a baby fair last weekend because the lady had asked if she could accompany her. Ara sent photos of pastel bumper beds with tents, air purifiers for strollers, and UV sterilizing machines shaped like doll ovens.

"I forgot, Miho said that your parents asked her to hold some

----

packages for you? They came by earlier and knocked on her door when they found you weren't home," says Sujin. "She didn't know your number, so she asked us to tell you."

The lady is silent. Then she sighs and says she was actually home, but she didn't want to speak to them, so she was hiding in her bathroom.

"They are trying hard already with this one, since they messed up so much with me," she says dryly.

I say that she looks like she turned out pretty good—doesn't she have a real job, and isn't she legally married and everything?—but she just smiles and asks me for some food delivery recommendations. "The baby always demands fried chicken at 1 A.M." she says, her hand on her bump.

"You know, fried chicken sounds really good right now," I say, and Ara claps her hands like a child.

"Would you like to come over to my place and we can order then?" the lady asks a bit nervously. "I have been meaning to ask you girls over for a while. You can have all my husband's whiskey that he left here. He will not be needing it anymore."

She says the last part with a small toss of her head. Ara nods and I say yes and Sujin says she will order and text Miho too.

"Oh," the lady says suddenly with a sharp intake of breath, putting her hands on her bump.

"Are you all right?" Sujin asks in alarm.

She stays still as if she is listening for something, then breathes deeply. "I'm okay. I thought it was pain, but I think it's gone."

I look across at her from where I am sitting. She looks forlorn but not despairing, and it is astonishing how calm she can be.

Ara moves so that she is sitting behind her and takes the lady's hair in her hands. She starts combing her fingers through it expertly.

The lady lets out a sigh—a tremulous release of a long day—which makes me feel lighter too.

"Do you . . . do you want to see a photo of my baby?" she asks in a shy voice. Sujin clamors yes and even I nod. The lady reaches into her jacket pocket and takes out a thin printout of a 3D ultrasound that is curling around the edges. It shows a tiny, opalescent face with closed eyelids and a miniature fist clenched near its mouth.

"Wow," breathes Sujin reverently, and we all gaze at the face.

"I haven't shown it to anyone," the lady says. "I haven't talked about the baby to anyone, really. So I need to practice." She tilts her head to consider this thought.

For a fleeting moment, as Sujin passes me the photograph and I hold this flimsy, curling image in my hands, I understand what it would be like to think only about tomorrow, instead of just today.

We sit in silence for a while, still staring at this photograph of new life, and then, in the distance, we see Miho walking up the street toward us. She is swaying a bit, wearing heels and a dress, for once, her new short hair resplendent under the light of the streetlamps, and I see men turning around as she passes them, although she does not register their gazes at all. Instead, she is looking abstractly toward us, probably thinking of floating frogs or a bed of snakes or something equally grotesque, I'm sure.

When she reaches our steps, she looks up and smiles ruefully. She does not express any surprise that we are out sitting on the steps like characters in some musical on Daehakro.

"Hey," says Sujin. "I texted you. What have you been up to, dressed like *that*?" Sujin indicates Miho's dress, a wispy cream dress with embroidered bell sleeves, which I recognize as the same one Shin Yeonhee wore to her film premiere last week.

"I'm a woman of mystery," says Miho, smiling impishly, and I re-

----

member what Sujin said about not having to worry about her. Miho walks up slowly, gives a familiar nod to Wonna, and then sits on the other side of me. She exhales, and I put an arm around her shoulders. "I'm hungry," she says, and I roll my eyes at her, the way I always do.

A fat drop of rain falls, and in alarm, I cup my hand over the photograph before handing it hastily back to the lady. Sujin's phone starts ringing, and when she answers, it's the delivery man who cannot find our office-tel and is asking for directions. The raindrops keep falling, more thickly now. So we all stand up to make our way upstairs together, as the sky starts crackling, taking aim at each of us and the drunk men stumbling by.

Acknowledgments

My eternal gratitude to my brilliant agent, Theresa Park, and her formidable team at Park & Fine—Alex Greene, Abigail Koons, Ema Barnes, Marie Michels, Andrea Mai, Emily Sweet, and Fiona Furnari. I am the fortunate recipient of their exceptional insights and efforts. As I tell her every time I see her, Theresa, thank you for changing my life.

I am completely indebted to my editor, Jennifer Hershey, for her patience, guidance, and vision. She made my book so much better with every round of edits, and somehow made it a soothing and pleasurable experience. To Kara Welsh, Kim Hovey, Quinne Rogers, Taylor Noel, Jennifer Garza, Melissa Sanford, Maya Franson, Erin Kane, Susan Brown, and everyone at Ballantine and Penguin Random House who worked on this book, and to my UK editor, Isabel Wall at Viking,

----

thank you for making my first publishing experience more wonderful than it ever was in my dreams. Much appreciation for Maria Garbutt-Lucero and Chloe Davies for their tireless publicity outreach.

This all began as a story in Binnie Kirshenbaum's workshop at the Writing Division at Columbia University. Her thoughtful reading and encouragement sparked the aspiration to continue this as a novel. To all the teachers I had along the way, thank you for recommending the books that you did, and for making me ponder time and story and suspension of disbelief: Catherine Tudish, Cleopatra Mathis, Heidi Julavits, Rebecca Curtis, Julie Orringer, and Jonathan Dee. Special thanks to Ed Park for wisdom, introductions, and spirited discussion of all things Korean and Korean-American.

While writing about these young women, I drew upon many topics that I worked on as the Seoul editor for CNNGo and later CNN Travel. My bosses, Andrew Demaria and Chuck Thompson, gave me a dream job and relentlessly whipped my writing and editing into shape every day. Thank you for the priceless training.

Min Jung Lee walked me through the storied corridors of Random House long before my book was ready, and after an early reading, told me that she was certain I would be published one day soon. Without her, I never would have had the courage to send out my manuscript.

Ten years ago, I first read about Janice Lee in an *Elle* magazine interview while sitting in a doctor's office in Korea. Little did I know that she would become such a critical figure in my writing career. Thank you, Janice, for your encouragement and generosity.

After moving back to New York, I was able to jump-start my rusty writing again thanks to the Columbia Fiction Foundry and weekly workshops at the Center for Fiction with Vanessa Cox Nishikubo and Cindy Jones. I am also grateful to Soo Kong and my immensely supportive Dartmouth Korea family led by the estimable

----

Dr. Michael Kim of Yonsei University, Henry Kim, Jaysen Park, Dr. Euysung Kim, and Kevin Woo. My talented journalist uncle, Chun Kyoung Woo, always answers the random questions I have with his thoughtful theories and introduces me to the coolest people in Korea.

Whenever I visit my uncle and aunt's house in Daejeon and stay up listening to tantalizing family legends, I am inspired to plot out another book. I really need to start recording those late-night stories.

For crucial feedback in times of need, special thanks to dear friends Jean Pak and Violet Kim, who read various versions of the manuscript.

Christie Roche, mommy friend, lifehack consultant, and daily therapist—what would I do without you? I owe you my sanity, or what's left of it. May the barrage of our daily texts and abrupt phone calls never dwindle.

For their beautiful souls and acts of generosity that often left me speechless in our family's dark times, and for all the laughter and overabundance of food in the good times, Annie Kim and Jeff Lin.

The friends of my parents who have been there for my family after my father passed away—thank you for all the stories, the support, the meals, and the love. I wish I could express my gratitude better in person.

My parents-in-law, Jun-jong Lee and Haesook Lim, have taken on our children in many crucial moments while I was writing this book. Thank you, 아버님 and 어머님, for loving and caring for them always the way you do, and for all your efforts for our family. Many thanks also for the warm support of the extended Lim family in Marlton.

Soon Hyouk Lee and Michelle Lee, for unparalleled love, guidance, and support as the stalwart backbone of our family. Nieces Maia and Aster are always paving the way for our girls and showing us how things should be done.

- - - -

ACKNOWLEDGMENTS

My brother, Chris, has always been overwhelmingly enthusiastic about my writing ever since I can remember. I love you and miss you so much—hopefully we will get to live on the same continent again one day. My sister-in-law, Jenny Jeeun, you are such a sweet and upbeat force in our lives—I always feel so blessed that you went from being a friend to joining our family.

For reading several libraries of books to me when I was a child, for staying up with me all night to prep for thirteen subjects throughout my Korean school years, for teaching me her high standards even though I cannot keep up with them, and for all her sacrifices for her children, I am wholly indebted to my extraordinary mother, Minkyung Shon. Growing up listening to her riveting stories and commentaries on life, I had no choice but to become a writer. My father, who I miss every day. I wish he was here to see me through this chapter of my life.

My little daughters, Cora and Avie—the source of all my extreme desperation and extreme rapture—you are ever-brimming wells of inspiration. Cora said to me this morning, "I love you more than anything," while Avie said, "I wub-EW!" for the first time, which summarizes my feelings for them exactly.

Finally, to my husband, Soon Ho Lee, who throws aside anything and everything he is doing to read revisions deep into the night and on morning commutes, who spends hours discussing characters and word choice and cultural nuances, who has supported all aspects of the writing of this book with inexplicable, steadfast faith—you are a wonder that I will never get used to. Thank you always.

He just wanted a decent book to read ...

Not too much to ask, is it? It was in 1935 when Allen Lane, Managing Director of Bodley Head Publishers, stood on a platform at Exeter railway station looking for something good to read on his journey back to London. His choice was limited to popular magazines and poor-quality paperbacks – the same choice faced every day by the vast majority of readers, few of whom could afford hardbacks. Lane's disappointment and subsequent anger at the range of books generally available led him to found a company – and change the world.

'We believed in the existence in this country of a vast reading public for intelligent books at a low price, and staked everything on it'
Sir Allen Lane, 1902–1970, founder of Penguin Books

The quality paperback had arrived – and not just in bookshops. Lane was adamant that his Penguins should appear in chain stores and tobacconists, and should cost no more than a packet of cigarettes.

Reading habits (and cigarette prices) have changed since 1935, but Penguin still believes in publishing the best books for everybody to enjoy. We still believe that good design costs no more than bad design, and we still believe that quality books published passionately and responsibly make the world a better place.

So wherever you see the little bird – whether it's on a piece of prize-winning literary fiction or a celebrity autobiography, political tour de force or historical masterpiece, a serial-killer thriller, reference book, world classic or a piece of pure escapism – you can bet that it represents the very best that the genre has to offer.

Whatever you like to read – trust Penguin.